*continued . . .*

# A Charmed Death

"A magical, spellbinding mystery that enchants readers with its adorable heroine." —*The Best Reviews*

"Entertaining . . . A fun mystery to read!" —MyShelf.com

# The Trouble with Magic

"A fascinating ride . . . A hint of romance with much intrigue, mystery, and magic in a small Midwestern town setting." —*Roundtable Reviews*

"A fun, witty whodunit . . . The characters are likable, the story flows easily, and the mystery and mystical elements are believable." —*Fresh Fiction*

"This new series is going to be a winner."
—*The Romance Readers Connection*

"The plotting is tight and the murderer came as a shock. The situations are funny and the characters charming."
—*Romantic Times*

# Where There's a Witch

## Madelyn Alt

BERKLEY PRIME CRIME, NEW YORK

**THE BERKLEY PUBLISHING GROUP**
**Published by the Penguin Group**
**Penguin Group (USA) Inc.**
**375 Hudson Street, New York, New York 10014, USA**
Penguin Group (Canada), 90 Eglinton Avenue East, Suite 700, Toronto, Ontario M4P 2Y3, Canada
(a division of Pearson Penguin Canada Inc.)
Penguin Books Ltd., 80 Strand, London WC2R 0RL, England
Penguin Group Ireland, 25 St. Stephen's Green, Dublin 2, Ireland (a division of Penguin Books Ltd.)
Penguin Group (Australia), 250 Camberwell Road, Camberwell, Victoria 3124, Australia
(a division of Pearson Australia Group Pty. Ltd.)
Penguin Books India Pvt. Ltd., 11 Community Centre, Panchsheel Park, New Delhi—110 017, India
Penguin Group (NZ), 67 Apollo Drive, Rosedale, North Shore 0632, New Zealand
(a division of Pearson New Zealand Ltd.)
Penguin Books (South Africa) (Pty.) Ltd., 24 Sturdee Avenue, Rosebank, Johannesburg 2196,
South Africa

Penguin Books Ltd., Registered Offices: 80 Strand, London WC2R 0RL, England

This is a work of fiction. Names, characters, places, and incidents either are the product of the author's imagination or are used fictitiously, and any resemblance to actual persons, living or dead, business establishments, events, or locales is entirely coincidental. The publisher does not have any control over and does not assume any responsibility for author or third-party websites or their content.

WHERE THERE'S A WITCH

A Berkley Prime Crime Book / published by arrangement with the author

PRINTING HISTORY
Berkley Prime Crime mass-market edition / July 2009

Copyright © 2009 by Madelyn Alt.
Cover illustration by Monika Roe.
Cover design by Judith Lagerman.

ISBN: 978-0-425-22871-5

BERKLEY® PRIME CRIME
Berkley Prime Crime Books are published by The Berkley Publishing Group,
a division of Penguin Group (USA) Inc.,
375 Hudson Street, New York, New York 10014.
BERKLEY® PRIME CRIME and the PRIME CRIME logo are trademarks of Penguin Group (USA) Inc.

PRINTED IN THE UNITED STATES OF AMERICA

10  9  8  7  6  5  4  3  2  1

*For Kristy and for Jen . . .*
*for always being there for me,*
*no matter what.*

If our personality survives death,
then it is strictly logical or scientific to assume
that it retains memory, intellect, other faculties,
and knowledge that we acquire on this earth.

—THOMAS EDISON

# Chapter 1

When a person has spent her entire life in the same small town, she starts to think she knows everything there is to know about it. That she has seen and heard and done it all, and no matter what happens, it is nothing that hasn't been seen or heard or done before.

I believed that about my Indiana hometown. I did . . . right up until the day I met my witchy boss, Felicity Dow, and began to discover the truth about Stony Mill's not-so-hidden dark side. Along the way, I also unearthed a few truths about myself.

My name is Maggie—Margaret Mary-Catherine O'Neill, actually, but I'm not a formal kind of girl—and one of my personal truths recently discovered is that I am an empath. A bona fide, natural-born intuitive capable of sensing emotion, both past and present, in the air around me. This means that I have a tendency to pick up strong emotional memories that linger near people, places, and things, whether those feelings are in the physical world or the world of spirit. Memories perhaps better ignored, or even forgotten. Too bad I didn't understand all of this sooner. It would have saved me from internalizing a lot of emotional heartache growing up that wasn't even my own.

And that was only the beginning, as I had been discovering. When I looked back over the last several months, I realized my abilities had been expanding. Whether I liked it or not—which also appeared to be a moot point. And the spirits who were making themselves known to me? I used to think ghosts and hauntings were no more than the products of an overly imaginative mind. Now, I'm not saying I'm psychic. But I will acknowledge that there is something more going on with me. No more sleepwalking through life, blissfully ignorant of the truth about the world around me.

I didn't have that luxury anymore. Things were changing. *I* was changing.

And I wasn't the only one experiencing oddities in my hometown. There were the other N.I.G.H.T.S., of course, a motley crew of ghost-hunting sensitives/intuitives I counted among my closest friends. But pay no attention to all the old stereotypes. You'll find no scarf-wearing, crystal ball–gazing pseudo-mystics here, only normal people living somewhat extraordinary lives. To me, that juxtaposition was part of my friends' charm. It proved one thing—that if none of us were quite "normal," at least we weren't alone in the experience. I, for one, couldn't have done it without them.

My name is Maggie O'Neill—empath, sensitive, and ordinary girl, and this is my story.


Dragon's breath. Well, that's what it felt like, anyway. The air, I mean. The month of June had baked us straight on into July with little respite in the way of rain, and my temper was slowly beginning to fray. Make that fry. Maybe that's why I was in such a black mood as I awoke that Sunday well before the alarm clock's bleeping beeps, the damp sheet wrapped like bindweed around my ankles. The remnants of a dream were still clinging to my cobwebby brain. *A stone building, water surrounding it . . . sunlight streaming down, warm and golden in the crisp air . . . the sky so blue above, as vivid as I could remember seeing it . . . and the eyes . . . oh God, the eyes, paler blue with just a hint of green . . . I knew them well. Whose were they?*

It was *that* dream again, the one I had been receiving in tantalizing snippets. Bits and pieces, flotsam and jetsam drifting through my consciousness time and again. Sometimes months separated the fragments, and sometimes they would be close enough together to actually almost, kinda, sorta make sense. "Almost" being the operative word. The bits and pieces seemed to connect, without being consecutive in any way. More like variations on a theme. It was only after years of having the same recurring dreams that I'd started to put it all together, the narrative of the story my mind was telling. Even then, I didn't believe what it was telling me. Couldn't believe. They were just dreams—what our minds liked to do for entertainment when the rest of the body was shut down for the night. SnoozeTube. They didn't really . . . *mean* . . . anything.

Of course, that didn't keep me from trying my darnedest to catch a glimpse of the face those eyes belonged to. It also didn't keep me from feeling desperately disappointed every time that I failed in my quest.

But that didn't matter. Because . . . "Dreams are nothing to worry about. Dreams are just dreams. Right?"

I posed that very question to my witch of a boss, Felicity Dow, the moment I set my things down and slid into my usual place at the gourmet tea and coffee bar I haunted at my place of employ. For several reasons: one, because as the proprietor of Enchantments, Stony Mill's best darned gift shop and secret witchy emporium, Liss had the best grasp of all matters that lay beyond the realm of normalcy of anyone in town; two, she had voluntarily served as my mentor in all things metaphysical since the moment I walked—er, fell—through the store's front door; three, because a part of me worried I was making too much of things; four, because another part of me worried that I wasn't making enough; and last but not least, five, because if Liss didn't know, who would? A rhetorical question, surely. Especially in this town.

I mean, what was the sense of working for a real, honest-to-goodness witch if you couldn't get the inside scoop on matters otherworldly—or not—when they presented themselves to you?

Lucky for me, Liss didn't seem to mind answering a never-ending stream of semi-intelligent questions from a struggling would-be sensitive. Liss personified grace under pressure. She was the kind of woman who never failed to take life in stride, even when she wasn't wearing the right shoes for the job. This morning she took one look at my pale, washed-out face, dark circles, and the wavy light brown hair that sprang out in all directions no matter what I did to tame it, and immediately set to work pouring out a demitasse of her favorite medicinal potion for sleepwalkers and talkers: espresso, steaming hot, ultracharged, and guaranteed to vaporize any remaining vestiges of cobwebs still clinging to overtired brains.

"There you are, ducks. This should do you some good."

There was something about her British accent that made me feel all cozy inside. It was like an instant shot of the warm-and-fuzzies.

Unlike her espresso. One sip of the stuff was more likely to give me a case of the nervy-and-janglies. I eyed it warily, took a deep breath, and wished it would magickally turn into a cup of Earl Grey on the spot. Still, I took it in hand and lifted it to my lips, determined to give it a try. "Thanks," I muttered around stiff lips—the stiffer, the better with this stuff.

Liss waited politely and made sure that I downed every last, bitter drop. "Now, then. What dreams are we talking about here?"

"Weird ones," I confessed. "Dreams where I'm not me—I mean, not the me that I am now, here, today, but another me. And yet it's still me. Only that doesn't make sense, does it." A statement, not a question. I knew it didn't.

"That depends. Have you been having these dreams often?"

She poured herself a cup of tea. Simple, neutral, non-traumatic tea that soothed one's system more than jolted. I gazed at it longingly as I shook my head in the negative. "Not often. Every once in a while, I guess."

"Is it a recurring dream? One that you have over and over again?"

"Well . . . I have had it—I mean, them—more than once. It seems to be part of a string of dreams that somehow feel as though they belong together if I can figure out how to put them in the right order."

That faint, neutral smile still hadn't left her lips. "And are you always the same you in them, this string of dreams?"

I bit my lip, remembering. "Always. A young woman. Blond, I think, with my hair in a long braid. Only it doesn't seem to take place in the here and now. And that's the crazy part."

"Not crazy. Not if you're remembering yourself from before this life."

That brought my chin up sharply. Not a good idea, when one was nursing a migraine and fighting sleep deprivation. "You mean . . ."

"You suspected it yourself, didn't you? Another lifetime? Another existence? Unless we're speaking of spirit contact through dreams here," she amended, her brow charmingly furrowed in deep thought. "It can at times be tricky to tell the difference."

Another surprise gift from the Great Beyond. Was I ready for this? I didn't even have a handle on the first ones yet. Wasn't being empathic and occasionally telepathic and newly aware of the spirit world enough? "Hm. I'm not sure I like either option. Do I get a choice?"

Liss laughed softly and reached out to cover my hand with her own. Her rings flashed in the focused beams of light from the recessed lighting, tastefully hidden in the rafters over our heads, which made the coffee bar glow like an oasis in the middle of the overflowing aisles. "I rather think we are the chosen ones," she told me, "not the other way around."

I'm afraid the face I made swung a bit toward the wry side of the spectrum. "So that's a no, then."

"Take heart, pet. Perhaps it is nothing more than dreams after all. Maybe there is no hidden meaning. Go with what your instinct is telling you."

That was just it. There was something different about these dreams, something very vivid and compelling that made me remember the details. Enough to recognize the fact that I'd had them before, more than once, and enough to fit them together like so many puzzle pieces. Something about them felt . . . important.

From the floor beside my bar stool came an insistent, chirruping *Merch!* that made me jump. "Minnie!" I leaned down to reach for the soft-sided pet carrier that was my constant companion these days. "I'm sorry, sweet pea. I wasn't thinking. I should have let you out first thing."

"I was wondering when you were going to let our dear girl out of there."

"Our dear girl" would be my beautiful kitten, Minnie, who had found her way into my life mere weeks ago and had instantly taken over. It wasn't just me, though—Liss seemed just as charmed by the little fireball of black fuzz, and had insisted that, as she was too young to spend her days alone in my apartment, Minnie should be the store cat while I was working. She didn't have to ask me twice. Minnie had accompanied me every morning since then and really seemed to be settling into her role. She spent her days learning how to walk on shelves without bumping things out of the way, which windows were best for viewing the birds and passing pedestrians, and, most important, where I hid her litter box. All the vital things in life.

I unzipped the carrier. With another funny meow Minnie scolded me for my forgetfulness as she climbed out onto my lap, all righteous indignation as she arched her back in a long stretch. I ran my hand down her back by way of apology, smoothing the gleaming fur and then scratching behind her ears. My reward was a motorboat purr, larger than life, as she lifted her face toward me. Her bicolored eyes, one blue, one green, sparkled like gems beneath the lights before she took a flying leap from my lap to the middle of the aisle and walked nonchalantly toward the back office.

*One blue, one green* . . . "Maybe that's what it meant," I mused, half to myself. Maybe Minnie's spirit or energy was coming through in the dream as the mystery individual. Maybe the dreams were simply an entertainingly symbolic confirmation that the two of us belonged together, she and I.

"What's that, dear?"

I shook my head. "Nothing. Nothing important, that is."

I was saved from having to answer any more questions when Evie Carpenter and Tara Murphy, our two young protégés and both sensitives in their own right, strolled through the front door. "Hi, Liss! Hi, Maggie! What do we have on the plate for the day?" That was Evie, an angelic blond ray of sunshine with a lightness of being that could rival any daisy blowing in the summer breezes.

"Cool it with the sweetness and light, wouldja, *E-Vil*?" Tara groused, shuffling around the corner of the bar and snatching at the first cup she could find. "I mean, jeez, it gets a little hard to take at the ass crack of dawn."

Evie just smiled and started to hum as she reached down to pet Minnie, who had reversed course the moment she heard the girls' voices and was now circling around Evie's ankles and gazing up at her intently.

The longer I knew the two of them, the funnier I found their differences. Tara was the yang to Evie's yin. It showed in her every aspect. Where Evie's hair was blond, Tara's was dark; Evie's long and free-flowing, with a sweep of bangs over one eye, Tara's shorter and chunky, almost as though she'd taken the scissors to it herself, and actually, I wouldn't put that past her. Evie was a morning person; Tara would sleep 'til two if no one woke her—and would still bite heads off until she got her shot of caffeine. Evie always looked on the bright side of things; Tara viewed the world-at-large as an adversary, ready to be squashed. Evie was all things Light; Tara, her polar opposite, right down to her quasi-emo makeup and predilection for Screamo Rock. But don't get the wrong idea. Tara also had a softer side to her that she hid behind all the hard-edged bluster. She just didn't want anyone else to know about it.

Tara plunked herself down on the nearest stool and rested her head on her hand and her elbow on the scarred wooden surface as she blankly stirred her iced mocha, heavy on the whipped cream. "Late night, sweetie?" I asked her soothingly. She barely lifted her glance in my direction and continued stirring.

"She had an argument with Charlie last night," Evie filled us in as she scooped Minnie up into her hands and settled on the stool to my right. "Because he's not spending enough time with her. I keep telling her that he's just got a lot on his mind right now, what with signing up for college classes next month and work and everything."

Teenage dramas. Boy, was I glad I had grown past all of that.

Tara glared at her. "Thanks for the spill, Evil. Jeez. Like they want to know about my man trouble."

Man trouble. Hee. Oh, if she only knew . . .

Evie pretended to be wounded. "I just thought maybe they could help. Give you some input. A shoulder to cry on. You know."

"Like I need advice from older ladies."

Older? Well, for heaven's sake, I was only twenty-nine. At least for a little while longer. "Oh, I don't know,"

I said, trying not to be insulted. "It's not like I don't remember what it's like to be seventeen. It wasn't that long ago, you know."

Tara gave me a sidelong glance that wasn't so much annoyed as it was completely and utterly dismissive. Which somehow made it worse. "No offense, Maggie, but, um, well, you aren't exactly a shining example in the relationship department, ya know."

Evie had just taken a sip from her cup of tea and spluttered into it. Liss turned away toward the cash register, but not before I caught the twitch of her lips that she was trying so valiantly to hide.

"Exactly what is that supposed to mean?" I bristled, really insulted now.

Tara had the decency to at least appear apologetic. "I'm sorry, but . . . well . . . you know."

And that's all she had to say. That was the trouble. I did know. It wasn't a secret that my most recent foray into the dating world with Tom—Fielding, that is, duly appointed officer of the law and recently named Special Task Force Investigator for the local boys in blue—hadn't exactly been the raging hot success that I had so hoped for. It wasn't even lukewarm. There just hadn't been time. He was busy. I was busy. We both had busy, busy, busy lives . . .

And I was making excuses. And what's more, I knew it. Because every girl in the world knows that a relationship needed to be made a priority in its early days if it was ever going to get off the ground.

And then there was Marcus. Marcus, who had become such a close friend, and whom I had been struggling so valiantly to keep at arm's length. Well, my efforts had been valiant, if not particularly successful. It had been easier when I'd thought him Liss's romantic property. Now, though . . . hm. I guess it was fair to say I was feeling more conflicted than ever. Why had I been struggling so, you might ask? I was beginning to wonder that myself. What was it about Marcus that made him the Kryptonite to my Superwoman attempts to resist my own weakening resolve? Was there something special about him? Or was it more that he represented everything that Tom did not?

Was I being played by my own mixed-up sensibilities?

I turned away so that I couldn't see the sympathy—not pity, never that—in their eyes. Give me liberty or give me death, but for heaven's sake, don't give me pity. I'm much too proud for that. "So, what's on the calendar for today?" I said, changing the subject and making my voice light and carefree.

"Before or after work?"

"After, obviously. Since we're all already here, for actual work, mind you, and Liss is *such* a slave driver."

"So sorry, ducks," Liss sang out good-naturedly without a shred of contrition as she sailed toward the front door to turn the sign over to OPEN.

"Well"—Evie climbed down from her bar stool and grabbed Tara's now-empty cup for a refill before the wannabe-Goth cutie could even register the need—"here's the thing. Tara's all up in arms about Charlie not having time for her—"

"With good reason," Tara interjected in her own defense.

"He's working construction this summer, you know," Evie continued without missing a beat. "So, what we thought we'd do is head on over to the Baptist church out on Wayne Road for the fundraising carnival."

I was following along word for word, but obviously I had missed something somewhere. A fundraiser instead of face time with the boyfriend didn't seem like an acceptable trade-off to me. Because I couldn't stand being the only one who didn't have a clue, I let my bewilderment get the better of me. "Wait, why the church?"

Tara sighed and gave me a look. You know the kind. One that said, *Do we have to spell everything out for you?* "The fundraiser is for the new wing they're adding on to the church," she said, as though I should already have known that.

Still missing something in translation. "*Ooo*kay."

Evie leaned over the counter and looked into my empty demitasse, grabbed it, then slick as a whistle turned to the espresso machine, refilled it, and had it back under my nose before I could say Timbuktu. Or even, no thank you. Urg.

"Charlie's working as a dirt laborer for the construction firm that's doing the job for the church," Evie supplied, helpful as always. "They're all supposed to show up there for the cook-off, and then there'll be a groundbreaking ceremony that everyone else is invited to watch. Most people there will be parishioners, but the fundraiser's open to the public, so it's okay if we show up, too."

Church fundraiser, huh? That hardly seemed like Tara's first choice for a fun Saturday afternoon's hijinks. "So, you're going to check up on Charlie, then? Make sure he's doing what he said he's doing?"

Liss coughed discreetly. "I'm sure the girls wouldn't dream of spying on Tara's boyfriend, ducks."

No, of course they wouldn't. Our strong, hard-as-nails Tara would never stoop to that kind of weakness. Our

Tara would kick 'im to the curb at the first sign of anything untoward. Go, girlpower.

"We're going," Tara said tartly, with an angry toss of her head, "to make an appearance. To show Charlie that he's not the only one with a life."

A life that still managed to revolve around someone else's schedule didn't quite qualify . . . but hey, who was I to judge? I made my tone neutral as I said, "Sounds like fun."

I soon forgot all about the girls' plans as I served a few early customers and Liss and I set about changing the window display at the front of the store. Liss had cooked up a fab idea for something fresh and different that involved switching out the antique furniture and adding in new, wrestling it into place between the two of us, draping and swathing and polishing it to perfection, and sprinkling it with clear white Christmas lights. Tiny fairies, diminutive masterpieces crafted by an English High Priestess of the Fey (known to us only by her Craft name of "Titania of the Woodland Green"), were strung from above, elements to be not so much viewed as discovered. Pretty little treasures. What we were left with was an enchanting Victorian fairyland, more than enough to bewitch anyone whose head was still filled with sugarplum daydreams. And really, what was wrong with that? A little fairy tale never hurt anyone.

We stood back, each gazing in satisfaction at the fruits of our labors. "Well. That turned out even better than expected," Liss said with only a hint of smugness as she wiped her dusty hands on a damp bar towel.

"I most heartily concur, Ms. Dow," I said, finishing off the round of back patting. "How *do* you do it?"

"I was, shall we say"—Liss cast her gaze playfully heavenward—"inspired."

"What do you think, girls?" I asked as Evie and Tara came up behind us.

"I like it," Evie offered.

"You like everything," Tara complained.

"Well, I do. I can't help it."

"It needs more sparkle. Another strand of lights or some glitter or something," Tara assessed casually. "Want me to put the sign on the door?"

"Sign?" I was tilting my head and squinting at the display, trying to see it through Tara's eyes. Did it really need more?

"The CLOSED sign. The noon siren went off ages ago. Didn't you hear it?"

I hadn't. I had been otherwise engaged, blissfully immersed in the artistic process. I glanced at the wall of antique and restoration clocks. Twelve fifty. Goodness. "Well, what are you waiting for? Don't you have places to go? People to see? A boyfriend to put in his place?"

Tara didn't need to be told twice. She was already grabbing her bag and heading for the door. Evie hesitated, torn between following her friend and her devotion to duty. "Don't you need our help shutting down and closing up the shop later?" she asked.

I waved away her concern. "We've got it covered. You two go on and enjoy the rest of your weekend."

The smile that spread over her face was as sudden as a ray of sun breaking through the clouds, and just as brilliant. "Thanks, Maggie. We owe you one." With a last scratch under the chin for Minnie, who was once again hovering underfoot, Evie waved at us and headed off to emulate her friend's disappearing act.

Liss removed the cash drawer from the register for counting. I headed toward the front door to turn the lock with Minnie scampering along at my heels, bat-bat-batting at me all the way. Little minx. I locked the door and scooped her up for a good ear rubbing as I carried her up the aisle . . . or, I would have returned up the aisle if a harsh rapping at the glass door behind me hadn't stopped me in my tracks. I turned to look, only to find Evie and Tara with noses pressed against the glass and hopeful and even, dare I say it, *ingratiating* smiles on their faces.

"Uh-oh."

# Chapter 2

I unlocked the door. "What's up?"

Evie and Tara rushed across the threshold. Evie turned me around and inserted herself under one arm, wrapping her arms around my waist, best-girlfriend style. Tara looked as if she might be thinking of doing the same thing, though in the end she decided to play it cool and let Evie handle all the sweet stuff while she fended off Minnie's relentless barrage of attention-grabbing tricks.

"Maggie? Do you think . . . oh, I know you're busy," Evie fussed, "but maybe do you think you could . . . oh, gosh, it just doesn't seem fair to ask, and if we had any other option at all, of course we wouldn't bother you, but . . ."

"For cryin' out loud, Evie, spill it, wouldja? It's not like Maggie's gonna bite our heads off or anything." That was straight-up Tara, proponent for the fast and dirty approach toward most things in life.

"Oh, I know. Maggie would never do that."

"Right. I try to reserve that for bats and old bosses. And old bosses who are bats," I quipped, laughing.

Liss scurried past us toward the coffeemakers. "What bats are those, dear?"

"Present company most definitely excluded!" I sang out, grinning at her.

"Can we get back to the really important things?" Tara interrupted. "Like whether or not Maggie can give us a ride over to the Baptist church."

Evie sent Tara a reproachful glance for her lack of tact. "What Tara is trying to say is that her scooter ignition is messing up. Again."

"What can I say? Big Lou said it was fixed."

"Which means that we don't have a way to get there today. I don't suppose you'd want to tag along with us, would you? It might be fun . . . Just think. Brats. Elephant ears. Hot fudge sundaes. Frozen lemonade. Cotton candy. All the good stuff."

What did it say about me that all of Evie's offered inducements were food related? Probably not as much as the fact that they were actually working.

Hot fudge. *Hmmmmm.* Talk about food for thought.

"First sundae is on me . . ." Tara just had to up the ante.

"Well . . . I do have Minnie here with me," I hedged, glancing down to where Minnie was playing with the ties on Tara's backpack.

"If you'd like to go with them, I'd be happy to keep the little dear here with me," Liss offered as she wiped down the outside of an oversized coffee vessel.

"Well . . . all right. I'll take you. But no complaints

from whoever has to sit in Christine's barely existent back-seat."

Evie and Tara looked at each other. "Shotgun!" came the simultaneous cry.

Evie grinned. "I called it first."

"Like hell, Evie. I called it before you did."

Before World War III broke out at my feet, I held up my hand. "One of you gets the passenger seat on the way there, and the other gets it on the way back. Easy peasy."

Tara raised her brows. "Easy *peasy*? News alert: no one says that anymore, ya know, Magster."

"Stuff it, Tara!" I said cheerily. Then to Liss, "You're sure you don't mind kitty-sitting?"

Liss scoffed. "Would I ever mind having the little sweetheart around? Go on and have fun. I have a million things to catch up on here. How does that sound, little one?" she asked, scooping Minnie off her feet. Minnie just gazed up at her with trusting eyes, seemingly entranced by Liss's face.

"Good. Great! Thanks, Liss!" Tara grabbed my arm and pulled me toward the office and the back door that lead to the alley parking before I could even give Minnie a departing chin scratch, with Evie bringing up the rear. I pulled my arm free with just enough time to snag my purse and car keys, and within moments the motor of my old VW Bug (long ago endearingly, if not originally, christened Christine) puttered into action and we were on our way. Evie and Tara had played an amazingly speedy game of rock-paper-scissors, a test Evie won to much grumbling on Tara's part. Evie took the front seat without further ado, leaving Tara to crowd into the diminutive backseat with her knees drawn up to her chin. I avoided looking in the mirror, because I could feel the thundercloud emanations rolling from her and I was afraid I would laugh. It's not that I couldn't sympathize, but . . . well, Tara on a rant could be very entertaining.

As we drew closer to the destination du jour, Tara forgot her annoyance with the heat and the tight quarters, even with the jarring ride over bumpy country roads. Her whole demeanor changed with every corn or soybean field we passed, becoming sharper, more focused, more intent as the sky-stabbing heights of an old church steeple loomed between distant treetops on the horizon. The sighting was soon followed by a series of handmade signs along the roadside that heralded the fundraiser one tantalizing word at a time:

*You're . . .*

   *Almost . . .*

      *There! . . .*

         *Who, Me? . . .*

            *Yes, You! . . .*

               *Ice Cream! . . .*

                  *Games! . . .*

                     *Godly Fun . . .*

                        *For The . . .*

                           *Entire . . .*

                             *Family!*

The fallow field next door had been roped off to provide parking, since the majority of the church's regular lot had been taken over by construction crews and heavy equipment. The makeshift lot was filled to overflowing with old-fashioned sedans, a few SUVs, and an extraordinary number of pickup trucks parked willy-nilly in the choppily mown field grass, almost all of them displaying the ultra popular "In God We Trust" specialty license plates to the world at large. Dodging jutting bumpers, I drove slowly through the chaotic disarray of vehicles, searching for a place to berth Christine for the afternoon that would still allow me a way out later, when the girls were ready to make a departure. Behind the roped-off area I could see a number of open-sided tents and tables, even a raised platform with bales of straw set around it in radiating half-circles for a makeshift open-air sermon hall. Fancy.

The old Baptist church that was hosting the afternoon's event was your stereotypical small country church that stood at one edge of what had once been a Depression-era crossroads community that grew up on the fringes of Stony Mill. Time had not been kind to the once-upon-a-time village—homes had fallen into disrepair, the corner store was gone, and the defunct gas pumps looked like something out of *Pleasantville*—but the need for the church had not dissipated in the same way. Instead, the pocket of Stony Mill Baptists had grown by leaps and bounds over the years. Some had stayed faithful to the old-style Baptist preachings of a vengeful God fond of fire and brimstone, and some had split off into other, more lenient factions, but the overall size of the congregation had grown incrementally, thanks in part to the charismatic tent gatherings spreading The Word back in the day. It was a universal truth that people might move from home to home around the county, but few felt comfortable in leaving their church behind and would travel miles, despite the price of gas, to attend their old tried-and-trues. And there was nothing more tried and true than a country church of stark white clapboard, double doors spread wide in welcome at the front, while the bell loomed, little more than a shadow in the towering steeple high above.

"I guess we'll park . . . here," I said, looping into a spot at the very end, which seemed easiest to manage. I had barely shifted the car into park before Tara was pushing against the back of Evie's seat.

"Come on, Evie!" She nudged the seat forward the teensiest bit again.

"Hold on and let me get out of the way. Sheesh!" Evie waited, standing dutifully aside as Tara climbed out. "Wait, don't you want your purse?"

Tara shook her head. "Nah, it'll just get in the way. I've got my cell and some cash in my pocket."

The two headed off like a shot toward where all the action was without even a wave or a backward glance, leaving me to shake my head after them. Ah, youth.

Left by the wayside, I dislodged my purse from the floor behind the passenger seat, dropping my keys into its depths before reaching across the car to roll up the window to within four inches of the top to keep the heat outside from baking the interior, and lock the door. More from habit than because I honestly thought there was a chance anyone might be inspired to steal my beloved, if slightly ragtag, VW Bug. Outside I spritzed myself liberally with aerosol sunblock, then slung my bag over my shoulder and set off idly toward all of the activity myself.

It was hotter than hot out. Hotter than Hades is what my Grandma Cora would have said with one of her trademark grim glances at the sky. The sun was beating down, the few clouds doing little to dispense it. I hurried over to where the tents were set up, not caring what entertainments would be found there so long as they were under cover. First things first: I found a frozen lemonade at a stand right by the edge of the parking lot and handed my money over with gratitude. It tasted a little too much like the kind of powdered lemonade you get out of a can, but the extra-large cup of smoothly ground ice was worth it. I sipped it slowly as I moved around the widespread gathering, indulging my favorite pastime of late: people watching.

And there was plenty of it to be had. One thing about church functions that I always found intriguing was the fact that people remained their usual, stressed-out, over-the-top, unlovable selves, despite the churchy goings-on, which one would think would ensure everyone's best behavior. Good, church-going families, all; and yet everywhere I turned, I saw more than one meltdown in progress. Some of them were even by the kiddos.

Was it the heat that was fraying tempers all over town? Because it definitely seemed to be a trend on the upswing. Just yesterday morning on my way into work, two men at the gas station I'd stopped by had nearly come to blows in front of me. Not over the astronomically rising prices at the pump, but because one didn't move his pickup out of the way fast enough to suit the other waiting his turn. And then there was the flustered call from my mom the day before. Seems she had gone to the grocery store only to witness a woman she knew from her own church group roughly handling her oldest daughter. A woman she had known for years to be the soul of grace and patience. Now, everyone knows that anybody can have a bad day. And teenagers have a tendency to push both boundaries and

buttons. But this was harsh, even borderline abusive behavior, and it upset the applecart that was my mother's
comfortable, small-town existence.

Because these were not isolated incidents. Because it
was happening over and over again, between people not
known to be violent. Longtime Stony Mill families that
were displaying the first signs of splintering and dysfunc-
tion. Normally that kind of thing, when it did happen,
would have been kept quiet. Family secrets better left to
sleeping dogs. Even the Stony Mill Gazette sometimes
agreed with that philosophy, burying select newsworthy
but scandalous local items behind the farmer's report on
page seven . . . but it did publish the police call report reli-
giously. Everything that was called in to Dispatch showed
up on those reports. Who, what, when, where, and why-
dunnit, even if it was as minor as rescuing a cat stuck in a
tree. The information it conveyed was better than a gossip
sheet.

Lately, the call reports had been running . . . long. Very
long. And not with lost pets. Filled with incidents similar
to the one my mother described, like the one I had witnessed myself. So many people, already on short tethers,
snapping for no good reason. Not to mention the deaths—
murders, actually. No wonder I rarely saw Tom these days.
He still had his regular duties in addition to serving as
leader of the special task force that had been created to
coordinate between law departments. That promotion had
guaranteed that any kind of a personal life Tom might have
been wanting to have would have to be put off for later.

Oh, Tom denied this. We'd talked about it before. But
even though he'd said mostly the right things, and even
though he had more than hinted that he would like our so-
called relationship to go somewhere—although the some-

where in question was clearly open to interpretation—the two of us never seemed to achieve liftoff status.

Maybe it was too much to ask right now. Timing, as everyone knows, is everything. History proved that particular Nugget O' Wisdom, over and over again. Knowing it was one thing. Accepting it, well, that was another matter entirely.

It was a sore subject with me, growing sorer by the day. Was it any wonder Marcus and his gentle but compelling flirtatious ways had held so much intrigue for me? Tom told me time and again that he'd like to deepen our relationship, but it was beginning to feel like lip service. And Marcus? Marcus went out of his way to make me feel I was important, without demanding a single thing in return. Everything he did said that he wanted me. But what did *I* want? I was starting to wonder if I knew. All the more reason to steer my thoughts out of treacherous waters and channel them into more calming venues. Deep within me was the sense that change was on the horizon, *must* be on the horizon. It would come whether I was ready or not. Going with the flow guaranteed an easier passing. At least, I hoped it did.

Sipping delicately on my frozen drink and relishing the cold burst of ice and lemon on my tongue, I cast my gaze around me as I wandered along through the makeshift stands. This was your typical, large-scale church money-raising event—all of the usual suspects were here. An ice cream tent that I was going to be making my way back to after the lemonade was gone. The white elephant auction, which was really just a way for people to clean unwanted gifts out of the backs of their closets, and who could blame them? It allowed them to be thrifty *and* charitable all at the same time. The pie toss (whipped cream–lined pie-*tin* toss might be a more apt description) was getting a lot of attention, as was the dunk-the-deacon tank. The poor guy getting dunked looked half-drowned, and boy, I hoped that suit he was wearing had been headed off to Goodwill, because it was a mess.

I moved on. Down the "lane" were more things for the kiddos, or at least the kids-at-heart: duck pluck, three-legged races, pin-the-wings-on-the-angel. Or how about the ever-popular throw-darts-at-the-devil? Just right for teaching the little ones to be ever vigilant in the war against Satan and his dark minions, complete with scary red demon face, horns, and flames. Just in case they weren't sure what to watch for.

Yes, it was your typical church fundraiser. Kids running happily amok, darting here, there, and everywhere, and making valiant efforts to evade the long-armed reach of parental law. Exasperated moms chasing after their sweaty, sticky kids with baby wipes in hand, looking frazzled and a little sweaty themselves as they made equally valiant efforts to collar their rowdy offspring. The dads for the most part let the moms do their darnedest to keep up with the kids while they looked after more important things, like talking sports teams and stats, and waiting for the one event they were actually looking forward to: the soapbox derby. Since it was a church function, the lemonade stand would probably not be offering a spiked variety, no matter how much the dads might want it to. Anything of that sort would have to come later, in the privacy of their own homes.

And I was pretty sure that it would. They might not be able to buy it on Sunday, but that didn't mean no one would partake, just as soon as their kitchen doors closed behind them. Their little secret.

At the end of the main aisle was the makeshift stage I'd noticed when I first arrived; at its center stood a podium with a sun umbrella attached to keep the rays at bay. The stage was surrounded by crescents of straw-bale seating as well as a bevy of collapsible camp chairs in a rainbow of colors. People were starting to filter in that direction as a soberly dressed man in a navy suit climbed up on the platform and approached the podium. He clapped a stack of papers down on the podium's slanted surface and began to fiddle with a microphone on a metal stand. I didn't need anyone to tell me that the man in question was the pastor of the Baptist church; the Bible he'd set down with the papers pretty much clarified that issue for me. This was not the place for me; if the quibbles I'd long had with the theologies taught at St. Catherine's were enough to keep me from attending Sunday morning mass, I certainly couldn't justify a Sunday meeting with the local Baptist assembly to my mother. *Time to back away, s-l-o-w-l-y.* I turned to head in another direction—any other direction—but instead found myself being shuttled along like a dried leaf floating on the currents of a fast-moving stream, taking more steps backward than forward, until I stood on the edge of the circle, receiving more than a few odd looks because I was facing in the wrong direction.

An antiquated sound system let out a rude squawk that made me jump. "Testing, testing," a deep and surprisingly pleasant male voice announced over the speakers. I sneaked a look over my shoulder. It was the pastor all right, all jovial good humor and blushing chuckles as he tap-tapped on the mike with a fingertip and then looked out at the crowd again. "Is this thing on?"

"We hear ya, Pastor Bob! Loud and clear!" some helpful soul from the crowd shouted.

"Ah, good. Thanks, Pete. You all know from worship, I'm sadly all elbows when it comes to technical things. Give me a pulpit and a fair-to-middlin'-sized room filled with a bunch of good-hearted folks, though, and I'm a-rarin' to go." Pastor Bob chuckled and gave the crowd a self-deprecating twinkle worthy of the best televangelist. For a moment, I wondered if he thought of himself that way. A tall man, middle-aged certainly, but still with a spare frame and a good head of hair to keep his age at best uncertain, he spoke with a mixture of warmth and down-home inflection that most people here seemed to receive with equally appreciative amounts of warmth.

"Why don't we just get things started here, then?" he continued in that same, gently humorous way. "For those of you who don't know me"—this received a gentle wave of laughter from the crowd—"I am Pastor Robert Angelis—Pastor Bob to those of you who do—and I'd like to welcome you all to our little get-together this beautiful afternoon in the middle of God's country. Has anyone ever seen better weather?"

It was a question without need of an answer, but of course there were a few catcalls of agreement from the ranks. Thank goodness for those helpful someones. Apparently no one else minded the steam rising from the grass—not to mention from foreheads. God's country was in dire need of a little rainy spell to cool things off a bit, in my humble opinion.

"Here at Grace Baptist Church, as you all know, we have been spilling out of our humble walls for quite some time. Not that we're complaining, mind you!" Another chuckle with a soulful wag of his head. "The good Lord knows, we welcome any and all souls who seek solace from the world within our doors . . . but it has presented us with a few challenges to be overcome. After consulting with the board of deacons and after helpful suggestions from many of you, we've taken a number of measures over the last years to try to accommodate the needs of our growing flock. Nevertheless, as you all know, we have at last come to the decision that we have outgrown our beloved church. Our white beauty. Our country clapboard queen."

Oh boy. It was getting a wee bit deep. Good thing we were outside.

"We already expanded her once, but that wasn't enough. The modern way would be to let her go, to build new and fresh a space that would accommodate all of our needs. But we refused to abandon her," the pastor insisted. "The good Lord didn't give us this sacred haven only for us to discard it when it no longer served our purpose. No, God wouldn't want a thing like that. He'd want us to be creative. He'd want us to be smart. He'd want us to use the brains he gave us, praise his blessed name, to come up with a solution that honored the gift of this old building. And, I'm happy to report . . . *that*"—he punctuated the word by slamming his palm triumphantly against the wood podium—"is *just* what we've done. Thanks to the work of a lot of good, decent, hardworking folk, we are now able to contract for a new expansion of our blessed church. A new wing to mirror the first addition . . . which, if you've seen the plans, will make the architectural layout into a complete Y. Y for Yahweh!" he enthused. "Not only will we have the space we so desperately require, but we will also retain the beauty and integrity of our original sanctuary . . . not to mention the beautiful courtyard garden my lovely wife, Emily, and my mother-in-law have worked so hard to put in. There's a whole lot of love and attention that's been lavished on this place by a lot of people. We are truly blessed here at Grace." He paused a moment to allow the crowd to reflect on that statement, a studied method of attack used to great effect by ministers, politicians, and high inquisitors. "But we're not done yet. We have raised enough to get us started and keep us going awhile, but we have a ways to go. So today, we need you all to dig deep into your pockets and enjoy yourselves. Both. Be sure to take your family to the ice cream social and the various auctions our Bible study groups have put together. Enjoy the music the choir has prepared for you. Enjoy the food. Enjoy the fellowship. Visit the garden. Just enjoy your time here today. Oh, and don't forget, the groundbreaking ceremony kicks off at three, and I'd like to personally invite you all to attend this momentous occasion in the history of our church. And once again . . . *Dig. Deep.*" He rumbled this last and slanted an impish but completely serious grin at the crowd.

A round of applause and chuckles broke out, but instead of climbing down off the do-it-yourself stage, he held up his hands to quiet them all. "Before we all head off into four different directions, why don't we take some time to offer our thanks to the great Father above."

All around me, people started backing up and reaching out to form a series of concentric prayer circles, linking hands. Now it really and truly was time for me to go—I didn't belong there, and it seemed dishonest somehow, an invasion of their privacy and space, to stay. I avoided the reaching hands and questioning eyes of the woman to my left and the man to my right and ducked my head. "Sorry, bathroom break needed," I whispered by way of explanation with an apologetic half smile, then turned and fled. The other parts of the event had all been closed down while the church's pastor had been offering up his take on the day. Where, oh where had Evie and Tara disappeared to? Wherever the work crews were hiding out, if I had to venture a guess. Which would be . . .

I hovered at the edge of the entertainment area, weighing my options. I could hide out in the porta potties—*ew*—or I could go back to the car and wait awhile until it was obvious that everyone had returned to the festivities of the day—*too hot*—or I could set out to try to find the girls.

Guess which one got my vote?

Most of the construction equipment was sitting idle in the church parking lot. I hadn't seen any men wearing grungy work clothes or hard hats around the assemblage, so I had to guess that if they were in attendance at all, as the girls had claimed, they were hiding out up by the church itself. Maybe in the courtyard garden the pastor had encouraged everyone to visit or in a fellowship hall somewhere outside of the afternoon sun. That second possibility was sounding better and better to me by the moment. I made a split-second decision to head that way myself.

I had nearly reached the church's neatly edged walkways when I heard raised voices in the vestibule. Raised and very angry.

*Ruh-roh.*

# Chapter 3

"What do you mean, what the hell am I doing here? I'm working here this afternoon, just as soon as the pastor gives the go-ahead for the groundbreaking. What are *you* doing here?"

"I go to this church. I have every right to be here."

"Well, sounds like we both have that right, then."

"I don't care. I don't want you here. This is *my* church. You don't belong here."

"I don't think you have much of a say."

"Oh, you don't think so? I can have you taken out of here anytime that I want."

"Right. 'Cuz you have connections, that it? *Sheee-it.* Give me a break, Ronnie."

"Why should I give you a break?" the female voice spat. "Huh? Because you say so? I'll give you more than a freaking break, Ty. I'll give you a—" Her last words were made unintelligible by fury and the sound of a scuffle inside.

Enough was enough. I rushed toward the widespread

doors only to see a petite woman who had vaulted herself in attack against a buff young man in worn, paint-smeared jeans, a plain T-shirt, and work boots, and was now being held at arm's length while she swung small, tight fists in his direction. She reminded me of a little bantam hen, squawking and flapping her wings at the big, bad dog threatening the chicken yard. Entertaining, but futile in the end. Neither of the two noticed me.

"Take it easy, Ronnie. Christ!" The man gave her a little push to get her away. "Back. Off! Jesus, there's no reason for this, is there? It's not like our split wasn't mutual."

Ronnie looked as though she were tempted to go at him again, then she seemed to reconsider and stood her ground, three feet away, her arms crossed tightly over her breasts, her face contorted in fury. "Mutual? Is that what you call that? Well, it's mutual now, dickweed. I don't need you, that's for sure."

"What's that supposed to mean?"

*Oh, Ty, buddy.* I shook my head at his dense response. *Don't you recognize when a woman is yanking your chain to preserve her own dignity?*

"Wouldn't you like to know?" Case in point—anyone with ears could hear the self-satisfied smirk in her tone. "But since you're asking . . . I have—what do you call it?—moved on. Onward and upward, I always say."

This situation could go nowhere but down from there. Time to defuse. Where were Tara and Evie when I needed them?

I cleared my throat noisily to alert them to my presence.

Neither seemed to notice.

"Am I supposed to care about the latest asshole you've manipulated?" The laugh Ty gave her was as self-derisive as it was mocking. "Hell, maybe I should care. The poor guy doesn't know enough to run in the opposite direction as fast as his feet'll take him. He will, though. It doesn't take long. We all run away, don't we?"

She swung at him again. This time, I didn't just clear my throat. To give them both pause, I hurried forward and put my hand on Ty's well-defined and quite muscular forearm. He had grabbed the woman's fist before she could connect with him, but had enough self-control not to be physical himself. You had to give him that.

It took a moment before she seemed to register that an intruder had witnessed her indiscretion. The frown glowering on her forehead deepened at the distraction; her gaze drifted left, toward me. With the realization that I was, in fact, there to separate them, she turned her attention back to Ty with an accusing sneer and yanked her arm from his grip. "You have to get a woman to fight your battles for you, Ty? You're pathetic. Why don't you just get on out of here? You're not worthy of walking the ground this church sits on. No woman"—she paused and challenged me—"would say differently, after what you put me through."

Ty-Boy said not a word. He gave her a long, measuring look, then turned on a worn, mud-encrusted boot heel and stalked off. Not toward the exit, as Ronnie-Girl would have preferred, but at least away from her and the conversation that seemed to have run its course. Thank goodness. I don't know what I would have done if things had gotten more out of hand. Ronnie-Girl watched him go, her upper lip still curled in a sneer of hatred and her fists ominously clenched as she followed his departure into the bowels of the church with her gaze.

I cleared my throat again. "Love. It's a bitch, isn't it?"

Her sneer transferred instantly over to me with a whip-like snap. "Get real. It wasn't love. It was never about love."

A hard-edged emotional signature shrouded her like spiny armor. She was as prickly as the proverbial porcupine, and those spines were projecting like crazy, seeking a means to an end. I held my ground, physically speaking, but instantly withdrew my own energy into myself and focused on making myself as small a target as possible, metaphysically speaking. Pulling my energy inward also served to strengthen my personal shields. Bonus.

For a moment, she stood there, stiff legged and stiff spined, wavering the slightest bit from the effort on the tottering platform sandals she wore—not your usual festival footwear. In that instant, I took in all of her, for the first time seeing her and not just her anger. In her low-rise boot-cut jeans and a pair of layered tank tops, she could have passed for any young woman on the go. Her body was certainly just as rocking, athletic with curves. Enviable. But her face didn't stand up on closer inspection. I would guess her to be at least my age, maybe even a few years more world-weary. It was all about the single line between the thin, arched brows and the tight muscle at the jaw. Her skin was passable but not great, a sign of too much partying along the way. And then there were the faint lines along her lips, which also weren't doing her any favors—either she was or had been a ritual smoker, or she held her mouth in perma-pout mode and it had stuck that way. All in all, my impression was of an attractive woman who had seen a lot of the world during her young years and now stood at that crossroads between those years and her future without a clue how to move forward to embrace it. Trying too hard to hold on to a youth that had left her behind.

And she was hostile. Lucky for me, I didn't feel the need to explore that. I pointed my thumb behind me, toward the exit.

"Okeydokey, then. Well, I'll just be going—"

She glared at me again, hard, then—unexpectedly—her shoulders collapsed inward, her entire tough-girl stance melting, and she heaved a sigh. "It was about sex," she confided. "Good sex, dammit. Sex I wasn't quite ready to give up yet. Sex, drugs, and rock 'n' roll. The big three." Her mouth twisted once but only briefly. "But that's okay. That's fine. I don't need him to define me or any of that to make me feel good about myself. I was made in God's image, same as him, same as everyone else. Pastor Bob's made me see that. He's been so good to me. His personal counseling has opened my eyes to a lot of things that I've never seen before. And one thing that I see crystal clear now is that Ty Bennett is a dick and a half, and I was too good for him then, and I sure as hell don't need him now."

She may recently have found God, but I couldn't help thinking it was only a cursory acquaintance. It was hard to reconcile her antagonism with the general Christian tenets of love, tolerance, and forgiveness. But perhaps I was jumping the gun with that assessment. Sometimes any real change in attitude takes getting used to. Like trying on a pair of stiletto heels for the first time—you might like how they look, and you can sure picture the end result, but it takes a good amount of practicing before you can walk around the block in them. Maybe her new-found faith would help her to adopt a forgive-and-forget attitude over time. One could only hope; her smoldering anger was enough to knock me over with its sheer force, even with protective shields in place.

"Well . . ." I offered soothingly, "it can sure seem that way when you're stuck down in the trenches, slogging away at the relationships and feeling like you're never going to luck into the guy you're meant to find. But I truly believe that everything happens for a reason, to help us to grow as individuals, and—"

"To help us grow? By cutting us down and beating our brains into submission?" She scoffed. "I don't think I need growing that bad, honey, but thanks anyway. Pastor Bob says we all have our trials to endure because God's just trying to see how committed we are to carrying on his legacy. He says that I'm doing God's work just by keeping on keeping on. Ty—well, he played his part in God's plan, too. Only too well."

So, her relationship with God was a way of getting over her breakup heartache. An interesting approach, but hey, whatever works. In any case, she seemed pretty up on this Pastor Bob guy. Maybe I'd been too harsh in my first impressions of him, allowing my own issues with organized religion to affect my judgment. Certainly he seemed to have plenty of fans among his parishioners. That had to mean something.

"Sometimes God's plans aren't readily visible to us until later on," I said, reaching into the depths for my own certainties about God, by whatever name he/she chose to go by. Most of my mother's church buddies would consider me a lapsed Catholic at this stage of the Game O'Life, but that didn't mean I didn't sense that there was something, or someone, bigger, grander, out there. The more I gave in to the otherworldly side of myself, the more I knew that to be true. "It's not like he lays it all on the line for us, in notation format and big, bold type."

"Oh, I don't know. Some lucky folks do have their information firsthand from the Lord," she said mysteriously, gazing off over my shoulder.

I was feeling more than a little out of my depths in this odd conversation. Why did I feel as though there was more unsaid than said? Which was saying a lot considering the previous TMI nature of the beast.

I felt my gaze being drawn to follow the path hers had taken. With luck she wouldn't notice me craning my neck to see, since she seemed to be held rapt by . . .

Pastor Bob, who had apparently finished with the prayer and was now walking up the sidewalk toward the church.

He didn't see us. Not until he climbed the steps to the open double doors and glanced up at the last moment. "Oh. Goodness. Hello there. Sorry, I don't mean to disturb—I didn't see you and your friend there." He nodded politely in my direction.

A change came over Ronnie in the presence of her minister. Her attitude, her posture, her entire demeanor softened. Maybe the church counseling *was* having the desired effect after all. "Hello, Pastor Bob. I saw you down there—you were wonderful, as usual. So eloquent. Everyone found it moving."

Pastor Bob ruffled his feathers. "Oh. Why, thank you, I did feel moved by the spirit of the Lord today in the presence of all these good people."

"I always feel the spirit of the Lord when I listen to your counsel, Pastor."

Did I think it was laid on a little thick out at the outdoor auditorium? Perhaps I spoke too soon.

Pastor Bob didn't seem to notice, or maybe he was used to such sentiments from his flock. "Anything I can do for you ladies? I was just heading inside . . ."

I spoke up. "Not me, thanks. I was just trying to find my friends."

Ronnie spoke up, too. "Actually, I was hoping you'd have a moment, Pastor . . ." She smiled her hope, as engaging and polite as moments ago she'd been hostile and fierce. "I could use some advice."

He paused. Hesitated, really. No doubt thinking about all of the details he needed to oversee for the rest of the fundraising event going on down the hill. "Oh. Oh, well, certainly, if it's an emergency. I always have time for those among my congregation who are in need."

"It's so important. It won't take long. Just a moment. Promise."

"Yes. Of course. I have a few minutes before I have to be getting ready for the groundbreaking . . . but only just." I caught the surreptitious glance at the face of his watch, too, before he swept an arm out to point the way.

She simply nodded solemnly and took the lead. I watched the two of them a moment, transfixed for no real reason. Then, coming to, I shook my head to clear the reverie and walked out through the doorway and into the brightly lit and overheated afternoon. Outside, the strangeness that had just gone down within the church doors seemed far and away, as though it might never have taken place at all. I was glad for that—I even stood there in the sunshine a moment, face toward the sky, as the heat burned away the vestiges of negative people energy still clinging to me and trying to find a home. I had lost my will to search out Tara and Evie right away. It no longer seemed imperative, with the prayer session out of the way. And yet I couldn't quite bring myself to venture back into the crowd, either. Maybe I would take the pastor up on his recommendation—to be sure to take a siesta in the prayer garden his wife and mother-in-law had spent so much time on. A little bit of quiet meditation time might be just what the doctor ordered. Maybe . . .

I walked down the walkway and turned the corner, pausing in the leafy, green-hued glow beneath a nice, shady maple tree. Just a hop, skip, and jump away, sweltering beneath the mirage-inducing rays of the afternoon sun, the fundraiser was picking up speed again, getting down and dirty. The white elephant auction was underway, and I had to say, Grace Baptist Church certainly enjoyed a gung-ho congregation, if the bidding wars currently in progress were any indication. It wasn't often that I'd personally witnessed that level of dedication to a community cause, that they would bid so boisterously on the regifting rejects from the back of someone else's closet. No fistfights or name-calling. Just the usual good-natured catcalls, ribbing, and teasing that accompanies organized competition. At least for the time being, it looked to be all in good fun. Still, nothing on earth could have convinced me to bid on any of the items I saw displayed there earlier. One could only assume the rest of the loot being sold was more of the same. Besides the various games, the other most popular experience going on was the father-son soapbox derby on the outer limits of the field. Neither really appealed to me. It looked as though I was going to be done with the festivities sooner than I had thought. Oh well, the afternoon had never been about me to begin with. Maybe it was better that I find a place to pass the time in peace. Peace and solitude. That was much more my style anyway.

I turned my back on the festivities and wandered slowly down the sidewalk that circled the old building. The line of old maples was a godsend, cutting the air temperature down appreciably so long as I remained in the shelter of their shadows. Behind the church proper, in a courtyard formed by an asymmetrical wing, I found the garden the preacher had raved about. It was bordered on the side nearest me by a tall hedge, to my left by the two-story stained glass window in the sanctuary, and opposite me by the oddly placed wing itself. It was unusual architecture, to be sure, but it must have made sense to someone at the time it was added onto the main building. Though, come to think of it, it was probably to preserve the stained glass, which faced the east and the morning light. It wouldn't do to have that covered by new construction.

I stepped forward through the open space in the hedge . . . and found a wonderland. Truly. Oodles and oodles of roses, swaths of lavender and pink baby's breath, soaring spikes of delphiniums, carpets of pinks, daisies waving in the breeze, coneflowers and sunflowers with their offerings of seeds, and more flowers that I could not name. Beyond, even more wonderful roses. The scent was heavenly, the colors divine. I could see why Pastor Bob was proud of this place. His wife and her mother had done an amazing job. A true labor of love.

I wandered along the hedge, for some reason hesitant to disturb the sense of peace within that prevailed despite the shouts and hoots that occasionally carried over from the raucous soapbox derby crowd. There was a bench there, in the shadow of the building beneath the stained glass representation of John the Baptist baptizing Jesus in the Jordan River, even though he knew him as the son of God. There was no morning light now to catch the oddly muted colors of brown and sand and milky blue—the sun had come round and cast a shadow catty-cornered across the garden space.

Mindful of the sacred air of the space, I whisper-walked my way over to the bench and sat down. Here the heat and steam of the day seemed to fade away like a bad memory. It was easy to forget the rest of the world, the rest of town, the breakdown in communications and just plain antisocial behavior that seemed determined to make every month a study in testing the depths of Stony Mill's weirdness capacity. It all seemed a million miles away, and that's the way that I liked it.

After a moment's thought, I reached into my pocket and pulled out the amethyst pendulum I had taken to carrying with me. It had been a gift from Liss a couple of months back, and far too nice to be given away willy-nilly, even though Liss wouldn't listen to my protests. Back then I hadn't known what to make of the gentle tracing of energy that I felt coursing through the faceted point from my first use onward, but with patient instruction from both Liss and our mutual Amish friend, Eli Yoder, it hadn't taken me long to discover I had a knack for this age-old method of divination and self-discovery. I didn't use the pendulum all the time, but I did like to meditate with the amethyst point held in my left palm. The energy of the stone meshed nicely with my personal energy signature and was a pleasant reminder that the natural world existed all around me and resonated through me.

I held it loosely in my palm, wrapping the short chain and balancing bead around my hand. Closing my eyes, I attuned myself to the energy almost immediately. I felt it first as a circular pattern in my palms that soon began to buzz and whir in sensation, not sound. I let the energy course through me, just gave into it to see where it would go. It was a good feeling. Warm. Powerful. The darkness behind my eyelids became more than dark. Black and inky but with a sense of movement. And then, injected into the blackness, colors that merged and blended, one into the other. This was the part of the experience I loved more than anything, this integration of myself into the energies. I smiled as I felt my heart lift. Following closely on its heels was a sensation on the crown of my head, a lightness or a lifting, as though my head and spine were being aligned by a helium balloon attached to my body. Ah, bliss. This was why I had stuck with the daily meditation regimen that Liss had recommended for me. This connection to the universe . . . there really was nothing like it. I could float like this forever.

I don't know how long I had been there, when . . .

"Excuse me. Did you need some help, miss? The heat getting to you?"

I opened my eyes, my moment shattered. Before me, bent forward at the waist with her hands on her knees as she peered at me, was an elderly matron wearing an oversized and frumpy flowered blouse that hung on her comfortable frame. Her round face wore a pinch of concern beneath the wide brim of a straw hat. "Hello," I said unoriginally, because I was somewhat off balance from the unexpected interruption.

"Heat getting to you, dear?" she repeated, her watchful eyes surveying my face closely. "It is another scorcher out, isn't it. I've been fighting it for weeks now. It takes a lot of toting to water this place, let me tell you." She wiped her grimy leather glove over her brow, effectively demonstrating her point and leaving a healthy smear of garden dirt in her perspiration. At her feet rested two large buckets filled to the rim with cool, clear water. "We don't have water access out here in the garden, but luckily we have a washroom at the very end of the hall there. Very handy, that."

"You must be the pastor's . . . mother-in-law, is it?" I guessed.

Her brow lifted. She smiled and quirked her head to one side. Her tight, iron gray curls made her look like an aging cupid. Minus the wings. "Why, yes, I'm Letty Clark . . . but how did you know? Are you new to the church?"

I inclined my head toward the assemblage of congregation to our east. "He mentioned you and the garden just a little while ago. And, well, large groups of people get to me sometimes, so I thought I would use it as my personal getaway. I hope you don't mind. I didn't know there was anyone here."

"No problem a'tall, dear, no problem a'tall. It's rather my own personal sanctuary, too, when I need to get away from the world. Although after today, I'm afraid it will be a bit busier and noisier for the rest of the year. The new wing is going up right over there, you know." She cast a fond gaze around the space that was obviously her pride and joy, then turned her face to the sky. "Beautiful day, even with the heat. Beautiful day."

"I'll say. The roses are wonderful. They're English roses, aren't they? Old style?" My grandfather had been a rose fan, once upon a time before his emphysema had cut short his gardening career. He'd taught me well . . . though he probably thought I'd heard not a word at the time.

She seemed pleased that I knew the difference. "Of course. No French floozies here in *my* garden. Blowzy petals and cheap perfume billowing everywhere? I don't think so. This is a place of worship. These English ladies are elegant and refined and restrained. Perfect, don't you think?"

"They are beautiful," I agreed. "My boss would love them."

"Oh? Is she a gardening enthusiast?" she asked with hope in her voice in the way that all green thumbs perked up at the first mention of a fellow devotee.

"A nature lover in the truest sense of the word." That was even more spot-on than Mrs. Clark would ever know, I thought as I pictured Liss in her high priestess garb, barefoot in the wooded glen in which she worshipped her beloved Goddess. "And yes, she loves gardens. Not to mention, she hails from the UK, so this place would be like a taste of home for her."

A beatific smile lit up her face. "Well, then. You must bring her by some day. Feel free to, my dear, any time you like. Gardens are meant to be enjoyed by those who understand and appreciate them."

We both fell silent for the moment, each in our own personal mind space. A perfectly lovely, soothing, companionable silence.

Which was broken only moments later by the drift of voices from the older branch of the soon-to-be "Y for Yahweh" expansion.

"No. *No!* I won't. Not again." A voice, male tones, but indistinguishable at this distance.

I froze, instinctively clutching my pendulum tighter, and trained my ears toward the building. I know, it was probably obvious, but I wasn't apologizing. If the last year had taught me anything, it was that it paid to stay aware of one's surroundings in this day and age—you never know when something *untoward* or even *abnormal* might happen. A girl can't be too careful. Not around here. Not lately. Besides, my older companion might appear to be absorbed in brushing away the mud from her hand trowel, but I knew without a doubt that she was listening as closely as I was. Her face had gone pale, her eyes darting surreptitiously toward the building, then back toward the tool in her hand.

All the windows in the wing had been opened to catch any stray breeze; the voice could have come from any of them. Many of these older churches still weren't air-conditioned except in the main sanctuary during worship only, and I would bet that was the case here as well.

The response that must have been forthcoming as a result of the man's outcry I didn't hear at all, but it was followed almost immediately by the male voice again.

"No, I'm sorry. You've misunderstood things . . . I regret that, but—" Something unintelligible here, then, "It's not . . . I can't do that . . . No . . . Stop . . . Damn you, stop!"

There was a crash, a shriek—more of indignation than pain, I hoped—and the sounds of a light scuffle. This, finally, mobilized my companion. She opened her mouth without a sound, turned away from me, froze (comically, one foot in the air), turned back to me, burbled, "Excuse me, I think I ought to go check to be sure someone doesn't need me inside," all on one intake of breath, dropped her trowel to the ground, and dashed off all hurly-burly toward the far end of the wing—arms flailing, knees pumping.

I'd never have guessed the old girl had it in her.

For a moment I didn't move. Mrs. Clark was on her way, after all, and I was loath to leave my glen of solitude.

*Except . . .*

Except I couldn't help remembering how swiftly things had spiraled out of control between Ty and Ronnie. And that got me to thinking. Could I be so sure that it wasn't the two of them at it again? Two hot heads could get into trouble so much faster than one . . . and Mrs. Clark was certainly no match for them. If it was them. Or even if it was anyone like them, for that matter. This weather was getting the better of everyone.

I was on my feet even before the decision had been finalized in my thoughts. But instead of taking Mrs. Clark's way, I decided I would take the counterstrike method, entering from the front of the building. After all, there was no telling exactly where those voices had emerged from, and for all I knew, the duo could be on the move.

Time to head 'em off at the pass.

I hightailed it out of the garden, racing toward the front entrance to the church. I couldn't exactly let an aging matron beat me to the showdown. I just hoped we weren't making a huge mistake. Domestic situations could be tricky. Sometimes one's aims toward being a good citizen backfired into busybody-hood. I had been accused of having a nose for trouble before—mostly by my mother, for whom trouble was something dirty to be avoided at all costs—but honestly, what is a girl to do when trouble jumps up and demands to be recognized?

She saddles up, leaps on that bronco's back, and prepares herself for the ride of a lifetime.

And with that thought and an overload of metaphors, I dug my heels in and pushed harder. No one over at the fundraising events seemed to notice me running, hell-bent for leather. Then again, that wasn't necessarily a bad thing. It would at least guarantee the adversaries a modicum of discretion and privacy. That way, even if they were angry for the interruption, maybe they would at least be grateful not to have their dirty laundry aired before the whole congregation.

Surely.

I had only just reached the corner of the building

when I saw a slim female figure run down the front steps, hands swiping furiously at her cheeks as she flew across the parking lot, darting in and out of the idle construction equipment, and heading off toward the crowd of revelers. Within moments, I had lost track of her entirely.

But that didn't mean I didn't recognize her.

Ronnie.

# Chapter 4

I didn't need to wonder whether she had been Part One of the heated exchange Letty Clark and I had overheard from the garden.

I just knew. The same way I knew that the cashier at the grocery store was having an especially bad night with her boyfriend and was on the verge of tears as she scanned my canned goods. The way that I knew when Liss had suffered a sleepless night even before I saw her with the supercharged demitasses of espresso as opposed to her usual herbal teas, healthfully caffeine free. The way I knew when Marcus was thinking things that made *me* feel supercharged with the energy that was pouring off of him. The way I knew Tom wasn't thinking those same things in quite the same, breathless way. I just knew. And as soon as I walked back through the doors of Grace Baptist, I felt the unmistakable, unsettled energy of her passing settle into my very bones as confirmation.

Girlfriend sure had *some* kind of power flowing in her

veins. Unfortunately I was only picking up on the negative. *Big time.* Anger. Resentment. Betrayal. Desire turned
aside. Fierce despair. And more ferociously than all the
others, hatred . . . but turned inward. Only I didn't know
whether she realized that or not, because I felt just as
keenly that it was being reflected from within toward an
outside source.

*Blame.*

The problem with being an empath, with only limited
glimpses at the more concrete facts and details that might
be available to a full-fledged clairvoyant, is, well, feelings are often hidden from the world and might not be
acknowledged by even the most self-aware individuals
among us. At least facts and details could be corrobo-
rated. The only way secret feelings will be confirmed is in
the extreme case of a nervous breakdown, or if by some
miracle the person generating the strong emotion might
for some reason feel compelled to confide. Hey, it happens. More often than you might think. Especially when
alcohol or guilt or some combination thereof is involved.

What that meant in this case is that I could feel the
rawness of the emotions, I could intuit some of the rest . . .
but I was lacking specifics. Like the cause for the uproar
itself. What had contributed to its being? What had
brought things to a head?

Wait a minute. What had brought *what* to a head?

Before I could begin wondering in that direction, I
headed into the church in order to meet up with Letty
somewhere in the middle—assuming I could even find
the middle—but as I paused in the foyer, I was distracted
by the purposeful sound of booted footsteps on the stairs
leading up from the basement.

I turned instinctively toward the sound. Almost immediately a head popped into view . . . followed by a manly set of shoulders. Arms. And yes, the rest was pretty manly, too.

Ty Bennett.

*Interesting.* Squabblers Part Deux?

He glanced at me, looked away, then glanced back. I could have sworn he blushed. "Oh, hey," he said. "I don't suppose you've seen—"

"She's down at the fundraising stuff," I supplied helpfully, quirking my head in the right direction.

He frowned at me, pulling his chin in. "Sorry?"

"You know." I looked around but saw no one, so continued in a low, confidential tone, "Ronnie. She's down at the fundraising stuff."

Again with the blank look. "Oh. Okay. Thanks for the warning."

Was he trying to save face?

"Actually," he continued, "I was looking for the rest of the guys on the construction crew. We were all down in the meeting area in the basement. You know, waiting for the bosses to let us know we were good to go. Cooler down there."

"You were down with the construction crew."

"Yeah. Then I . . . well, I guess I lost 'em."

I squinted at him, not hiding my skepticism.

He grimaced, shifted his weight from foot to foot, then lowering his voice, admitted, "I, uh, had to hit the john."

My cheeks flushed hot. "Oh."

"I guess I was in there longer than I thought."

Well, if *that* wasn't too much info . . . "Oh," I said again.

"When I came out, they were gone. I thought I heard voices, so I came up here to meet up with 'em."

He'd heard voices, too. Maybe he wasn't part of the contentious twosome Letty and I had overheard.

Or maybe he just didn't want us to know that he was.

I couldn't say as I blamed him, were that the case. It's embarrassing to have your dirty laundry aired out in the open. Especially twice in one afternoon, in front of the same nosy neighbor. Not that I was one. Honestly, I don't live anywhere near them. *Ba dum bum.*

"Well," I told him, "I haven't seen anyone else in here."

"Huh. I guess they must have ditched me as soon as I locked the john door."

"Ah. Well, I hope you find them."

"I'd better, or my crew leader'll have my hide. Guess I'll go wait by the equipment. Groundbreaking's supposed to start anytime now, anyways."

Ooooh. Just my kind of fun.

All right, so I'm kidding about that. Really I could think of little less exciting than watching piles of dirt being moved around. It also meant my peaceful little escape in the garden probably wasn't going to be peaceful for long, either.

As Ty left the cool shade of the lobby for the sunstroke-inducing glare outside, I turned my attention back to the selection of closed doors leading off the foyer, wondering how to go about locating the rear wing. *Through the sanctuary? Surely not. Maybe this door . . .*

The door opened inward. I turned the knob and pushed it open, hoping to find a hall stretching toward the rear of the church. To my relief, I did. I also found Letty Clark six steps away from the door, disheveled, pink cheeked, and winded. Startled, I blinked at her.

"Did you find them?" she demanded.

I thought I was surprised before, because finding her there behind Door Number One was just a little too strange, but this question floored me. "Didn't you?"

She shook her head. "No. They disappeared before I got there. Did you see anyone come this way?"

I hesitated only a moment before saying, "Um . . . no. I didn't see anyone come this way."

I don't know why I felt compelled to lie . . . and yet I found the fib rolling off my tongue. Calmly. Without guilt. Because while there was no real reason to keep secret from her the identities of the two people I had witnessed separately emerging from the church, there was no real reason to tell her, either. Because whether I knew them or not, and despite the fact that they had chosen a fairly public place for their battleground, Ty and Ronnie's problems were their business and theirs alone, and I felt they deserved a chance to let the snarling dogs of their emotions settle down on their own. Without expanding their viewing audience by a party of one.

Letty frowned. "I don't understand. They must have come right past you."

The way she was peering at me made me nervous. She was too suspicious for my own good. "They must have been faster than me, I guess. Unless there's another exit from the hall?"

Now it was Letty's turn to pause. Did I imagine the hesitation before she answered? Or just misinterpret it? "No. No exit from the wing, other than the one I came through."

"Hm. It's a mystery, then." To get myself off the hook,

I glanced at the time on my cell phone. "Well, it seems as though the groundbreaking should be next on the schedule."

Letty was still muddling over the missing pair and didn't respond. Instead she wandered away with a vague mutter about "people not respecting the office of the Lord." Truth be told, I was a little relieved. It allowed me to slip away unnoticed.

And I did. Immediately. Exit, stage left.

Back to the throng of fundraisers, in hopes that I could spy Evie or Tara somewhere in their midst.

It didn't take as long as I thought it would. I caught sight of Tara first, standing off to one side of a group of people who had gathered around a plain, unadorned table situated somewhat in the middle of the event. Almost instantly I knew something was up. Tara's dark head was raised, her shoulders back, her feet braced, looking for all the world like she was about to storm the castle. Evie huddled by her side, whispering away, and I saw Charlie there with them as well. He bracketed Tara on her opposite side with a hand on her shoulder and seemed to be trying to steer her away. Without success, I might add. Which didn't surprise me. When Tara had her mind set on something, she was the very definition of an immovable object.

I made my way over. "Hey, guys. What's going on?"

Tara barely flicked her eyes toward me. "Hey, Maggie," she said, her calm tone at odds with the strained position of her shoulders. "You're just in time."

"In time for what?"

"Oh, don't ask," groaned Evie.

"Why not?" I asked, wondering what was over the shoulders and heads of the people in front of us.

"Because I'm about to raise some hell," Tara replied, digging in her toes and straining forward against Charlie's firm grip. "Just as soon as Charlie lets me go."

"Come on, Tare," Charlie urged. "It's not worth it, and you know it."

"Oh, I disagree," Tara sang out with a kind of icy cheerfulness that sent chills down my spine. "I think it's very worthwhile to knock these sanctimonious pricks right on their asses."

"Shhh," Evie hushed her with a quick glance around those nearest. "Someone will hear."

"Maybe they should hear. Maybe then they'd realize what pious little nits they really are."

"I don't think it's going to matter to them, Tare," Charlie told her. "Come on, let's just get away. I'm gonna have to get to work any minute, and you know I can't leave you here if you're all worked up like this. Come on."

I didn't know what had gotten Tara all het up, but whatever it was, I had a feeling I wasn't going to like it. "What is going on?" I asked again.

With a sour twist turning her mouth, Tara yanked her thumb toward the table setup. "See for yourself."

I edged my way closer to the table, squeezing in between broad shoulders, big beer bellies, and baby bumps.

"Are you looking for the end of the line?" asked a stringy-thin, middle-aged woman who looked a little too much like Miss Gulch from *The Wizard of Oz* for my taste. I'm sure she was a nice enough person anyway.

"The end of the line for what?" I whispered back.

"For signing the petition."

"Petition?"

But the woman had moved ahead and didn't hear my

question. I pushed and prodded along until I finally had a clear view of the panel-board sign that said:

GRACE BAPTIST CHURCH, JOIN WITH US!

WE, THE CONGREGATION OF THE FIRST EVANGELICAL CHURCH OF LIGHT, INVITE YOU TO JOIN FORCES WITH US! DARK FORCES ARE THREATENING STONY MILL. SATAN'S FOLLOWERS ARE EVERYWHERE, BUT NEVER BEFORE HAS THAT BEEN MORE OBVIOUS THAN HERE IN OUR OWN BELOVED HOMETOWN IN THE LAST YEAR. JOIN WITH US AS WE STAND STRONG AGAINST THE DEVIL WORSHIPPERS WHO HAVE INFILTRATED OUR MIDST. GHOST HUNTERS AND WITCHES? OCCULT PRACTITIONERS? WHAT'S NEXT? WE THINK YOU KNOW. WANT TO HELP? SIGN OUR PETITION.

Oh my goodness. First Evangelical, the refuge for Reverend Baxter Martin's followers. And I had a pretty decent idea of who they meant by their whole devil worshippers charge. Not good, not good. And if the crowd around the table was any indication of support, this was very, very not good.

Just over two weeks ago, Liss and Marcus had been outed as practitioners of magick by my little sister, Melanie. My own flesh and blood. They had been helping Mel with a little . . . problem of the supernatural kind, and with Mel on pregnancy bed rest per doctor's orders, there had been no other option than to perform the banishing ritual in front of her. We had to protect her and her family from the dark entity that had wormed its way into her home. It was a noble cause, and a successful one . . . until

Mel returned the favor by exposing the truth about Liss, Marcus, and the rest of the N.I.G.H.T.S. to her good friend, and my high school nemesis, Margot Dickerson-Craig. Margot Craig, who was married to the editor of our local newspaper, the Stony Mill Gazette. Margot Craig, who never heard a piece of scandal she didn't want to pass on. It was the worst possible choice of a confidante. And from there the news had spread. It was scary how fast . . . but that was a small town for you.

I backed away nervously. I didn't think anyone had recognized me, but it was only a matter of time before people started putting faces to names, even outside of the Enchantments environment.

*Well, I told you about getting involved in these kinds of things . . .*

It was the voice of my grandmother. My late grandmother Cora, who these days served as the voice of my conscience. She always had, even when she was still alive. I just happened to hear her more clearly than ever now. "Stuff it, Grandma C," I grumped under my breath as I made my way back to the kids.

Tara was still rooted to the same spot with her two bodyguards at each elbow serving to keep her from attacking, rather than the other way around. She had her arms crossed, and with her wide stance and wild, dark hair, she looked a bit like a Celtic warrior of old, energy high, preparing herself mentally for battle. "Well?" she demanded.

I took a deep breath and let it come out as an exhausted sigh. "I saw."

"Well, what are we gonna do about it?"

"*We*"—I looked her hard in the eye—"aren't going to

do anything about it. *We* are going to let Charlie go off and do his job while *we* move on before *we*—meaning *you*—get into any trouble."

Tara opened her mouth, looked me in the eye, saw I meant business, then slammed her mouth shut.

Charlie's relief was huge. "Thanks, Maggie," he said, "I owe you one." He glanced over his shoulder, back toward the parking lot. "In fact, I'd better get going now or I can kiss this summer job good-bye." He lifted Tara's mutinous chin and stared pointedly into her eyes. *"Be good."* Then he gave her a little peck on the mouth and took off like a shot, pulling a beat-up baseball hat out of his back jeans pocket and tugging it down over his head as he ran toward the assembling construction crew.

"Be good, be good," Tara muttered under her breath. "What kind of useless-ass advice is that? That's like saying, 'Go right on ahead and spout your hate wherever you please. Just be sure to floss. Residual hate is bad for your gums.'"

I laughed in spite of myself but squelched it when I saw her face. "Yes, well, sometimes rising above is the only way to stop the hate from spreading. It's not what anyone expects, and it does make them stop and think," I said as I steered the girls safely out of earshot of the people mingling as they waited in line to sign the petition. At least there were others who were passing the petition table by with discomfort etched on their brows, I noticed gratefully. Not everyone here felt the same way. There was solace in that. "Come on, let's go."

"I don't know that they're capable of thinking for themselves, Maggie," Evie murmured in all seriousness. "I really don't. And I think that might be part of the problem. From what I've heard, First Evangelical is lead by a real radical conservative pastor. I know a couple of people from school whose families attend. It makes the Pope's views on sin look weak by comparison."

We made our way up the central aisle. I had to admit, my heart was no longer in staying for this fundraiser. Despite the air of purported good humor, there had been far too many undercurrents of something else off and on throughout the afternoon.

The darkness.

I could feel it still, circling around us, sweeping about on the breezes in the treetops and through the struggling corn in the distant field. Searching. Seeking.

Testing.

Truth be told, it was always there. Some days I did better than others at ignoring it . . . but it was always there. I was starting to come to terms with that. Once I had been certain that Evil-with-a-capital-E was nothing more than evidence of the mind-freak control issues of a certain religio-paranoid populace. I'd thought that Evil Incarnate was something invented to keep people in line or at least toeing it fifty percent of the time. But I'd seen evil up close and personal, and I'd recently been rethinking my opinion. It was the fact that it actually *was* incarnate that scared me. It resided in the hearts of people. People I'd known. People I'd shared a downtown sidewalk with. People I'd driven past on my way to work. People just like my mom and my dad or my next-door neighbors. Regular, run-of-the-mill, everyday kind of people. But unlike most Stony Millers, I didn't think evil had a particular face or name. It wasn't some guy with cheap horns and a snarling mask trying to get you to sacrifice virgins to him. It was far more subtle and insidious than that, and that was what gave it strength. It was a force that simply *was*, is, had always been, and always would be lurking about, somewhere nearby in the shadows.

Where it was going to show its face next . . . that was the question.

I shivered in spite of the midafternoon heat.

"So. Did you girls actually want to stay for the ground-breaking?" I asked, hoping against hope the answer would be no.

Evie shook her head. "I think I've had enough of this place." She turned to her friend. "If that's all right with you, Tare. You don't think Charlie will be too disappointed if we leave, do you?"

"Nah. It'll be fine. We're supposed to meet up later this evening anyway."

"So you pinned him down?" I teased, trying to lighten the overall mood.

"Was there ever any doubt?"

With Tara, nothing could ever be in doubt. She was a force to be reckoned with.

Except when we finally reached Christine, I discovered someone had blocked me in with their rear fender thanks to the angle at which they'd parked their behemoth extended-cab pickup. With another car directly in front of me, I was quite stuck until the owner of one of the two vehicles decided it was time to leave as well.

"What should we do?" Evie asked me.

I shrugged. "Grab some frozen lemonades and go watch the groundbreaking after all, I suppose. Unless you'd rather listen to the testifying at the outdoor podium or take in the soapbox derby extravaganza?"

"As if," Tara sniffed.

"Lemonades it is."

With extra large versions of the frozen treat in hand, the three of us rounded the corner of the church. The construction zone had now been roped off, and a small group of parishioners had gathered at the edge of the nylon cord fence to watch as a hardhat-wearing worker bee waited in the cab of his monster machine for the go-ahead to dig in and get this groundbreaking started. Just on the other side of the barrier, I saw the dark-suited figure of Pastor Bob running here and there as he consulted with the leaders of the crew. When he ducked under the cord and joined a tall, thin woman in the small crowd that had gathered, I knew we were getting down to business.

Thank goodness. The sooner this was over, the sooner I got to go home. It might only be to Minnie and a *Magnum, P.I.* rerun, but things could be worse—after all, I could still be babysitting Mel.

It was always most productive to look on the brighter side of life.

Pastor Bob pulled a portable microphone out of his pocket. "Friends! The time has come! If you've gathered with me and Emily here today, then I thank you for sharing this momentous occasion with us. It's certainly a special day, and I know that we all thank the good Lord for allowing us the means to tend to the needs of our flock in this way." He bowed his head for a moment as though overcome with emotion . . . but why did I get the feeling it was mostly for effect?

*Cynicism, Margaret, is never becoming in a young woman . . .*

Grandma C was in rare form today.

*And neither is snark, missy.*

Sigh. Trouble was, Grandma C was probably right.

My first impressions of people can often double as spot judgments. Pastor Bob was flamboyant, but that didn't mean his heart wasn't in the right place.

"Would anyone else like to say a few words?" Pastor Bob was asking.

I held my breath, but no one stepped forward. Thank goodness. Much longer in this heat and I was either going to have to purchase yet another frozen lemonade or else go 'round and chase down the perpetrator of that bad parking job myself.

"No? That's fine, that's fine. I'll just give the crew the go-ahead, then, and we'll get this show on the road." He snapped a smart if somewhat dramatic salute toward the work site foreman, who in turn spoke into the walkie-talkie in his hand. The end result was the sudden roar and deep rumbling of the payloader as the operator started up the engine. Around us, members of Pastor Bob's flock began extending their hands to each other and swaying back and forth as the familiar strains of a hymn began among them. Drawn by the thunderous growl of the machine, or perhaps by the hymn itself, the crowd around us also swelled.

Evie and I kept our heads together and our hands molded around our cups (ooh, frozen fingertips), our lips surrounding the plastic straws. Tara, on the other hand, crossed her arms and stared down anyone who got too close.

That's my girl.

Everything went really well for a while. The big earth-moving machine made quick work of the first couple of strips along the crust of the ground, to the cheers and high-fiving of the crowd. Push, scoop, reverse, re-situate. Laborers and backhoes stood at the ready, chatting good-naturedly amongst themselves and waiting to really get down to business.

"Everyone knows the crew has a lot more to do with the grading of the site and all," a short, squat, motherly type with a freckled upturned nose told me. "But Pastor Bob told 'em to give everyone a show, just to make things fun for everyone."

I smiled and nodded politely. A show, huh? I supposed it made little difference to the construction crew. They got paid either way.

But I'll bet the unusual crunch that came next as the rear of the payloader dropped down suddenly sure as heck didn't make their day.

"What the—?"

The payloader's rear was cocked at a strange angle, with one tire lower than the other. Its rear wheels spun, throwing clumps of crumbling dirt every which way as it sought purchase in the newly exposed earth. In the next instant, the entire construction crew burst into action. The operators manning the idling machines shut them down and leaped from their high perches in the same motion, hitting the dirt running. The laborers, Charlie included, threw their shovels and other implements to the ground and met the operators in the middle, where the payloader was still struggling.

Everyone around me was whispering together. Pastor Bob looked on at first in confusion, then concern, as he realized that the crew had encountered the unexpected. He said something to the thin woman next to him, handed her his suit jacket, then ducked under the cord barrier, rolling up his sleeves as he hurried toward them.

"What's going on?" someone in the crowd shouted out.

"Need any help, Pastor?"

Pastor Bob waved his hand to turn down the offer but kept going until he stood beside the crew foreman. While the foreman shouted terse orders into the radio to the operator on the payloader, with the crew on standby, the minister shuffle-hopped from foot to foot like a boy waiting for permission to use the bathroom.

Taking advantage of my attention being fixed on the scene unfolding before us, Tara ducked the barrier and ran over to Charlie's side. I opened my mouth a moment too late to catch her, nimble minx that she was. No one except Charlie seemed to notice her there, and Charlie had little success in waving her away.

I watched on, riveted by a sudden overwhelming sense that there was something out there, something major.

"Outta the way, boys!"

With a little fancy footwork and maneuvering and a spurt of movement that made the payloader's rear end scramble, the machine operator finally righted the rig. The machine bucked to one side, making everyone jump back, too, before it became obvious that the operator had everything under control. He shut it off and jumped down out of the cab. In an instant, the entire crew had surged forward and formed a circle around the trouble area.

"Whatcha got there, Pastor Bob?" bellowed a big-bellied man in an outdated Hawaiian shirt that was as loud as he was.

"I don't think he heard you, Ned," another man laughed to my left. "Say it a little louder, why don't ya?"

Ned obligingly put his hands to his mouth. "WHAT-CHA GOT THERE, PASTOR BOB?"

I don't think Ned did sarcasm.

"Is anyone going to tell us what's going on?"

The crowd around had grown larger as more people

drifted over from the other areas, drawn by the noise and the tension.

"I think they've forgotten about us," a freckled woman with a strong, Southern-ish twang fretted.

"Well, what's saying we can't get a closer look?" someone else asked. "I mean, they're not digging. There's no machinery runnin' . . . So?"

Evie and I looked at each other and shrugged. So, indeed.

In a flash the barrier was set aside and the crowd stumbled forward over the rough ground and unrazed hillocks. We descended upon the work crew like a swarm, driven by curiosity to the area the men had not moved away from and still seemed to be surveying in bemusement. Evie touched my arm and pointed to Tara, standing there among the men. The two of us worked our way to her side.

"What is it?" Evie whispered, stretching up on tiptoes and craning this way and that.

She was too short to see over the shoulders of the two men in front of her. I was at a slightly better vantage point to see the hole, three feet across, where the machine's weight had broken through the crust of the earth . . . and the blackness yawning away beneath it.

"Oh, wow."

"What on earth . . ."

"Is it—"

"Maybe it's a cave!" an excited kid cried, visions of treasure no doubt dancing in his head.

"Everybody stand back!"

"Whaddaya think, a sinkhole, maybe?"

Sinkholes were common in the area, most occurring when pockets in the limestone base that made up the bulk of the area's foundation collapsed inward upon themselves due to the continuous trickle over time of groundwater. They were a problem for some, difficult to control once the sinking had begun. But this . . .

"Here's the flashlight you wanted, boss man."

One of the guys had retrieved a high-powered beacon from his pickup truck and slapped it into the hands of the crew foreman, who immediately got down and laid himself flat on the dirt, heedless of any damage to his plaid cotton short-sleeved shirt or jeans. He slid toward the edge of the hole and reached his arm down over and in. "What do you see?" he asked the members of his crew standing closest. "Anything?"

"Nothin'," someone responded. "Can you hang it down in there farther?"

Unfazed, the foreman scooted even closer on his belly and risked life and limb, in my opinion, to look down inside. Air was swirling up out of the hole—I felt it on my face. Dank. It made my stomach clench.

"Well?" Pastor Bob said urgently. "What is it? What's down there?"

"Huh." The crew foreman rose up on all fours, then pushed upward to his feet with an athletic thrust. He tucked the flashlight under his arm and briskly dusted off his hands. "Reverend . . . I think you got yourself a problem."

The throng of parishioners leaned forward as one. Avid curiosity burned on the overheated airwaves, a mirage form of thought and speculation.

The tall, pale woman who had stood by the minister's side and taken charge of his suit coat only moments ago appeared just as suddenly by his side now. "What is it, Bobby? What's down there?"

The pastor shushed her and turned toward the crowd.

"If you all don't mind, I think it might be a good idea for you all to go on now. Just go on about your business, have some more fun at the events across the way, and let me take care of this with the work crew."

"Aw, come on, Pastor Bob. It's our church, too."

At the murmurs of agreement all around, he relented. "All right. Let's have it, then, Tim."

Tim the Foreman looked him in the eye. "Oddly enough, it looks like a buried room. A shelter of some sort. Maybe a storm cellar."

Pastor Bob's breath came flooding out, a chortle of relief. "Is *that* all? Phew. I thought maybe it was something serious."

Tim nodded matter-of-factly, his expression otherwise neutral. "The question of the hour is . . . why was it covered over?"

Pastor Bob froze, his brow furrowing. "Why—"

"And then my next question would be, why are the walls and ceilings covered with crosses?"

# Chapter 5

Behind them, dirt and rock suddenly sprinkled down into the unseen space below. I froze. For a moment, I thought the ground below our feet quivered, and more air came rushing out, no doubt as a result of the falling debris.

Evidently I wasn't the only one with worries. One of the men leaped into action, waving his arms at everyone. "Back! Everyone . . . get . . . back!"

There was a frantic scrambling, punctuated by a couple of screams as people let the fear go to their heads. Some took off running for the safer ground of the fundraiser, some for their cars. A few intrepid souls stayed where they were. As much as fear tended to stifle curiosity, for some, curiosity was just as remarkably effective at stifling fear.

Tim the Foreman rocked into action. "Troy, I want you and Mike to rope off this area. I want it to be completely protected. No one goes near the area until we know exactly what we are dealing with here." He tossed an apologetic glance toward the minister. "Sorry, Reverend, I don't mean to rain on your parade here, but until we can assess the situation, I'm afraid that we're not moving ahead with the work today. No tellin' what else we might find out there. I'm gonna have to get an engineer out to assess the structural situation at hand, and I'd like to get someone out here with a small sonar reader, just to be sure we're not going to run into any more surprises like this one. I, uh"—he paused delicately—"I expect you're going to want to have a look at that room once we've determined it's safe."

"I . . . yes."

"In the meantime, we're gonna have to declare the site sealed."

Secret rooms covered in crosses . . . ooh, scary. I would have loved to have stuck around—you know, for curiosity's sake—but there was no hope to that end. The buried bunker was a guaranteed lost cause for the rest of the day. The girls and I waved to Charlie, knowing it would be a while before he was released by his foreman. Tools to put away, machinery to secure. We made our way out to the temporary parking lot in the field and back to Christine to compare notes.

"Should we leave, do you think?" I asked.

"I don't know about you, but I'm done," Evie said. "Tare?"

Tara was still gazing back toward the church and the construction site. "Did you guys feel it?"

"Feel what?" Evie asked. "The cave-in? I felt it. The ground trembled. My stomach dropped to my toes. We're lucky no one was hurt here today. It could have been so much more than just the payloader wheel breaking through."

"It wasn't just a cave-in," Tara stated flatly. "Maggie, what about you?"

I thought back. It had all happened so fast, but . . . "There was something," I said, remembering. Or at least, I thought I did. "I felt . . . a rush?" I was searching for the right word and not finding it. "Air moving past me. Like wind, but not."

"Yeah. Like a *whoosh* of something, right after the guy stuck his arm in there with the flashlight."

"But you don't think it was just air?" I knew the answer to that even before I finished the question.

"No. Do you?"

"Well, I don't know. I wasn't really thinking about it."

"Well, turn your brain back on again for a sec," Tara groused, "because I think I'm right."

That's our Tara. Always the diplomat. "Fine. So if you don't think it was air, or a cave-in, what *do* you think it was? Energy? Spirit?" I was just joking for the most part, but the look on Tara's face stopped me in my tracks.

"Yeah," she said in a flat tone. "I do. But I don't think it was a nice one, whatever it was."

I didn't want to believe her, but how could I not? I'd felt the rush myself. The vibration. I had just preferred to see it as natural at the time. Now that I thought about it, I couldn't believe I didn't pick up on it immediately myself. "What about you, Evie?" I asked.

She shook her head. "But I could try, if you want me to."

Tara looked at me. "You know, it wouldn't hurt any of us to do a little bit of psychic digging. Whaddaya say, Maggie? Care to try it and see what we find out about that hole?"

I was a little nervous about that look in Tara's eye. Tara was the adventurer in our little group of metaphysical wanderers. Our very own little no-holds-barred, take-no-prisoners general of occult exploration. Whenever she was all set to jump right in, that was a good indication it was time to take a step back and consider the situation a bit longer. But Evie answered before I could.

"Well, okay. Only . . . not here. I think I'm getting a little bit tired of all this sunshine. It's giving me a head-ache."

"You, tired of sunshine?" Tara teased.

"Where to, then?" I asked.

Tara met my gaze. "How 'bout your place?"

"My place. Right. What . . . *exactly* . . . is this little explorative venture going to entail, Tara?"

"Oh, a little of this, a little of that. Why? You scared, Fluff?" she said with a grin.

Fluff. As in Fluffy Bunny, her favorite gibe when it came to me, not very kindly referring back to those of Pagan faiths who focus on all things light and, well, fluffy, to the exclusion of all else. A bit like the Pagan version of being scared of the dark. She was right. I was a little afraid of the dark, and yes, I did tend to try to focus on keeping things light in my life, wherever possible. But that didn't mean I didn't think it merited attention. I just preferred not to address it to its face if I could help it.

And was that so bad? But then maybe I was just con-fusing myself. Polarity of all kinds—light and dark being just one—is the nature of the beast, the circle come 'round and back again. I believed that. It was one thing I could believe in, without the least bit of ethical struggles or logical concerns.

Tara and I weren't so different really. We just had different approaches. Different comfort levels.

"Not scared, no. Just . . . cautious," I told her. "You get that way once you get to my age. Sad fact of life actually."

She tossed her head, superior with the confidence her age allowed her. "Boldness in life is for the young."

"So is learning from one's mistakes," I reminded her sweetly.

She stared me down, all dark-eyed glower and teenage bluster . . . then broke out in a sheepish grin. "Yeah, *whatevs*," was her good-natured reply. "So are we gonna do this or what? I got a little time to kill before meeting up with Charlie *latahh*."

I didn't have much of a choice . . . but then, what else was I going to do with the rest of my afternoon? "Who gets the front seat?"

That would be Tara, and she wasn't about to let Evie forget it. She had her hand on the thumb-button door latch before the question had finished rolling from my tongue, an evil eye at the ready should Evie attempt to usurp her rightful place. She needn't have bothered. Evie wasn't the type to overstep her boundaries. She took the backseat without comment, easing in with the grace of a ballerina.

Outsiders witnessing the entire exchange might have seen Tara as overbearing and even rude, but those of us in her inner sphere knew her for her fierce loyalty to her friends and family, her willingness to stand up for what she knew was right, her steadfast dedication to justice. She really *was* the modern embodiment of the Celtic warrior princess of old. She also had a wicked good sense of humor that evidenced itself when you least expected it.

Between the two girls, one might perceive Tara to be the leader, but I'd seen her follow Evie around, avidly listening as they compared notes on their metaphysical experiences and abilities. There was a level of mutual respect and trust between them that was really nice to see in teenage girls these days. I'd seen worse—far worse. And so had Tara, poor girl. It made me glad that she and Evie got along so well.

Every girl needs a true BFF.

The ride home to my place didn't take long. We stopped off first at Enchantments to pick up Minnie, who had firmly wrapped Liss around her furry paw by plastering her soft little body across Liss's shoulders. My shameless baby hussy. Liss was on the phone when we got there, so I knew I wouldn't have a chance to fill her in on the afternoon's events.

"Well, that's just wonderful, darling. I'm so proud of you." A pause during which she winked and waved at me, then, "You know, if you're looking for a new site to study, you could always come to America. I'd love to have my favorite nephew under my wing for a while, and then there has been all of the activity here that I've been telling you about. Mm. Well, just think about it. Yes, I'll keep you posted. Now, tell me about that young research assistant of yours. Don't play coy, it doesn't work with me, remember?"

I undraped a yawning Minnie and tucked her in the crook of my arm before blowing a kiss of thanks toward Liss and tiptoeing out the door. Minnie settled in for the ride on Evie's lap, sprawling in the carefree, utterly relaxed way that only very young creatures of all kinds can master. The girls were hungry, so we decided to order in pizza once we got to my apartment. Ten minutes later we were pulling up in front of the aging Victorian on Willow Street. Just me and my two—just then, Minnie lifted her head and gazed at me with reproachful, bicolor eyes—er, make that three shadows. I lead the way around the side of the house to where the sunken steps to my basement apartment could be found.

Tara eyed the stairs with surprise. "You live in a basement?"

I fought the urge to apologize or explain. It was what it was. "Yeah."

"Cool."

I let us into the apartment and reached inside for the wall switch before entering. "Let there be light." One of the quirks of living in a basement apartment: you always had to have a lamp burning, no matter what time of day it was. "Home sweet home. Come on in."

Evie set Minnie down. Minnie ran straight for the cupboard where I kept her food and sat down, giving me her "urgent eyes." "What, are you hungry, girl?" I asked. When I didn't move forward right away, she rose up on her hind legs and pawed at the cupboard door, then sat back down and repeated the process. "All right already. Keep your fur on."

"Does she do that every time?" Evie asked.

"Pretty much. Unless she decides she'd rather have what I'm having, in which case she won't touch her kibble. She plops herself on my lap and tries to work out which way she needs to preen for premium cuteness."

Minnie rolled over on her back at that, paws poised just so, inviting anyone and everyone within to come over and pet her, and maybe, just maybe, feed her, too. She knew how to work it.

"So, girls. Have a seat, have a look around, whichever

you'd like. I need to check messages. It's a little early for pizza, but if you want to decide on a place to order from—"

"Giovanni's. Defs," Tara opined, sliding her finger along the books and magazines atop my bookcase. "Best deep dish I've ever had. Almost better than chocolate."

"Better than making out with Charlie?" Evie teased, peeking into the fridge. I hoped I'd remembered to clean it. Ah, well. She'd live.

"Let's not get too carried away," Tara objected with a giggle that was delightfully, if atypically, girly. She plopped herself down in my favorite chair.

"Well, at least you've got your priorities straight. I on the other hand can't manage to get a decent date." Evie sighed.

"Oh, I can't believe that," I scoffed. Evie? Blond, beautiful, smart, delicate Evie? It was absurd. What teenage boy wouldn't be after that?

I punched the button on my answering machine to play the messages that were blinking there. The machine was on its last legs, taking forever to initiate the message list. I couldn't see throwing it out and buying new, though, not until it was done for. Midwestern frugality, I supposed. Then again, it had been on its last legs for two years. At this rate, I might never be rid of it. Some of these ancient hand-me-downs lasted forever.

"It's because she doesn't want the ones who are interested in her, and because the one she's interested in won't even look her way."

"Ta-*ra*!"

"What one?" I asked, looking at Evie in a new light. "You haven't mentioned anyone to me. I'm hurt."

The machine beeped at last. "Hello, Margaret, it's your

mother calling. I didn't hear from you yesterday, so I thought I would check in with you and make sure that everything is all right. You know I worry if I don't hear from you. Your sister's home nurse is working out well. I'm disappointed that the two of you didn't use this time to bond more closely together, but at least I know that she and the girls are being well taken care of. I of course am still visiting every day; I would hope that you could find it in your busy schedule to visit as well. She is your sister after all. How is the job search coming along? Well, that's all, dear. Your father sends his love. Grandpa said to tell you that his blood work came back right as rain. He's been chasing after the widow woman across the street in his wheelchair again. She's twenty years younger than him at least. I think he scares her. That man." She sighed, long-suffering and exasperated. "Well, good-bye, dear."

That was my mom for you. At least she hadn't inserted a question about my love life. Such as it was.

"Job search?" Tara asked, narrowing her eyes at me in sudden suspicion. "What's that supposed to mean? You ditching Liss at the shop?"

I shook my head. "Of course not. It's just my mother. She thinks she can strong-arm me into giving in to her need to control my life. She was none too happy to hear about Liss's and Marcus's forays into the occult."

"Thank goodness my mom works in the city," Evie said. "She doesn't hear much in the way of gossip; she's too deep into her spreadsheets, even when she's home." She'd found a tub of Ben & Jerry's in the freezer—Cherry Garcia, the real thing, not frozen yogurt—and was now feeding driblets of it to Minnie with her pinkie, in between spoonfuls. "I like your grandpa, by the way. He's just a big, lovable goofball."

I grinned. "I'll let him know you said so. He'll be thrilled to know he's conned yet another pretty young thing into thinking he's harmless. Now, back to this so-called 'one' . . ."

Evie blushed.

"Never mind, Evester. Maggie's hardly one to talk."

I was more than used to Tara's taunts, but I pretended to be affronted. "I beg your pardon."

"She has Marcus following her around like a puppy dog—"

Marcus was hardly a puppy dog . . .

"—and she keeps wasting her time with Deputy Iron-britches himself instead."

*Ironbritches?* Just who'd been bending her ear? And how in heaven's name could they know that we'd never . . . that he hadn't . . . that we . . . "I'm going to assume you mean that in a completely complimentary way," I said, my cheeks flaming.

"*Whatevs.* We all know you haven't been getting any, Maggie." Tara looked supremely smug. "It's written in the angst on your face."

"Yes, well, my love life"—*or lack thereof*—"is none of your business, now, is it."

The machine beeped again. "Hey, Maggie. It's me." *Tom.* My eyes widened, and then I cringed. *Too late to stop the machine now.* "Hey, I guess you're out. Just my luck. I feel like I haven't connected with you in days. I know, my job, my fault." He sighed. What was it about people sighing into my answering machine lately? I was beginning to feel like Debbie Downer. "I guess I'll try you later if I get the chance. Okay. Bye."

"See what I mean," Tara whispered to Evie. "Not exactly Mr. Hot Stuff, is he?"

I turned away, smarting as much from the message as from Tara's blunt assessment. "I'll just look up the number for Giovanni's."

Behind me I heard an indignant "Ow!"

"You hurt her feelings!" I overheard Evie whisper. I missed Tara's reply entirely as I busied myself digging through my junk drawer for the little-used phone book. It was probably for the better.

The answering machine beeped a third time. I could have sworn I'd seen only two lights blinking?

"Maggie-May-I." My heart fluttered against my will. It was Marcus's voice coming across the old machine, deep throated and full of the kind of promise a girl longed for in her wildest daydreams. "Sorry I haven't been around much the last week or so, sweetness. Things got busy, and actually . . . well, I've been filling out paperwork. Uncle Lou has finally convinced me to start back with college courses again this fall, and I have a lot to do to catch up with the admin stuff. The band . . . it pays the bills for now—well, that and my knife sales—but . . . I guess it can't last forever. So. Yeah. Going back for my degree when classes start up again. Wish me luck." He paused as though weighing his words and thoughts. "I'll call you again later. I was hoping . . . I'll just call you later. Talk to you."

At least there was no sigh attached.

Now it was my turn to blush—which I did . . . furiously—as I flipped through the Yellow Pages. I cleared my throat. "*Soooooo*, Giovanni's." I peeked over my shoulder at the girls; I couldn't help myself. As expected, waggling eyebrows, times two. "Oh, for heaven's sake, stop it."

Tara smirked. "I rest my case. If you were actually getting some, you wouldn't be so defensive about it. Iron-britches or my cousin. Which one would I choose? Hm, hm, hmm." As an afterthought, she revised that: "Assuming in that situation that Marcus wasn't actually related, o' course."

Of course.

Without a pause for breath, she asked, "By the way, got any paper?"

Grateful that she was at least off the subject of my love life, I handed her a pad of sticky notes and a felt-tip pen. "Here you go. What do you girls like on your pizza?"

"Everything!" Tara said.

"Cheese!" Evie said at the same time. With a deferring glance toward Tara, she amended, "But I can pick everything off with no problem."

I laughed. "Gotcha. One deep dish with everything, coming right up." I placed the call, arranging for delivery. It was a little on the early side for dinner and on the well past for lunch, but teenage stomachs didn't seem to work on the same timetable as their adult counterparts.

Hanging up the phone, I turned around to find Tara and Evie kneeling on the floor on either side of my coffee table. Spread out in a circle were the letters of the alphabet, the numbers zero through nine, and the words "yes" and "no."

"Okay," Tara said, brushing off her hands in the universal gesture of a job completed and a job well done. "Now all we need is a glass. The table is nice and slick, and no seams, so it should work out fine."

"A homemade Ouija?" I knew my face was reflecting my skepticism, the experience with Mel fresh in my mind. "I don't think . . ."

Tara headed toward the kitchen and grabbed a wineglass from my under-the-counter rack. The cut glass goblets had been a gift from Grandma Cora, back when I graduated from high school. "For your hope chest," she'd told me at the time. Grandma C had always been big on gifts for the old hope chest. Never mind that at the time she was giving wineglasses to someone who couldn't yet legally drink.

Tara waved away my concern. "It's no big deal. Is it, Evie?"

I turned my gaze on Evie, who blushed. "Well, um, I . . . I don't think it's going to hurt anything, honestly, Maggie. We have the three of us, you know, in case any-thing negative tries to get through, and we all know what we're doing . . ."

"You've done this before, you two? Together?" I knew Tara liked to play with the Ouija, but I had no idea Evie had been playing with it as well.

Tara shrugged off my question. "It's no biggie. Really. There is nothing to worry about. Come on, Maggie— would I lie to you?"

Did I have a moment to think about that?

I could "just say no" . . . but I had a feeling if I did, they would just go off and Ouija by themselves. At least with me there keeping a watchful eye, things couldn't get *too* out of hand.

I plopped down on the sofa and folded my arms. "What do you want me to do?"

"Well, for one thing, you can get rid of any bummer energy you've got goin' on," Tara said with a measuring glance. "Loosen up, for the god's sake. It'll be okay. *Trust.*"

Somehow I found it hard to trust my spiritual well-being to the willful actions of a teenager. Sue me.

"All right, have it your way." I closed my eyes, shook my head a little bit and shook my hands at the wrists, letting my breath huff out of me. It might look goofy, but it was a tried-and-true method that worked like a charm. With a last purposeful swipe down the length of each arm, I opened my eyes again and tried a smile. "Better?"

Tara shrugged. "It'll do. Put two fingertips on the glass. You, too, Evil."

"Just like with the pointer, I'm guessing?" said Evie, complying.

"'Xactly. Now center yourselves. Find your place. Just like when you're meditating. Now, I'm going to ask my Guides to protect me from any and all negative influences. You can do the same either out loud or mentally; makes no difference either way. Both ways work."

I most fervently and earnestly requested protection from my Guides. Other than with the pendulum, I'd not been in contact with them on a conscious level, but I had no doubts that my Guides—or angels, if you prefer—were in fact an influence on my life. They were out there somewhere, working away in the background. I was still trying to figure out how to work with them, or how to step aside completely and let them do their job without me mucking things up.

"Everyone ready?" Tara asked.

"First question: who is Maggie here going to marry?" Evie asked quickly with a grin and a giggle. Obviously she was less worried about the use of the homemade board.

"Well, that wouldn't have been *my* first question, but . . . *whatevs*."

The glass zipped smoothly to the letter M.

"Very funny," I said wryly. "Which one of you pushed it?"

"Not me!"

"I didn't push anything," Tara said indignantly. "No

one better be pushing the glass. The whole point of this is to be able to trust the response as not coming from us, *capisce*? All right, then. We will skip Evie's nosy-ass question, since it has *nothing whatsoever to do with the church weirdness*. Sorry, Eves. No offense. Anyway. Just like a séance here."

Séance? Had we said anything about a séance? It was one thing when Liss was leading a foray into the beyond. I wasn't sure I was entirely comfortable with this . . .

Still, what could happen? It wasn't much past four thirty in the afternoon. Daylight was filtering through the small windows, and we had the lamps in the living room turned on high. It didn't eliminate all the shadows in the room, but it was a good start.

"We're going to think together, back to the churchyard construction site, because we're going to send ourselves back there. I want you both to retrace your steps. Really see it in your mind's eye. Feel the crunch of the dried-out grass beneath your feet. The heat from the sun on your face. Taste the lemonade on your tongue. Remember the faces of the people you passed. Got it all in your mind? Are you really seeing it? Experiencing it again? Good," Tara said in an even tone that was surprisingly soothing. "Now go back to the moment the excavator broke through the crust of the dirt, when we moved to stand with the crew, to see what was happening firsthand. There was an energy there at that place. Focus on that energy. Really focus . . ."

I was beginning to feel . . . unsettled. My stomach . . . it felt as though the muscles were tightening in my abdomen, from the very core of me all the way up, like an elevator moving up in its shaft, floor by floor by floor. Tightening. Gripping. Closing like a vise. My breathing had grown shallow; no matter how hard I tried, I couldn't seem to draw a deep breath into my lungs. I could only get so much air, and I was starting to see stars, I was starting to see . . .

Next to me, Evie moaned.

I came back into myself, just the teensiest bit. Enough to realize that the wineglass beneath my fingertips was quivering, ever so slightly.

I opened my eyes and looked at Evie. Her eyes were squinched together hard, making the middle third of her face a mass of furrows and lines.

"If there is anyone here with us now who would like to make a connection with us, someone with information about what happened at the churchyard, then we invite you to speak. Use the glass to give us your message," Tara intoned, taking no notice of Evie.

But I noticed. I could feel her tension traveling through the glass and up my right arm, settling itself at my shoulders until they felt knotted and tight. I breathed deeply. Normally I would have gathered my own energy and pushed back to keep the stray tendrils from infiltrating my own . . . but this was Evie we were talking about here. Whatever she was experiencing, it was better that I didn't close myself off, just in case. Two intuitives are better than one when it came to protection.

"There *is* something here," Tara said, her eyes still closed.

"Evie, are you okay?" I whispered. Waves of energy were coming through the glass, either from Evie herself or from something that had joined the party.

She didn't answer. Her head had fallen forward, her chin dropped down toward her chest, and her pale bangs fell in a wispy curtain over her eyes. Her fingertips rested lightly on top of the overturned glass, but the nail beds had gone white, as though she was applying great pressure.

The glass lifted on one side, then set itself back down. I blinked at it. Had I actually seen that?

*I had.*

# Chapter 6

I yanked my fingertips from the glass. "Tara, snap out of it. Something's wrong." I reached out and put my hands on Evie's cheeks. "Evie, honey. Look at me."

Tara pulled her hands back in her lap and rubbed them together as though trying to scrub away dirt. She was looking at Evie now, too, and biting her lip. "What happened? Why is she like that?"

"Aren't you supposed to be the expert at this Ouija thing?" I snapped. I'd probably regret that later, but right now all I could think about was Evie, and I didn't like what I saw. Evie's eyes were unfocused but open, her breathing shallow. I brushed her hair out of her eyes, willing everything to be all right.

"She's never done that before," was Tara's defiant answer. "Come on, Evie, whatever it is, switch it off. Just like we've talked about, remember? You're in control. Flip that switch."

"Trouble." The word sprang from Evie's lips, and all

of a sudden her eyes flared open, clear as the morning sky. Her gaze searched out mine. "Trouble."

Relief flooded through me. I could have hugged her, but instead all I did was pat her maternally on the cheek. "Oh my goodness. Oh, thank heavens." And God. And the Goddess. And all the angels and Guides and Guardians, for that matter. I was an equal-opportunity gratuitist. "You scared the bejeebers out of me for a second there, Evie." Then I paused, frowning. "Wait. What do you mean, trouble?"

"There's something wrong with that . . . that place," she said. She still looked like she was in that half-dazed state of trance, where threads from the astral were tugging at your energies, pulling you in.

I frowned. The glass jumped again. "Evie, take your hands from the glass."

She blinked drowsily at me. "Hm? Oh, sure. Sorry." She slipped her hands back into her lap, leaving the overturned wineglass on the coffee table with its surround of alphanumeric sticky notes.

"Eves, what did you mean that you think there's something wrong with that place?" Tara asked a little impatiently. "What did you get just now?"

Evie turned dreamy eyes her way. "I think something bad is going to happen."

Such a strange voice, so sleepy and sweet and calm. So preternaturally wise with the kind of knowing I recognized. It came with the territory, the knowing. The intuition. Thanks to my own so-called gifts, I had come to understand with a resigned sense of certainty that, whatever the underlying cause of the Very Bad Things that had plagued Stony Mill in months past, it was not done with us. Whatever it was that had gotten into people, whatever was making them go a little crazy. Well, crazier than usual. I knew without a doubt that the murder of Joel Turner was not going to be our last, and I knew it in a way that only another sensitive would understand. So that left only the question that I gave voice to now: "When?"

She lifted her gaze to mine. "I don't know. I don't know when. And I don't know what."

"What did you see?" Tara pressed her.

A tiny frown marred Evie's brow. She shook her head. "A jumble of images. I don't know for sure. Darkness, closing in. A pale moon of a face with blank eyes. Tiny little bones. And I felt . . . pain. Pain and terror and anguish all mixed up together in one sickening, horrible spiral."

Tara thrust a cup of water at her, and Evie took it, gratefully gulping down a mouthful.

A knock at the door made everyone jump.

"Pizza!" I said. Relieved to have something normal to do, I leaped to my feet and headed for the door. "Tara, there are plates in the cupboard to the left of the sink and napkins on the table. Evie, you stay put." I scooped up Minnie on the way to be sure she didn't try to escape out the soon-to-be open door.

I turned the knob and gave it a yank, swinging the door toward me. "Hi, what do I owe y—"

"Well. Let me think. What . . . *exactly* . . . can I get away with here?" Marcus waggled his eyebrows at me over a pair of black shades, a playful grin spreading across his face. He tipped his shades down, blasting me with the full effect of killer blue eyes that had no problem taking my breath away. "I mean, if you're offering up the opportunity—very generous of you, I might add—then it seems the least I can do is take full advantage of it." He let his gaze drift down to my mouth and reached out to tuck a stray curl behind my ear. "Hello, sweetness."

Yup. No breath available. None whatsoever. Heart was working just fine, though. Even at double-time.

From the living room came a lively tag-team effort of, "Hi, Marcus!" in full, blooming harmony.

I cringed.

Openly surprised, Marcus removed the soft look from his face and leaned sideways to peep around me. "Well, well. If it's not two of my favorite girls in the whole world, all together in the same place," he said. He flicked his gaze back in my direction. "Make that three," he whispered for my ears alone. Then he laughed as Minnie reached up a paw to him. He shook it gently. "All right, four. I'm easy."

"I-I wasn't expecting to see you today," I stuttered, thankful for sturdy doorknobs and the support they so obligingly provided. Once, not too long ago, he'd kissed me thoroughly up against this very door. I still hadn't fully recovered.

His lips quirked on one side as he glanced pointedly at my tight grip on the door. Of course he'd noticed. He noticed everything about me. That's what made him so damned dangerous. "I guess this is just my lucky day."

Thinking that perhaps it was a good thing after all that I'd brought the girls home with me, I followed him dazedly into the apartment, where Evie seemed to have fully recovered from her strange episode and was now giggling openly with her darker-natured compadre.

"Cousin," Tara said with a nod of acknowledgment, smirking.

"Little cousin," Marcus countered solemnly. "I didn't see your scooter outside."

"It's acting up again. The Loumeister is going to have to look at it again."

"I can take a look at it for you if Uncle Lou has too much going on." He slipped off his shades and tucked them into the collar of his T-shirt. "Well, well. What do we have here? A good-ladies-behaving-badly get-together?"

"Well, if we were, you wouldn't be invited, now would you?" Tara replied smartly.

He laughed. "Good point. Was Miss Maggie here taking part?"

He gave me a sidelong glance that had me blushing. Again. Or was that still? "Um . . ."

"I'll take that as a yes." On a more serious note, to Tara he said, "You did protect yourselves?"

Tara looked insulted. "White light, protection from my Guides, yadda yadda. We didn't have any problems . . . well, except for Evie . . ."

Marcus narrowed in on that loophole fast. He looked at the three of us, one at a time, ending with Evie. "What kind of problem?"

Faced with having to admit her experience to Marcus, a grown man she had never quite owned up to having a bit of a schoolgirl crush on, Evie clammed up faster than you could say Timbuktu. Or even Terre Haute. Seeing her hesitation, I stepped forward and told Marcus what had happened at the church, what had happened with Evie here in the apartment, and what she'd said she'd seen.

"Hm. Interesting."

Was that all? He didn't seem overly concerned. Maybe I *had* been making too much of things.

"So you're thinking that the cave-in was caused by something paranormal?"

"No," Tara answered for all of us. "Not the cave-in. Obviously that was caused by the weight of the machine and the vibration of the ground. But there was something that we felt out there, after the cave-in. We were just trying to figure out what it was, that's all."

"Why don't we all try it, then?" Marcus surprised me by asking.

"What, here?" I blurted. "Now?"

"Why not? There's safety in experience."

Well, I didn't know why not, but I knew I had felt a little strange about using the Ouija at all—the many horror stories and warnings I've heard over the years, I suppose, not to mention my relatively way-too-new acquaintance with the spirit world itself—but using it with Marcus . . . well, let's just say I already felt exposed with him in the vicinity. My inner world laid altogether too bare.

"Besides"—leaning toward me, Marcus murmured for my ears alone—"I'd like to get a feel for how Tara is using this, whether she's using it responsibly. Will you trust me?"

Taken aback by the simple request, I could only nod in assent. Suddenly it didn't seem like too much to ask at all.

We both took a seat on the sofa. Briefly Tara told him how she'd lead the mini-séance, thankfully skipping over Evie's initial silly question. "And then when we were all focusing on the things we'd experienced out there, that was when Evie had her visions."

"Except they were all mixed up. Flashes. Not a running dream," Evie clarified. "Flashes, one right after the other. And they were so intense, I couldn't get a grip on them, but I couldn't ease back, either. Does that make sense to you?"

He smiled and chucked her under her chin to ease her anxious question. "Perfect sense. No worries, hey?" He thought a moment. "Why don't the four of us try again to make a connection with the spirit or energy that you sensed there, whatever it was, and see what it has in mind. Maybe together we can make sense of what you were seeing."

Minnie jumped onto the table and walked across the sticky notes as though she wanted to remind everyone that she was involved in this, too. Evie and Tara giggled and argued back and forth between the two of them over who should hold her next.

"Do you really think this is wise?" I whispered to him with the girls' attention drawn away. "I mean, Evie sensed something bad, as did both I *and* Tara. That's three separate negative impressions. Are you sure we should push this?"

His eyes held mine, but he didn't lower his voice, as I had. "What do you think the best way to conquer fear is? To face it head on and know in your heart that you are strong enough to overcome it . . . *before* it gets to you. There is no better way. And you know as well as I do that, as intuitives, we are by our very natures prone to observing the negative forces that are out there while they're in action, whether we want to or not. Right now, we don't know what that entails exactly. Where it's stemming from, or why. I think every bit of knowledge we can get our hands on is going to help us to understand what we're dealing with. That's got to be a good thing."

I sighed. "All right. Let's get this over with."

"Tara? You lead?"

Tara nodded, took a deep breath, and shook out her hands to ground herself. "Okay. Just like before . . ."

Except it wasn't just like before. The glass moved

almost immediately this time, as soon as we'd all provided a looped connection through our fingertips on the glass. The energy was unreal, humming through my body like a power station on high and vibrating the glass until I thought it might sing. There was no need to go into a meditative trance—it was as though the energy that we had tapped into before knew we were coming and was sending out a welcome wagon.

Time would tell whether that was a good thing.

"Interesting," Marcus murmured. "Everyone be sure to shield. We don't want any mishaps if we can avoid them."

I was actually getting fairly good at shielding. It came as second nature to put on that cloak of Teflon, to protect oneself from hurtful words, hurtful feelings, hurtful thoughts . . . but how does a girl know if her protective measures are strong enough to withstand an attack from the astral? Belief and trust? I couldn't help wishing there was a more definitive answer than that.

"Okay," Tara said quietly but firmly, "if there is a spirit here who followed us from the church this afternoon . . . well, we know you followed us, that's not a question . . . the one who wants to give us a message . . . speak through the glass this time and tell us who you are."

We were all watching the glass, focusing on our fingers and the energy traveling through them, and reaching out with our minds. I felt that same viselike squeezing of my core. I breathed as deeply as I could, but it was so hard. Dimly I watched the glass begin to move, slowly at first, then gaining speed. Circle after circle. My eyes widened, and I surged back to the present.

*E* . . .

Once the first letter had been selected, the glass began

to slide about in a frenzy of movement, from one letter to another, then came to a stop.

*E-L-I-A-S*

"Hello, Elias," Tara said. "Are you a spirit connected with the Grace Baptist Church?"

The glass moved to the sticky note marked "yes."

"Are you a spirit of the Light, Elias?" Marcus asked.

The glass circled but did not indicate a single letter.

"Hm. Not liking that," I fussed.

"Elias, why have you come here today? Why did you follow us?" Evie asked, her voice soft but firmer than I had expected. The girl had a core of strength that came through for her when she needed it. "You came here today because you followed us, didn't you?"

*L-O-N-L-Y*

Misspelled, but its point was clear.

"Was your spirit released somehow from the room that was exposed by the big machine today?" Marcus asked.

Again the glass moved to "yes."

"Were you tied to that room?"

*Yes*

"Why were you tied to that place?" Tara, this time.

No answer, only circular movement.

"Did you once live on the land that the church stands on?"

*Yes*

"Well, that's something," I said. "Elias, were you a farmer?"

*No*

"A woodsman?" Evie guessed.

*No*

Well, this was getting us nowhere. I thought of a new tack. "How old are you, Elias?"

*H-O-W-O-L-D-A-R-E-Y-O-U*

A shiver zipped up my spine. There was something strange and confrontational about that response. Why wouldn't he just tell us his age?

"He's a child," Marcus guessed. "It's a game he's playing with us."

I felt ashamed suddenly for jumping to conclusions. It was the fear again, that instant, inbred fear that a youth spent with ruler-wielding nuns and catechisms had propagated to the minutest of molecules within my makeup. Whether it made sense or not, that fear was still there. It was something I constantly struggled with.

"Was there something you wanted from us?" Tara asked the spirit.

I felt the puff of a breeze wafting across my face, down the back of my neck. The temperature in the room when we had started was cool—it was always cool down here in my apartment. But the air around us seemed to have chilled considerably, and it was swirling, ever so gently.

Slowly the glass spelled out *F-R-E-I-N-D-S*.

Wistful. He *was* a child. And apparently not always the best speller. "Elias, don't you have other friends? There are others on the Other Side who are waiting to help you cross."

*D-E-A-D*

"That's true. They have passed over. But they are there to welcome you home—"

*No*

"There is a light, a very bright light that is there. The others—your family—they are waiting for you there, within that light. Can you see it there? Can you look—"

*No*

The atmosphere in the room was getting thicker,

heavier. My stomach muscles had coiled up as tight as a constricted snake. The movements of the glass were at their strongest, boldest.

"Don't you want to go be with your friends and family?"

*No*

"Why not?"

*D-O-N-T-L-I-K-E*

"You don't like your friends and family?"

Circles but no answer.

"Why not?"

More circles.

I was getting a little impatient. So far, we hadn't learned anything, really, about why he had followed us. "Elias, what is that room that was uncovered? Why was it closed off the way that it was? Buried?"

*S-E-C-R-E-T*

"It was covered over in secret, or it bears a secret?"

*Yes*

Hm. Interesting. "Which one?"

Circles.

Tara asked, "Elias, do you have a message that you want to give to us today?"

*T-R-O-U-B-L-E*

We had gotten that already through Evie, so it wasn't news. "What sort of trouble?" Tara pressed.

*B-A-D*

Bad trouble. Well, I suppose almost anything that most of us considered to be trouble was bad by the very definition of the word.

"Trouble in the past that you want to share? Or trouble in the future?" she asked.

*W-A-R-N-Y-O-U*

"Warn us?" Tara narrowed her eyes with a thoughtful tilt of her head. "Warn us about what?"

*U-L-C*

"Ulc. What does *that* mean?" I asked, looking to Marcus for insight.

"I'm not sure. The glass isn't moving as quickly now. Maybe he's used up his allotment of the energies in the room and needs to rest."

"I know!" Tara said, hopping up and down in her seat—a real feat, considering her fingers were still lightly positioned on the glass. "U-L-C. You'll see. See?"

We saw. It made sense, but I had to ask, "Why won't you just tell us what we should expect, Elias? If you're so interested in warning us?"

*U-L-C*, the glass spelled out again. Then, *U-L-C-U-L-C-U-L-C-U-L-C-U-L-C-U-L-C-U-L-C-U-L-C-U-L-C*.

"We'll see. You can't tell us more. I think we got it," Marcus said wryly.

He shifted to a more comfortable position on the sofa, and his knee bumped the outside of my thigh. The touch was so unexpected that I couldn't help myself: I started and bit my lip as my pulse leaped ahead like a racehorse just out of its docket.

Lucky for me my fingertips were still connected with the glass, because otherwise it might not have spelled out *M-A-R-G-A-R-E-T*.

Did I say lucky? My jump-started heart nearly failed. But the lucky part of this particular twist of Ouija fate came into play because the movement of the glass distracted Marcus enough that he didn't even notice my reaction.

"Is that for you, Maggie?" Evie asked, her brow furrowing prettily.

"I don't know why it would be. It must be another Margaret. It may not be so common now, but at one time it was very popular. At least, that's what my mom always told me whenever I complained about it."

But Evie wasn't convinced. "Elias, do you have a message for our Maggie?"

*A-R-O-S-E-B-Y-A-N-Y-O-T-H-E-R-N-A-M-E-W-O-U-L-D-S-M-E-L-L-A-S-S-W-E-E-T*

A lovely sentiment but cryptic as hell, in my opinion. "Honestly, I don't see how any of this relates to me."

*T-O-M*

Now, *that* got my attention. I stared at the glass, not really wanting to believe that I was receiving messages from the Great Beyond. Personal messages. From a spirit I knew absolutely nothing about.

"I guess you were wrong," Tara said, eyeing me curiously.

"What do you mean?"

"No need to get defensive, snookums. It was just an observation."

The glass began to move outside of its circular path again: *B-E-C-A-R-E-F-U-L*.

Be careful. Be careful of what? Of whom? Of Tom? Is that what the spirit meant? Why was he reaching out to me to begin with?

*T-R-O-U-B-L-E*

The last thing that the glass spelled out was *S-I-S-T-E-R*, then it stopped just as suddenly as it had started and the air around us returned to normal. All except for the scent of lavender and licorice, which came and went so suddenly it might never have been there at all.

We all stared at the glass, wondering if it was only a brief reprieve. I know I half expected it to start circling again with a vengeance, but it didn't. With a communal glance around the table, the four of us as one let our fingers slide from the glass. But none of us relaxed back into our seats.

I was the first to find my voice. "Well, that was interesting."

Marcus's brow was drawn in a frown. "Interesting, yes. But I don't know if I'm okay with it."

I looked at him with surprise. "What do you mean, you don't know if you're okay with it? You said you *were* okay with it."

"I did. But that was before I started to think you might have a spirit trying to attach itself to you," he said reasonably. "Don't look like that—it can happen to anyone. We can handle it."

Sure it could happen to anyone. Anyone who was messing around with a Ouija board, that is. "Why would it be trying to attach itself to me?" I asked. "I'm not anywhere near the strongest sensitive in the room. Evie is. And you, Mr. Medium."

"I prefer Mr. Expert. Mr. Medium is so . . . average," he quipped, cracking a smile.

His attempt to lighten the burden of my fears worked. I fought the smile twitching about the corners of my mouth, but in the end they won out. I was never very good at keeping laughter inside. "Very funny."

"Thanks, I thought so."

"But your ego is completely beside the point."

"True. Sad, but true. Honestly, I don't know why he'd choose to attach himself to you. Maybe he likes your energy. Maybe your energy signature is all sparkly and swirly to those on the other side. Who knows?"

"Maybe he followed Evie and picked on you because

your energy is all over this apartment?" Tara offered.
"You know . . . the predominant energy of a new place?"

"He *is* lonely; he said so," Evie chimed in. "Maybe he
just likes you."

"Maybe." But if that were the case, why wouldn't the
frown pulling at my forehead go away? I couldn't help
but feeling there was more to Elias than first meets the
eye. Or the Ouija.

Minnie woke up and stretched, then wandered over to
sit by the door, yawning widely. I wasn't surprised when
less than a minute later a knock sounded on the door.
"Pizza delivery!" a muffled voice cried. And not a moment too soon. How long could it take to make and de-
liver a pizza across Stony Mill for goodness sake?

The four of us spent the next couple of hours gorging
ourselves on heavenly deep dish, and hashing and re-
hashing what the girls and I had experienced at the
church site and what we had all just experienced with the
church spirit, Elias. Add in a pinch of giggles and a
healthy dose of good-natured ribbing, and the time
seemed to fly by.

During a lull, Tara leaned back and patted her con-
cave, teenage stomach. "I am stuffed! I'll bet I gained
five pounds with all the pizza I ate." She glanced at the
small windows, where the smallest measure of daylight
still shone through the short, gauzy sheers I'd hung when
I first moved in with the hope of admitting as much light
into the rooms as possible. It was difficult to gauge time
of day when living in a basement. Somehow the earth
that surrounded the walls seemed to swallow up as much
daylight as it did sound. "What time is it, Maggie?"

I glanced at the clock over the stove. "Almost eight
o'clock. What time did you girls need to be getting back?"

"Eight o'clock?" Tara wailed in a completely un-Tara-like fashion. "I was supposed to hear from Charlie by seven! I wonder why he hasn't called." Marcus rolled his eyes. She dove for her purse and dug within. Not finding what she was looking for, she stirred the contents around some more, then ended up dumping it all out on the table amid the Ouija sticky notes. "Ohmigosh. My cell phone. I can't find my cell phone."

"Don't panic, Tare. It's got to be around somewhere," Evie said reassuringly. "When do you remember last having it?"

Tara thought a moment. "At the fundraiser. When I called Charlie's cell to see where we would find him. But my cell isn't in my bag."

Evie shook her head. "You weren't carrying your bag, remember? You left it in Maggie's car because you didn't want to carry it."

"Hey! That's right! I put the phone in my pocket." Tara's face brightened considerably. "Maybe it fell out in the car. Maggie, can I see your keys to go check?"

I tossed them to her. "Have at it, chickie."

Evie handed Minnie to me, then she and Tara ran out of the apartment and up the stone steps. They had returned before I even had a chance to get uncomfortably comfortable with Marcus.

"Nope, not there. Argh! Just my luck."

"I'll bet you dropped it out at the work site, Tare. Either that or in the church where we were waiting with Charlie." Evie nodded to herself. "We could do a Finder's Spell."

"Why don't you just look for it first, before you resort to magick?" I asked them. "You know, be normal first, then magickal second."

Tara shot me a measuring stare that was more curious

than aggressive. "Maggie, why are you so afraid to use magick? It's not like it's going to hurt anyone. The old Harm fits here, you know. It's not a big deal. Trust." Then she paused a moment and relented. "But in this case, since I know where I've been and it shouldn't be too hard to backtrack, I probably don't need to. It would take too much time anyway, and I really need to find it fast."

Marcus had leaned back against the sofa to watch the interplay between us. "You're both right, you know. It depends on the situation. It's at every witch's discretion and judgment."

Appeased, Tara backed off and was suddenly as sweet and smooth as Annie Miller's sugar cream pie. "So, um, Maggie? Do you think you could take me back out there to look for it? I hate to ask you," she said quickly, "but Big Lou will kill me if I've lost it. It won't take long, I promise. Witch's honor."

"I have a better idea," Marcus said. "Why don't we all go out to look. Four sets of eyes have got to be better than two."

# Chapter 7

Something made me think that maybe, just maybe, Marcus was doing his best to extend our impromptu get-together. The thought left me feeling . . . confused. But the afternoon had been completely harmless, just friends enjoying friends. Exchanging pleasantries.

Contacting the spirit world.

Okay, so mostly harmless. I knew some people would disagree with that assertion, believing any and all but all's well that ends well. It had been an interesting experiment, to say the least. Chalk it up to experience and understanding.

"We could all go in Christine," I offered, trying not to laugh as I pictured the four of us squeezing into the tight confines.

"I have a better idea," Marcus said. "I've been trying to get Maggie to go for a ride on the back of my bike for weeks. Why don't you girls drive the old Bug, and Maggie and I will follow? If that's all right with you, of course, Maggie."

Tara leaped at the notion. "That's a great idea! I could really use some practice on an old stick shift anyway. It took me forever to get the hang of it in Driver's Ed."

"Me, too," Evie said. "My dad won't let me touch his old pickup truck, though. And he only uses it for fishing and hunting anyway."

Poor Christine. This was what she'd been reduced to? Still, I relented. "Fine, but you have to take care of the old girl. She needs lots of TLC. She's not as young as she once was, you know."

"Kinda like you, right?" Tara asked in an innocent voice. "Kidding! Just kidding. Honest!"

Tara used my phone to call Charlie's cell. He was still with the construction crew. He said he'd been trying to call her and offered to meet us out at the church to help look for Tara's phone.

"Come on, Granny," Marcus teased. "We'd better get a move on. It might take you a while to swing your leg over the back in your rapidly deteriorating state."

The ride through the golden dusk along quiet country roads was nice. Peaceful. Even the helmet flattening my hair to my head and the mosquitoes and lightning bugs smacking into me along the way didn't dim the sense of complete freedom I felt riding on the back of the bike. And the man guiding the bike, whose long muscles I could feel as we leaned into every turn? Bonus! A sinful bonus, perhaps, if you believed in that sort of thing—but a bonus nonetheless. I even had to hang on.

The churchyard was quiet when we arrived. Though the tents and tables still remained, the area was abandoned. Long shadows stretched across the area from the tall steeple and the windbreak of old maple trees, ever-deepening shadows that reached dark fingers toward the expansion project area.

Tara maneuvered Christine to a surprisingly smooth halt in the parking lot, parking her beside an old, beat-up Volkswagen Rabbit. Marcus pulled up alongside her. I withdrew my hands from the supple muscles at his waist before the girls could notice, and buried them beneath my thighs.

"Any ideas where you want to start looking?" Marcus asked the girls.

"The church meeting room in the basement," Tara said. "We were sitting down there with Charlie for a while, waiting around for the groundbreaking to start. I could have left my cell on a table. We didn't really go into the actual fundraiser except to walk through, and I did have my cell with me after that. Other than the church, I guess it would be out at the excavations." She glanced up toward the church, then indicated the Rabbit with a jerk of her thumb. "That's Charlie's. He must be up there looking already."

"Tell you what," I said. "Why don't you two go find Charlie, and Marcus and I will head over to the parsonage to let them know why we're here and what we're doing. The church might be locked. We might need someone to let us in."

Tara nodded. " 'Kay. I wouldn't have thought of that. Good thinking. Come on, Evil."

Was that a compliment from Tara? Would wonders never cease?

The parsonage was situated off to the left and behind the church itself, and was connected by a nicely maintained walkway. Marcus and I headed in that direction, walking slowly side by side. After the close proximity of the motorcycle ride, I felt the separation from his energy acutely. More so than was all right to feel. Neither of us spoke, and yet I heard thoughts and wonderings that could have been his in my head . . . and what's more, I think he heard mine. The farther we walked along the path, the closer he seemed to edge toward me. Did I reciprocate? I wasn't even sure anymore.

I knocked on the cranberry red front door of the parsonage, a small colonial-style farmhouse with symmetrical windows on the second floor that looked a bit like eyes looking out over the mouth of the porticoed entrance. The door opened to the thin, pale woman I had seen with the pastor earlier. Thin—I would almost say gaunt, seeing her from close up. Pale hair and pale eyes also contributed to the overall bloodless look of her. She wore a thick, comfy bathrobe with a nightgown peeping out from beneath, and a towel wrapped turban-style on her head.

"Yes?" she asked, tilting her head at us in confusion. "Can I help you?"

"Um, hi there. I'm sorry to disturb you. My name is Maggie O'Neill, and this is my friend, Marcus Quinn. I just wanted to let you know that my friend thinks she might have dropped her cell phone while we were here at the fundraiser earlier today, and we were hoping to be able to look for it. Do you mind?"

"Who is it, Emily?" a strong female voice called from farther back in the house.

"Nothing, Mother . . . just a couple of people who lost something at the fundraiser and were wanting to look for it," she answered over her shoulder with an apologetic glance toward me and Marcus. "I was just about to go out with them to help them look—"

The unseen female bustled around the corner. It was

Letty Clark; I recognized her from earlier, even without her all-encompassing straw hat. "Don't be ridiculous, dear, you'll do nothing of the sort. You're exhausted from today. I'll go out with them." She was already grabbing a big, black flashlight and throwing a light sweater over her shoulders. The flashlight would come in handy, but she needn't have bothered with the sweater; though the sun was now dipping down toward the horizon, the blazing temperatures of the day certainly hadn't dropped by much.

"Well . . . if you're sure you don't mind . . ."

"Of course I don't mind, dear. You're my daughter, and you know as well as I do that you're unwell. It's my job to take care of you."

"I'm much stronger than you think I am," the woman fussed with a small frown, but she still gave her mother's arm an affectionate squeeze as she passed by.

"Nonsense. You've had your bath, and I've made you a cup of tea. Chamomile. It's cooling for you on your bedside table. You go on and get in bed. I'll send Bob in when he gets back."

Letty accompanied us along the walkway toward the front of the church. "Do you know where you need to be looking, dear?"

"Well, the girls have gone out to the excavation site, and Marcus and I thought we'd—"

Letty interrupted me. "They shouldn't be out there alone, with that hole, in the dark! They could get seriously hurt. We don't even know if the ground is stable yet. We'd better go and get them out of there."

I wasn't quite sure where that would leave Tara if we didn't find her cell phone elsewhere, but we'd have to cross that bridge if we came to it.

With Letty in the lead, Marcus and I followed her rather speedy trajectory along the concrete path leading around the church. We had just reached the corner of the church when my own cell phone rang. Letty continued on while I paused to locate it in my purse. The screen on the outside of my phone read, "Tara-Cell."

I flipped open the case. "Oh, good, you found—"

"Maggie?" It was Evie's voice, trembling and urgent. "Maggie, you've got to come quick! Ohmigod. Ohmigod, ohmigod, ohmigod."

My eyes flew to Marcus, but his gaze was already searching mine out. In the background, I heard Charlie's and Tara's voices, all running together over the airwaves. I couldn't make out what they were saying. "Calm down, honey," I said to Evie. "Take a deep breath. What's wrong?"

"Just come over here, Maggie. At the construction site around the churchyard. Come over here—quick."

The phone call ended. Marcus touched my shoulder. "The girls?"

My gaze searched out his, urgently. "At the construction site."

I didn't even have to tell him that we were needed. He took off like a shot, outpacing Letty in seconds and leaving the two of us to follow in his wake. Running was okay so long as we were on the concrete pathway, but once we left it, the roughness of the field made a faster pace treacherous. The beam from the flashlight was flaring crazily this way and that, jostled by our gait. Up ahead I made out the darker shapes of the girls and Marcus. I headed in that direction, using their shadows as a focal point to guide us.

I was panting by the time we arrived by Marcus's side. "What is it?" I asked.

Marcus didn't answer, but asked Letty, who had kept up admirably for a much older woman, if he could borrow the flashlight. She cradled the heavy light protectively against her body for a moment as though she worried he might leave her stranded out there in the dark, then handed it over.

"Stay here," he told me. Letty seemed to think the command applied to her as well, for she remained by my side, wringing her hands.

Evie rushed to my side and threw herself at me. "Oh, Maggie, thank God you and Marcus came out here with us. And Charlie, too. I don't know what I would have done if Tare and I had found this on our own," she babbled against my shoulder. "I really, really don't. Oh, it's awful. Just awful."

Marcus was down on his knees in the dirt, poking about while Charlie held the flashlight for him, with Tara cradled securely against his left side. They were behind the ropes that had been erected, closing off the excavation site from the chance interloper. In fact, they seemed to be right on top of where the payloader had accidentally broken through the crust of earth.

I took a gentle step backward, holding Evie out at arm's length and prompting her to look at me. "What is it, Evie?" I asked quietly. "What did you find?"

"A-a woman," Evie said, sniffling. "Oh, Maggie—her hair is just full of blood, and she's not breathing. Charlie called the police, but . . . she's dead! I know she is!"

Letty was wringing her hands, suddenly looking very much an old woman. But she surprised me then by stepping forward and putting her hands on Evie's shoulders, gently turning her away. "Come along, dear. Let's just go sit in the garden and get away from this for a while, hm?

You shouldn't have to be seeing all of this." She raised her eyebrows at me, looking for my approval. I nodded, sending her silent thanks with my eyes.

"I'll send Tara up in a few moments to sit with you, all right, Evie?" I tried to sound as reassuring as possible.

"All right." As she allowed herself to be lead away, I heard her tell Letty, "I should probably call my parents. They're gonna have a cow . . ."

My nerves were all a-jangle. I gave myself a mental shake and took a few deep breaths to ground myself and send the excess energy back into the earth where it could do some good. With that done, there was nothing else to do but to duck under the rope myself in order to meet up with Marcus, Tara, and Charlie.

Tara was glued to Charlie's side, but all of her concentration was drawn and focused on Marcus, still crouching down several feet away. I touched Tara to get her attention. "Evie's in the garden sanctuary," I told her, my voice barely above a whisper. Hushed, in honor of the dead. It seemed only right. Even the summer cicadas seemed to have silenced themselves for the occasion.

Tara pressed her lips firmly together. "I'm staying here with Charlie."

I nodded, knowing she was not going to be swayed. Stepping carefully, I picked my way over to Marcus's side. He turned and peered at me, his mouth grim. Off in the distance, sirens wailed, making their way closer.

Wordlessly, I put my hand on Marcus's shoulder and leaned down to see what we were talking about here. Charlie obligingly manipulated the light beam.

Oh my stars and garters.

It was Ronnie.

"I saw her, earlier today," I told Marcus once I had

found my voice. "Here, at the fundraiser. Was she . . . was she killed?"

His lips moved in a kind of wry smile that brought no joy to his eyes. "Well, if she wasn't, then she'd better have one heck of a good explanation in a suicide note somewhere, because inquiring minds are gonna want to know."

The beam from the flashlight caught in the sticky red gleam in her hair. I winced.

"There appear to be bruises on her throat, too," he added. "Not a nice death."

Not nice at all.

The sirens and popping lights from emergency vehicles screamed along the same country byway we'd traveled less than a half hour ago, pulling into the area with the kind of speed and precision customarily reserved for high speed chases and dead-drunk idiots with no ability to comprehend their own looming near-death experience. They were all over us within seconds, a swarm of movement, searching lights, squawking radios, and barking voices. I had expected Tom to be among the new arrivals, but there was no sign of him amidst the men and women assessing the body and setting up a perimeter.

"What about it, Dawson? Anything?" It was Jim Johnson, one of Tom's departmental cohorts, putting the question to the EMT who had taken up Marcus's post next to the body.

The EMT pulled the stethoscope from his ears. "Nothing. Not a blip, not the faintest breath. Zero vitals. I would say we're too late, but by the looks of that"—he nodded to indicate the wound to her skull—"I would say she never stood a chance. Off the record, mind you. The ME will have to determine all of that."

Johnson nodded and turned to the four of us. "I'm going

to need you all to step away from the area." He indicated the line of trees along the walk. "Over there would be fine."

"A friend of ours is waiting in the garden with the pastor's mother-in-law," I mentioned.

"That would be fine, too."

"Jim—" I waited until he turned to look at me before asking the question on my mind. "Where's Tom? I thought he'd have come out, too."

"Not on duty, and must be out of range 'cause I can't reach him." Voice neutral, without judgment. "It happens. I've left a voice mail for him. I'll do the preliminaries for him and hand it over as soon as I can."

I didn't quite frown, but I couldn't help wondering where Tom had disappeared to. No wonder I hadn't heard from him.

The four of us stood along the tree line for a while, watching in silence while the emergency and police crews did their thing. With Tom absent, it didn't surprise me at all when more police and sheriff's department cruisers pulled up. Lights only, no sirens. I was glad for that—I was getting a splitting headache.

I recognized Chief Boggs, that twenty-plus-year bastion of the old guard and frequent customer at Annie-Thing Good, as he hurried toward the roped-off area. And was that the county sheriff trying to elbow him aside to take the lead? I'd heard buzz before that there was no love lost between the two, despite (or should that perhaps be *because of*) the fact that they shared space in the Municipal Building in town. Boggs was always in the spotlight, giving press conferences for the Stony Mill Gazette and actually calling them "press conferences"; Sheriff

Reed had been rumored to view his colleague as being far too forthcoming and rash.

"It's my crime scene, Boggs, not yours," the sheriff was saying as they passed twenty feet from us.

And never the twain shall meet? Arguments already—not a good sign.

"Fielding works for me, not you. I have every right to be here."

"It's county business, not town business. And Fielding's supposed to be cross-departmental, or had you forgotten that a portion of my budget goes toward his salary as well? Not to mention the fact that he's not here, in case you hadn't noticed. I have another deputy on the way. He'll take over from Johnson, then get with Fielding."

At least there was no question between the two of them that Tom was the man for the job. That was good to hear. Despite the issues that stood between us, I was still proud when someone spoke of him with respect. He deserved that.

The night was so quiet that even from where we stood, the ongoing conversations could be easily heard.

"Another murder. Christ. What in God's name is this town coming to?"

Reed relented in his annoyance long enough to say, "Just the state of things everywhere, I guess. No one's immune. Not even Stony Mill."

"We can't even chalk it up to gangland shootings or some such nonsense," Boggs fussed. "What is it? Drugs? Drink? What has gotten into people? Christ, I'm gettin' old."

"Good people gone bad, I guess. Maybe it *is* time for you to retire."

"I'm going to pretend you didn't say that."

Bickering aside, they were right. They knew enough by now to realize that things were going very wrong in our small town. They just didn't have a clue how wrong.

And for all of the gifted intuitives the N.I.G.H.T.S. could boast among its members, neither did we. We had worries. We had feelings. We had fear. We had doubts. What we didn't have was proof, and neither did we have a true understanding of where everything was headed. While the sheriff himself worked the crime scene, Chief Boggs and Jim Johnson headed over to us for questioning. Evie and Letty Clark came down to where we were all congregating.

Boggs spoke first. "Which one of you found the body?"

Charlie hesitantly raised his hand.

"Put your hand down, son. We're not in a classroom. Mind telling me what you were doing here? Looks like the party down the way ended a while ago."

Charlie nodded. "It did. I'm on the excavation crew. We found the . . . the hole that the . . . the woman is lying in."

"Well, it wasn't the hole that did that to her, I gotta say. What did you say you were doing here?"

"I didn't, I guess," Charlie said, looking confused. "I came to help Tara here, my girlfriend"—Tara hugged him closer at that—"find her cell phone."

Boggs nodded, his eyes watchful. Despite the Mayberry-cop persona he liked to purvey most of the time, I got the impression that he didn't miss as much as people might think. "Now—forgive me if you were about to tell me this, but—why would her cell phone have been here?"

"I dropped it, I guess," Tara said, uncharacteristically

deferential. "Earlier today. Evie and I were visiting with Charlie here at the church fundraiser before the work crew got started."

"Evie, huh?" Boggs said. "Which one of you's—"

Evie raised her hand to breast level and gave it a weak, royal wave.

"Ah. Another high schooler." He squinted at the three of them. "I take it the three of you were together when you found the body?"

Charlie shook his head. "Not really, sir. I found it—her, I mean—a couple of minutes before the girls got here."

"And then you called us."

"And then I called you."

Boggs stared him up and down a moment longer, then gestured behind him for Johnson. "And you three," Boggs said. "What's your business here?"

Letty Clark drew herself up and sputtered, "Why, I live over at the parsonage, officer."

"Chief."

"Chief, then. My son-in-law is the pastor of this fine church. I came over to help these young people find the girl's cell phone. It was only as we reached the church that we received the call from . . ." She looked to me.

"Evie," I supplied. "The kids had just found Ronnie out there and called for me and Marcus to hurry over and . . . help."

Boggs's attention caught. He peered at me. "How did you know her name?"

*Uh-oh, Maggie. Explanation needed.* It wouldn't do to be listed as a person of interest, even temporarily, given Tom's already testy views of my so-called knack for sniffing out trouble. Of course I didn't actually sniff it out. It just had a way of finding me, over and over again. Why? I wish I knew.

Just lucky, I guess.

"I saw her here at the fundraiser this afternoon," I explained. "A couple of times, actually."

"And what time was this?"

I thought back. "Well, the first time was fairly soon after our arrival. No later than two, I would guess. Maybe even earlier than that. Sorry I can't be more specific—I wasn't exactly watching the clock."

He nodded, working his jaw as though he was chewing an unseen amount of tobacco. "What was she doing when you saw her?"

"Arguing," I told him.

I had his interest, that much was clear. "Arguing, eh? I don't suppose you know who she was arguing with?"

"She called him Ty. He was an employee for the construction . . . crew."

As one, we all turned to look at Charlie, who gaped back at us in openmouthed surprise. Gradually understanding dawned. "Ohhhh. I think you mean Ty Bennett?"

"Yes," I said, "I'm pretty sure that was his name."

"And what was the nature of their disagreement?" the chief pressed.

"Well . . . it was personal."

Chief Boggs just looked at me. "Miss . . . ?" He let the question trail out for me to fill in.

"O'Neill." He must have forgotten that we'd been introduced not just once but a couple of times over the last eight months by his very own Special Task Force Investigator.

"Miss O'Neill. This woman's life was taken by someone tonight. Do you really think that anything in her life can be considered personal and off-limits at this point in time?"

Well, when he put it that way . . . "I suppose not." I glanced shyly around at everyone in our little group. "I would just prefer that it goes nowhere else. If everyone can agree on that . . ."

"I wouldn't tell anyone," Evie promised.

"Me, either," both Tara and Charlie said at the exact same moment.

One by one everyone nodded, right down to Letty Clark. I cleared my throat, ready to fulfill my part of the bargain. "They were arguing about their broken relationship. She was very bitter and fierce with him, ordering him out of the church. Her church. She said he had no right to be there."

Letty looked troubled by the revelation that the woman who was killed was presumably a part of Grace Baptist's own congregation, but she said nothing.

"The argument got quite physical. She was pushing against him and hitting him with her fists. They broke it up when I made my presence known, but . . . well, I guess you had to be there. I was scared for a minute that I wouldn't be able to stop them from going at each other."

Chief Boggs had been making notes as I spoke, and now his pen paused over the spiral notebook. He glanced up at me. "Anything else you remember?"

"Well, she did say a little more to me after he disappeared into the church. The gist of it was that their relationship was very sexual in nature." I blushed, because I could feel everyone hanging on my every word. Lowering my gaze so that I didn't have to look any of them in the eye, I continued. "But according to her, she had grown past that. She was done with him. She'd found God or something through this church, and she was moving on to better things."

Chief Boggs had a thoughtful expression on his face. "Was she? I wonder."

It was frighteningly easy to see his point. Especially as the camera flashes in the background behind him turned the scene wonky with an unearthly strobe effect.

"Anything else?"

I cleared my throat. "Actually, yes. Later in the afternoon, I was visiting with Mrs. Clark here out in the garden—this was before the excavation started, you understand—and we overheard an argument coming from somewhere in the church. I thought it was in the existing wing addition. All I heard was a man's voice protesting something. There was even some kind of a scuffle, judging from the sounds that came drifting out through the open windows. Mrs. Clark went to try to intervene, and I headed in the other direction, figuring one of us would be able to find them if we were moving in opposite directions."

"And did you?" he asked.

I shrugged. "I did see Ronnie leaving the building in a hurry. I only saw her from the back, but I think she was wiping her eyes. Maybe crying? I have no way of knowing for sure, but I had the feeling that she could very well have been part of the scuffle."

Boggs scribbled some more. "What about anyone else? Mrs. Clark, Miss O'Neill said that you had gone one way to try to intervene with whoever was doing the arguing?"

Letty Clark nodded. "Yes, sir. I decided the closest route would be to enter the church from the far end of the addition."

"And did you see anyone or anything?"

"No. No one." She gave me an odd look. "Miss O'Neill didn't mention that she had seen anyone emerging."

"No, I didn't," I admitted. "Mostly because of the argument I'd already witnessed. I felt that it was private and should stay that way. You know how gossip travels around this town."

She sighed. "True. A pity that people like to talk so. Perhaps the good Lord should have added that to the stone tablets he saw fit to provide us. The eleventh commandment. Might not have been a bad idea."

"Uh-*huh*." Boggs didn't even look up this time. "Did either of you see or hear anything else? Anything at all?"

When Letty demurred, I sheepishly raised my hand. "One last thing before I left the church, trying to find the girls here. As I was leaving, Ty Bennett came up the stairs from the basement."

"Bennett again, huh?"

"Yeah." I didn't much like telling him about Ty Bennett and whatever beef he'd had with Ronnie. I had a bad feeling about it, like I was saying too much or putting too much of an emphasis on the encounters I'd had. But what could I do? Facts were facts, and Chief Boggs had asked for the truth. I couldn't *not* tell him. "He said he'd been waiting in the air-conditioning with all the other guys on the construction crew in the big assembly room in the basement until it was time for them to get the machinery ready to go for the groundbreaking."

"It's true," Charlie offered. "We were all down there for a couple of hours. Better than waiting out in the hot sun, let me tell ya, when you're gonna have to be working out in it. There's no real reason that we needed to be here so early anyway, but the pastor asked, and they were paying us for it, so we all came. All of us were glad for the extra bucks, since we were gonna be working today anyway."

Boggs frowned. "So you're saying that he was down there with you all the entire time?"

"Well, no. I mean, it's hard to know really, when you've got a bunch of guys—"

"And girls," Tara pointed out.

"And girls," Charlie corrected automatically, as though used to that kind of intercession, "all together, messing around, laughing, talking. Well, I mean, who knows if anyone goes in or out."

"He said he had gone out to use the bathroom, and when he came back everyone was gone," I volunteered. "He was looking for everyone, wondering where they had gone."

Boggs accepted this without comment, the scritch-scratching of his pen on paper his only response. After a moment, he asked, "Anyone have anything else to offer?"

We glanced around at each other, all of us shaking our heads in the negative.

"Nothing at all? Miss O'Neill, which direction did you say that the victim headed toward when she left the church?"

"She was headed off to return to the fundraising events, from what I could tell."

"And that was at what time?"

Time was just not my forte. I squinched up my nose, considering. "Three? -Ish? I'm sorry, I'm just not certain."

"And that was the last that you personally saw of her."

"Until I saw her lying over there in that hole, yes."

Boggs turned his attention to Letty. "And what time did the fundraising events finish up?"

"The end to the excavation pretty much put a real

damper on any kind of a celebratory mood we were in," Mrs. Clark responded in dry tones. "Too many questions, too much curiosity, and no answers to any of it. Once everyone figured out they weren't going to be allowed a close-up look, they started drifting away. We started closing down around five o'clock. Everyone was gone by six."

"And all of this can be verified by your son-in-law, Pastor—"

"Robert Angelis. Yes, it can."

"Is he here? I'd like to speak with him, if I could."

With a regretful shake of her head, she said, "I'm so sorry, Chief. He was pulled away on a welfare call this evening. He's been gone since, oh, five, five thirty."

"Ah. I see. Tomorrow, then." He looked up from his notebook. "What about your daughter? I'm assuming she lives here with you both."

"Yes, of course. My daughter . . . well, of course you can speak with her if you like, but I can assure you that she went from the fundraiser straight to a hot bath, and from the bath to her bed. My daughter is unwell, you see. She shouldn't be distressed or overtired in any way. She has been under doctor's care for a while now, and—"

Boggs waved her concerns away. "I won't need to speak with her tonight, Mrs. Clark. But if there's a way for me to speak with her when she has rested . . . just to get a confirmation of a couple of points here . . ."

Mrs. Clark could see she had little choice. "Of course," she concurred.

"Now, about this excavation . . ."

As the only representative from the crew present, Charlie took up the tale, explaining to the chief about what had happened during the groundbreaking ceremony and what his crew foreman, Tim Kendall, had seen below-ground, that the site had been closed due to fears of instability—this made Chief Boggs's eyes bug out—and that excavation had stopped immediately, to be resumed only after engineers could be called out to review the situation.

Boggs took down the foreman's name from Charlie, then said, "That about covers it for now. Mrs. Clark, you are free to go on back to the parsonage now, but the rest of you—I'll need your name and contact information so that I can get in touch with you. Once I have that, you're free to go. I'll be needing official statements from all of you, so we can talk later about the best time for each of you to come down to the station."

Mrs. Clark waved her hand toward the garden. "If you don't mind, Chief, I'll just watch from over here for a while. I promise I won't be in the way. I often sit in the garden when I'm troubled, you see. I find it very sooth-ing."

"Fine, fine."

Charlie, Tara, and Evie went first, volunteering their home phone numbers without reservation, other than Tara's whispered, "My dad is gonna kill me for this!" Mar-cus, next, gave only his cell, since he often worked either in his workshop in his garage or with the band.

When it was my turn, I asked, "Chief Boggs? What was her last name?" At his questioning glance, I explained, "It seems wrong to keep referring to her as just Ronnie, somehow, considering that I didn't actually know her."

"Maddox," he answered. "Her name was Veronica Maddox."

I nodded and gave him my cell number but told him it

would probably be easier to find me at Enchantments. I gave him the number there, too.

Boggs's pen stopped midscratch. "Enchantments? That store down on River Street . . . the one that's owned by the witch?"

# Chapter 8

I drew myself up with as much dignity as I could muster. "Felicity Dow is the owner of the store, and whatever she is or is not is pretty much up to her, now, isn't it?"

Boggs grunted. That could have meant yes, or it could have meant hell, no—I wasn't too sure.

Finally we were able to leave, and I breathed a sigh of relief.

"Who'da thunk the store would get a reaction like that!" Tara said, sounding impressed as we trudged in the dark back to the car and Marcus's bike. "For a second there, I thought he was going to go all whoop-ass on you."

"Don't exaggerate, Tara," I said, feeling the edginess of annoyance grate at me. It had been quite a day.

"Seriously. First the stupid Church of Light, and now the Chief of Poh-Leece. You'd think that Liss was the freakin' Jezebel of the Cornfields or something."

"I have never been so glad to get out of a place in my life," Evie confided to us.

"The church?" I asked, distracted.

"No. The garden. Bleah. I didn't like it." To demonstrate her point, she lifted her shoulders up and made
herself shudder.

Well, I wasn't all that big on bugs myself, but the garden had been quite nice, I'd thought. Chalk it up to personal differences of opinion. Or maybe she was just
reacting to the whole stumbling-over-a-dead-body thing.
It made sense.

"So . . . who's riding with me?" Marcus asked.

I couldn't help noticing that he was looking at me
hopefully. I pretended to be digging through my bag and
said, "Well, I guess probably Tara should go with you,
and I'll take Evie home."

"Oh," he said. "Okay."

"You know, because it's late now."

"You're right. It is."

I heard the disappointment in his voice, but what
should I have done? Guilt was an emotion I was quite familiar with. Not comfortable, but familiar. And already I
was thinking about Tom and our issues with timing. We
really needed to talk, he and I . . .

Frowning, I fumbled with my key ring. "So . . . thanks,
Marcus, for coming over, and for coming with us tonight."

"Well . . . you're welcome, Maggie."

We were both being so formal, so stiff, it was almost
laughable. Except it wasn't funny. The tension between
us was a physical thing hanging in the air. What had happened to the easy candor we usually enjoyed as friends?

"The night would have been even more horrible without you here," I offered, trying to regain it.

"Thanks. I think."

Evie coughed. "Hey, Tara. Did you see this over here?" she asked, grabbing her friend's arm and pulling her over to look at one of the machines left behind by the on-hold construction crew.

Marcus watched them go, shaking his head. "Wow. That was obvious."

I laughed in spite of my discomfort. "They should work on their excuses. That was far too implausible. Pure high school stuff. Go figure."

He studied me a long, serious moment, searching my face. His directness had always thrown me for a loop, and this moment was no exception. I lowered my gaze, keeping it focused directly on the ground at his feet, so I knew exactly the moment he took that single questioning step toward me. My breath caught and I instantly backed away. When he didn't move again, I was forced to bring my gaze up to look deep into the all-seeing eyes I had been trying to avoid.

Marcus shook his head again. The smile he wore was just the teensiest bit regretful. "Still scared, Maggie?"

*Am I ever. Only of myself, not of you.* I shrugged.

"There's no need," he whispered, making sure no one could hear but me. "We're friends, yes?"

I could barely find my voice. "Always."

Friends who wanted each other but who kept dancing around that fact.

He nodded. "Always."

I knew he was well aware of the boundaries I had forced myself to reiterate just now, and I knew he respected that. It would mean that I'd have to be strong for myself, to forgo the relief of collapsing into his arms to take the edge off the anxiety the night's events had reintroduced into my life . . . but it was for the time being necessary. Where we would be in the future remained to be seen . . . but I knew I couldn't with any conscience move into a future at all without trimming up a few loose ends. Not without losing all respect for myself.

Turning toward where the girls hovered, watching us from the corners of their eager little eyes, I called out, "Ready, Evie?"

Tara said something under her breath to Evie before they headed in our direction. I had a feeling it was either pitying or exasperated in nature. Tara's expression as she picked up the spare motorcycle helmet that had flattened my hair earlier pretty much said it all.

I got into my car and rolled down my window as Evie circled around behind to the passenger side. "Marcus?" I said softly.

"Yeah?"

"Thank you."

No further explanation was required. With him, it was always that way. He always seemed to understand, even when I was still muddling through myself. "Anytime."

"Bye, Tara," Evie said with a lackluster wave. "See you tomorrow. If my parents let me live, that is," she amended gloomily.

I headed to Evie's house first, asking whether she'd like me to come in and explain things to her mom and dad. She declined. I had a feeling she wouldn't be telling them much. At least not yet. After dropping her off at the curb and waiting for her to get inside, I made my way home to my apartment, still mercifully well lit, and Minnie, who spent the next ten minutes scolding me for being gone and leaving her alone for so long. She seemed to have made the most of her time alone by knocking the stack of magazines off the end table and scattering them to the four winds. And then there was the toilet paper puddle on the floor in the bathroom, the entire length of which bore the distinct signs of claw and tooth marks.

With a weary sigh I picked up the magazines, tore off the length of toilet paper and wound it up, setting it aside, then picked up a still chirruping Minnie and took her off to bed with me. Soothed and happy, Minnie was out within minutes of my turning off the bedside lamp, but I stayed awake longer than I would have liked, unable to rid my mind of the body crumpled in that weird hole and the image of crosses, crosses, crosses nailed to the walls in every direction, filling my vision as it spun 'round and 'round and 'round in exhaustion.


It was not a good night.

Dreams again. Wild, wacky, and weird. Filled to the brim with flashes of things better left unthought. I don't know when I fell asleep, but the next thing I knew, I was rolling over and slitting one eye open to squint blearily at the glaring lights from the digital clock on my bedside table. Six forty-five. Which meant my alarm was going to go off in ten minutes. Yawn. I rolled over and covered up my head with my pillow.

Then promptly flung it off when I started feeling like I was breathing in cotton.

The second I did, I felt a weight on my chest and a scratching rasp on my chin. I opened my eyes again. I could only just make out Minnie's loving tongue very attentively whorling around on my face from the dim glow emanating from the light that I always left on in the kitchen. For security purposes, you see. Not because I was afraid of the dark.

And if you believe that, I have a bridge to sell you.

Minnie sat up to blink at me when I folded back the covers and got out of bed. Her head cocked to an inquisitive slant. I told her, "Some of us have to get ready for work, snuggle bug, and can't laze about until it's time to walk out the door." She just yawned, then rolled herself up into a fuzzy black ball. I don't think she believed me.

I went through my early morning routine, yawning widely through my shower, through my breakfast of toast with honey and cinnamon, through deciding what outfit I could possibly wear that would keep me as cool as possible through the July swelter and yet still look professional and put-together enough for the store. I settled on a light cotton sundress that came down to my ankles, with a tissue-weight shrug to cover my bare shoulders and upper arms. I'd been air-drying my wavy hair, which had a tendency to be unruly, especially in humid conditions. Like summer. All three-plus months of it. What to do, what to do? Finally I settled on twisting the back into a mass of smooth loops and securing them all at the base of my skull, creating a large kind of bun (but not). The clips and a goodly amount of spray gel kept it fully contained against the weather. Satisfied, I studied the final effect in the mirror: calm, cool, and collected. Success!

Running back into the bedroom to check the time and to grab my essentials of cell phone, lip balm, and sunscreen, I gasped when I saw the time. "Eep! How did that happen?" My things weren't on the dresser tray where I always leave them. "What the heck? Minnie, have you been acting up again? Go on. Cough 'em up, you little minx." Not even a peep of an answer. I sighed, then got down on my hands and knees to look under my dresser. Nothing. As I pushed back up on my hands, I saw a dark shape move past me in my peripheral vision. "I suppose you've come to apologize," I halfheartedly grumbled at the kitten I knew I'd find doing her best to be cute if I looked that way. "Well, you can just forget about that, missy, until you show me where you've hidden everything. Come on." Normally Minnie would have bumped up against me by now, purring and rubbing. She might even have jumped on my back, claws dug in for balance. But she did neither of those things. Which, I had to say, was . . . unexpected. I glanced over at her, where I'd seen the dark movement.

She wasn't there.

Frowning, I sat back on my knees and glanced around the room. Minnie, aka Mini Minx, was still lying all curled up in the middle of the unmade bed, completely zonked.

Something else was hovering where I had thought I had seen Minnie, though. I saw it now, thickening into a sort of nebulous mist. Small at first, but as I watched, it seemed to grow larger, so slowly that I wouldn't have recognized the change at all if I hadn't looked away to locate Minnie. My mouth fell open as I locked my gaze on the shifting mass of energy. I sat back on my heels, unwilling to take my eyes off it for even a moment.

"What are you?" I whispered. At least I thought I did. Or was it possible I only thought it?

Before the mist could answer, a second black shape, darker and more solid, launched through the air in a blur. It landed smack dab in the center of the looming mist blob, then spun around wildly, dispersing the energy that had been attempting to gather. The solid black blur flipped its body around again—I should have known, Minnie to the rescue!—and faced me, a delightfully mischievous look on her face. With a ferocious growl, she twitched her fully bristled tail back and forth, raced around the room in one complete circuit, then came about and very docilely climbed into my lap and began to purr.

I cupped her chin in my hands and lifted her face up to look into her eyes. "You are a very special girl, you know that? You just chased that spirit energy away. You did! You awesome, awesome girl!"

I guess Liss was right about the protective qualities of cats. I should have known she would be. My Liss was always right. Always.

I really liked that about her.

With the unexpected energy of the intruder successfully *poofed*, I was feeling on top of the world. Invincible. Ready to face the day and anything it might present to me. Given the events of the weekend, who knew what that might be?

I had a feeling it might include Tom. And not in a good way.

The thought sunk my confidence levels, just a tad, but it couldn't be helped. Gathering up Minnie, her carrier, and my bag, I hurried out the door, giving a last considering glance at the light switch as I went. Naaah. I wasn't feeling *that* gutsy. The lights would stay on today, just as they had since I first discovered the truth about the spirit world that touched our own with a little too much familiarity.

I had just enough time to stop in at Annie-Thing Good, Annie Miller's hopping little café, to pick up the standing order the store had for her plate-sized apple fritters, raspberry ganache pie, turtle cheesecake brownies, and blueberry popovers. Baked fresh, just for us, bless her ever-loving baker's heart. The woman was a veritable witch with a mixing spoon. Maybe even in more ways than one.

I parked Christine across the street, because all of the spots around the café were taken, seeing as how we were smack in the middle of the early morning rush. I rolled the windows down for Minnie, to be sure she'd be okay for the five minutes I'd be inside. "Mind things for me while I'm inside, sweet pea. I'll be right back."

I ran across the street, dodging traffic, and pushed through the glass door to the always delightful tinkle of brass announcement bells. Delicious smells wafted together throughout the outer limits of the establishment, the kinds that made you instantly think of buttery pastries and gooey cinnamon confections and instantly *not* think of the effects such items might have on your, um, bottom line. I was faced with these innocent little indulgences day after day—I *knew* how dangerously seductive they could be.

I considered myself a saint, actually, for every day that I managed to resist. St. Margaret the Resolute.

St. Margaret of the Growling Stomach was more like it.

"Hey, Maggie," Annie called out as she bustled around behind the counter for the line of people in front of me. "How's it going this morning, hon?"

"Peaches and cream," I said breezily. Evidently she hadn't heard about the situation at the Baptist church, and I wasn't about to be the first to break it to her. It would get out soon enough anyway.

"Be with you in a mo'," she said, assembling an order with all the grace and intricate movements of a choreographed ballet.

"No hurry."

I settled in for the wait, knowing it wouldn't be long. It was never long. Annie was a whirlwind in the kitchen, a dynamo behind the counter, and a ray of sunshine to anyone who needed a lift. She would be breezing up with the pastry order before I even had time to yawn in boredom.

"I heard they have an engineer scheduled to examine it today."

My ears perked up as I caught the middle of a conversation between two men in front of me.

"I heard something more."

The first man quirked a brow. "More about the cave-in?"

"Beyond the cave-in. About a situation that went down last night."

Two men chatting away like old hens might have struck me as funny. Trouble was, I knew exactly what they were talking about, and humor was not even an option. So people were already talking about it. I wondered which of the people involved last night had been spilling the beans.

"Let's just say," the second man continued, "that this town appears to be experiencing more than its share of *non-accidents* of late."

Non-accidents. How very PC.

"What did you hear, Randy? And how?"

"Let's just say," he said again, "I have my sources."

"Aw, come on."

Randy smirked but didn't relent. "You can read about it in today's edition."

Something clicked in my brain. A realization: Randy must be Randall Craig, editor in chief of the Stony Mill Gazette. He was also married to my least favorite person in the entire world, Margo Dickerson-Craig. And if he knew about the whole dead-girl-found-at-the-church (may she rest in peace) thing, I had to assume Margo's sources were hot on the trail as well.

I pretended to be engrossed in a piece of cat-fur fuzz on my shirtfront while I took a sneak peek at Margo's husband from the corner of my eye. Funny—he didn't look henpecked. Randy Craig was a good-looking man. Youngish in appearance, but I had heard from Mel that he had a good fifteen years on Margo. He also had a slickness to him that I associated with people on the make, and whether the pursued is money or power or women did not seem to matter. Maybe with newshounds, that just went with the territory. Even when said newshounds were very small potatoes indeed.

The two men went on to less intriguing conversation, leaving me to obsess about my fur-dusted shirtfront for real. Finally it was my turn at the counter. "Just picking up the regular," I told Annie.

"Got it right here for you."

Annie-Thing Good was a new establishment by Stony Mill standards, which usually meant a lengthy breaking-into-the-conservative-market period, but the café had found an immediate customer base because of one thing: Annie herself. Not only was she a fabulous chef with inventive ways of making everyday comfort food stand out with her signature gourmet flair, but she was also the perfect small-town café owner: friendly but not intrusive, bustling but not too busy to lend an ear, and when you needed a smile, her freckled face and wide grin could light up the world of even the most diehard pessimist. Annie was a great start to anyone's day.

She slid the white cardboard box across the counter to me. "I don't know how you manage to do this every day,"

I said after making sure that there wasn't anyone waiting behind me. "They must take hours to prepare."

Even without makeup and with her fuzzy strawberry hair all a-frazzle, Annie was pretty in a mom-next-door, fresh-faced way. "I haff my vays," she said with a wink.

Magick with a wooden spoon? I had to wonder at that. "I can only imagine."

"I threw in a couple of pieces of lemon raspberry tart," she said, putting a hand to her hip in an all-work, no-play kind of way. "Let me know what you two think. I'm considering adding it to the menu and I need a couple of guinea pigs."

"Oh, hey, count me in whenever," I said with a laugh. "I can be a pig, guinea or otherwise, as well as the next girl."

Annie nodded but fell silent. Which, in Annie's world, was not normal.

"What's up?" I asked.

It took her a moment to gather her thoughts together. Or was it her courage? Both impressions were coming through to me, equally strong. She glanced around the shop and lowered her voice to make sure that the few customers sitting at the tables wouldn't overhear. "Maggie . . . you know that normally I wouldn't butt in, and if you feel like I'm butting in then just tell me, because you know I hate that, and . . . gosh, I would hate for you to think that of me, and . . . but if it were me, I would want someone to bring it up to me, because . . . well, it could be nothing, and I know how sometimes it's easy to misinterpret things, and I would hate for it to be that, I really, really would, and—"

"Annie?"

She looked up at me blankly. "Hm?"

"Why don't you just tell me? It would make you feel better, I think."

She nodded, but in truth she looked miserable about it, and it was starting to make me nervous. "All right." She took a deep breath. "Maggie, how are you and Tom getting along?"

Why was everyone always asking me that? "Oh. Um, well, okay, I guess. We've both been a little busy, and, well, Tom's been a bit preoccupied. With his job and everything. You know. Just life. Honestly? I haven't seen much of him lately, but up until last week I was spending all of my evenings at my sister's, you know, and we just haven't had a chance to touch base yet." And then, because my excuses were hitting sour notes on even *my* ears, I looked her squarely in the eye. "Why?"

She cleared her throat and dropped her gaze to the countertop . . . then grabbed a damp towel and began swiping away at the already spic-and-span surface before saying, "Well . . . I guess I just wondered, because . . . well, the truth is . . . I saw Tom last night."

Was *that* all? I relaxed and felt my tension ease a bit. "Oh. I heard he was off last night, but I didn't get a chance to talk to him, with everything that happened out at the . . . with everything that happened. Where'd you see him?"

She stopped swiping. "At Casa D's."

"Casa D's," I repeated, I must admit, a bit blankly.

"Yeah. It's that nice Mexican restaurant in North—"

"Yes, I know," I said. *Casa de Mil Sueños*. It was one of my favorite places. Tom had taken me there on our second date, I remembered, and it had been a favorite of ours ever since.

That worried feeling in the pit of my stomach? It started up again with a vengeance.

One look at my face and Annie started scrubbing away with the towel again. "I stopped by there with a gentleman

friend of mine for a late night appetizer fest. Sometimes
you just don't want to cook, you know? And, well, Tom
was there. I don't think he saw me. He was at a table
toward the back of the restaurant, by the fountain, and we
were in a booth toward the front." Her hand stilled, and
she bit her lip. "Maggie, he was with someone."

I stared at her.

"A woman. He was with a woman."

# Chapter 9

I couldn't do anything except blink. "I see." Except I didn't. Because Tom was so upright and straitlaced that he would never dream of seeing someone else while he was seeing me.

Would he?

*You aren't entirely innocent in all of this, Margaret Mary-Catherine O'Neill*, Grandma C's voice in my head whispered.

My thoughts flashed to Marcus and the kiss we'd shared a month or two back. The tension from last night, and what it could have led to, had I invited it? No, I wasn't innocent . . . but I was trying hard to do the right thing. I just hadn't found the opportunity to square everything away.

*You could have tried harder.*

I bit my lip. Yeah. I could have.

*He is a man.*

He was, in fact, that. But that was no excuse, I thought, frowning.

*And you haven't exactly come to an agreement between you.*

That was the truest statement of all. Neither of us had committed without the shadow of doubt hanging over our heads. Neither of us had been completely honest about what was holding us back, although we'd been coming closer to an understanding of it. And the whole thing with Mel had happened, and then the fire at the feed mill and Marcus there by my side, quietly offering me strength and protection, and everything had just . . . fizzled quietly on a back burner, waiting for one of us to get brave and open up the line of communication again. But I'd been busy with Mel and at the store, and when he phoned, it had seemed so halfhearted, and . . . and then there was Marcus.

*You have to decide what you want.*

I knew that.

*Who you want.*

Yeah, I knew that, too.

In theory.

I swallowed my misgivings and uncertainties and gave Annie a grim smile. "Thanks, Annie. I mean it. Thank you for telling me."

She nodded. She understood me perfectly. "Anytime, honey. If you need someone to talk to, I'm here for you."

My best friend, Steff, was even more accommodating when I called her from a quiet corner of Enchantments' upstairs loft during a lull at the store later that morning. "You need someone to TP his house?" she asked. "I haven't done that in years, but if you need a posse, I'm your girl."

I laughed. A weak chuckle, but it was something. "It

hasn't rained in weeks. As payback, it wouldn't be worth a damn. Way too easy to clean up with no rain."

"Hm. I see your point. Dueling pistols at twenty paces? I could be your second."

"You don't like guns, remember? For that matter, I'm not too fond of them myself."

"Guns are guns. I don't care about them one way or the other. It's people who use them for their nefarious ways."

"True." I sighed. "Besides . . . I really don't think I have the right to say anything."

"Marcus?"

"Mm." My noncommittal way of affirming without actually saying anything.

"Maggie O'Neill, you hussy!" she teased, laughing.

"Well, I wouldn't go so far as to say that," I protested, my cheeks blazing. "It was just a kiss. And a little harmless flirtation. And a fair amount of hinting on his part that I for the most part have managed to downplay. Other than the fact that I am, um, feeling it more than I probably should. I mean, he is fairly . . . intriguing. And—"

"So, which one of them do you want?"

That was the problem. I didn't want to hurt anyone, and making the decision I felt hovering on the horizon was going to mean *someone* was going to be hurt. "Steff?"

"Yeah?"

"I think I'm in trouble."

"I know. It's a bitch, deciding sometimes, isn't it?"

I didn't know. I'd never had the problem of deciding between two men at the same time before now. But based on the way I was feeling right at this very moment, I'd have to say Steff knew what she was talking about.

"For what it's worth, hon, I think you've already made your decision. You just haven't put it into words yet."

Oh.

"So," Steff moved on breezily, "while you're deciding that, why don't you also give some consideration to when you might be able to find some face time for your dearest, oldest friend? And when I say oldest, I say that in the most nonliteral way possible."

Yet another thing to feel guilty about. "I haven't exactly been the best best friend lately, have I?" I accused myself gloomily. Minnie stared at me from her perch on top of a glass counter, pawing at the air to get my attention. When I didn't reach for her, she walked around in four concentric circles, then sat down where she could pout and watch me more comfortably.

"No, but neither have I. We've both been on the preoccupied side of things. Me with Danny, you with work and Tom and, well, Marcus, and your sister and—gee, Mags, no wonder you're feeling confused and pulled in different directions."

"Well, if we can't find time for our best friends, there's got to be something wrong with that."

"I completely agree."

"How about next weekend?" I suggested. "I'm off big-sister duty now since Mel decided hiring a nurse-slash-nanny was the way to go. Thank goodness. I thought my nieces were going to run me ragged, but instead Mel was the biggest culprit. Boredom and a busy husband do not make for a happy bed-bound mommy. The girls were precious." They were, too. That was the biggest surprise. I actually missed seeing them on a daily basis. The new baby was due in the next month or so, too. Another niece or nephew to ward off those pesky little longings I attributed most often to the advancing biological clock and a dose of the maudlin and hormonal.

"Next weekend sounds great! I work Saturday, but I'm off by three thirty."

"Think Danny will let you out of his lecherous sights for an evening? If not, you can bring him with you, so long as you both agree not to paw all over each other in front of me. It's embarrassing," I teased.

Steff laughed. "Well, I *guess* we can control ourselves for a coupla hours. Assuming he even wants to crash an all-girl party. I have a feeling he might just demur."

"Well, if he does . . . we'll always have Magnum."

Some days, I nearly convinced myself that Magnum was destined to be my only true love. But when you already had perfection, maybe it was greedy to want more. Even when said true love existed only in that form via the time-lapse magick of TV reruns.

Sigh.

"Maggieeeeeeeee?" Evie's voice drifted up the stairwell.

"Whoops, gotta run. I'll talk to you later, Steff."

"Later, gator."

I hurried over and poked my head out over the gallery rail. "What is it?"

"Liss just got back."

Ooh. I hurried down the stairs. I had arrived at the store this morning in the nick of time after stopping in at Annie's, only to find that Liss herself had been there and had left already for a quick trip to City Hall to fill out a form that would allow the store to be a vendor at the town's Scarecrow Festival this fall. The note she left for me said that she expected to be back in an hour; it was now just after eleven. The line at City Hall must have been longer than she'd thought it would be.

Minnie trailed me down the stairs, a black blur at my feet. She seemed to think that a trip down the stairs meant a foot race she needed to win, every single time. Most of the time, I let her.

Evie appeared out of nowhere to scoop up an unsuspecting Minnie into a furry ball against her chest, which allowed me to win the race to Liss after all. As I passed the counter, I saw Tara sitting on a stool, blowing bubbles with her gum and texting fast and furious on her cell.

I pushed through the purple velvet curtains to the back office. Liss was standing there in the muted light of the office, her back to me, but I knew instantly that there was something wrong.

Something *else* wrong, that is.

"What's up?" I asked her. "City Hall certainly took their time, didn't they?"

Liss turned and sat down in the antique barrel-shaped desk chair with a sigh. "They turned me down," she replied matter-of-factly . . . and yet the matter-of-factness of her tone did not hide from me her disquiet.

"What?" The thought hadn't even occurred to me. This was a small-town festival. They were always hungry to get vendors to participate. "Why on earth—?"

"Limited slots . . . not the right kind of product . . . some opposition to the store in conservative quarters . . . there will be children at the festival . . . There were other reasons mentioned, but they were equally vague and meaningless."

My eyebrows had risen more and more with each statement. So had my indignation. "Just what do they think we sell here? Antique pornography? Do they expect us to man the booth as dominatrixes and force whips and fuzzy handcuffs on the children of Stony Mill?"

"Oh, my dear, it's not what they know we sell—the various antiques, the crystal decanters, the scented lotions, the chocolates. Nothing like that. It's what they don't know that worries them. Very offensive. At least *I* am."

"You?"

She sighed, fiddling with the chain handle of the silk frame purse she still held in her lap. "Not Felicity Dow, businesswoman, so much as Felicity Dow, town witch. Despised universally for my religious practices and beliefs." Her smile was a little sad, but a smile nonetheless as she straightened in the chair and briskly dusted off her slacks. "But no matter. These things happen for a reason, and it's obvious to me that I have work to do here in this town. Just what that work is, I can't be certain, but it will be revealed to me in time. Of that I have no doubt."

The Witch Factor. And that was it entirely. I felt my spirits sinking. "Oh, Liss. Oh, damn. I'm so sorry. I feel like this is my fault. It was my stupid sister who let the cat out of the bag."

Liss shook her head. "It would have happened some other way, if not for Melanie. The timing was the key. It was meant to happen precisely when it did. If there's one thing I'm certain of in this universe, it's that some things are meant to happen. It's the other little things along the way that are decided by all of our decisions and actions."

Well, *she* might have found it in her heart to forgive Mel, but I wasn't feeling anywhere near that magnanimous. Mostly because I knew Mel for what she really was. I knew what motivated her, and in this case I knew how shallow that motivation was, because that was the kind of existence my sister led. She was the ultimate small-town trophy wife, and she reveled in the quality of life and the social status that being an up-and-coming lawyer's wife afforded her. For Mel, the universe was all about her. She was the star at its center, and she insisted that everyone else come into alignment with her. The problem with that was, she was constantly competing for status with other trophy wives in her tony subdivision, and that usually spelled trouble . . . of the gossipy kind.

And the trouble this time was, a friend of mine was the unhappy target, with the potential for backlash to come at her in a big, possibly even dangerous way.

Liss rose from the chair and began to put her things away in the closet where we kept coats and sundries. "Never mind all of this now. It will work itself out. How was your Sunday afternoon?"

Tara poked her head in through the curtain. "Did you tell her, Maggie?"

Liss raised a brow as she gazed back and forth between Tara and me. "I take it the festival was more eventful than you had expected." *But in what way?* the continued lift of her brows seemed to be wondering.

"A dead girl at the church!" Tara burst out with a force equal to that she used to come through the velvet curtains.

Liss looked at me quickly. "Another body?"

What she really meant was, *Another murder?* I could only nod.

Evie joined us with Minnie draped over her shoulder, vulturelike, as Tara spilled the details. "The festival was pretty sucky when all was said and done, so Evie and I found Charlie and hung out while Maggie did her thing, and then the payloader thingie broke through the ground and nearly fell in this hole that was created by its weight, which made the excavation schedule pretty much shut down because they wanted to make sure it was safe, and then Evie and I went over to Maggie's to wait for Charlie, and wow, the whole Ouija thing, which was pretty eventful in itself because I think Maggie drew something to her when she was out at the church, and Marcus showed up—did I mention that?—and then I couldn't find my phone and we decided I must have dropped it out at the church, so we all went out there, Marcus included, and we all split up, and of course Charlie met us out there, but he got there first, so yeah, Charlie found the body, and she was kind of beat up around the head and he wouldn't let us look, and then Maggie and Marcus showed up, and then the police, and so . . . yeah."

When Tara decides to spill, she really spills.

"Well." Liss looked back and forth between the three of us. "That was quite some night."

I nodded.

"And what does our dear Tom say about all this?"

The mention of Tom brought my conversation with Annie back full force. "I don't know," I said, my voice a bit more terse than I would have wanted it. "I haven't heard from him yet."

"I see." And I got the feeling that she really did, which was even more embarrassing. Me and my messed up love life. "Marcus was there?"

I nodded again. It seemed to be all I was good for.

"He was," Evie answered for me, "the whole time. I don't know what we would have done without him and Charlie."

"*Pfft*. We would have done exactly what we did *with* them," Tara scoffed. "We would have taken care of business."

·

"All of that happened after you left here yesterday afternoon?"

"All of it. After the cave-in, that is. Crazy, isn't it?" I had found my voice, so I proceeded to explain to her with a little more clarity all that we had experienced and knew as fact. "The crew foreman looked down into the hole as much as he could," I finished up. "He said it looked like there were crosses all over the walls and ceiling. Weird, huh?"

"Hm. Very unusual indeed."

"The room or root cellar or whatever it is, wasn't something that the pastor of the church knew about. He seemed as surprised as everyone else."

"Extraordinary."

"And then the spirit that followed Maggie home popped up through the Ouija," Evie added excitedly. "He kind of scared me. Not as much as that garden, though. Still gives me the shivers."

"What are you, plant phobic?" Tara teased. "That's a really weird thing to be afraid of, Eves."

Evie shrugged. "I can't help it. It felt . . . off. Haunted. Lots of weirdness all wrapped up in a pretty package. I didn't like it."

"Perhaps you were experiencing the same spirit that followed the lot of you to Maggie's home," Liss suggested.

"Maybe." But Evie didn't sound convinced.

The bell at the front of the store jingled. "Hidee ho, ladies! Anyone here?"

Marian Tabor's voice boomed through the store, loud enough to wake the dead—thank goodness we didn't have any of those here. I went up front to greet her. "Hiya, Marian. How goes things at the library?"

Marian Tabor was the town librarian and aunt to both Marcus and Tara. She was also one of my mother's oldest and dearest friends, one of the few who did not balk from standing up to her . . . which made her a rarity in my book. Today her hair was teased to French-twist perfection, and her penchant for animal print was in full force: she wore a purple cheetah-print blouse that made her breasts appear even larger than usual . . . which was in truth rather startling and made it difficult to look directly at her for any length of time.

"Oh, you know. Same old thing. Books in, books out. Ol' Bertie and the Librarian have been going at it, but I just give them the business and they settle down. The important thing is that they don't frighten the patrons with their antics."

Bertie and the Librarian. Bertie being Boiler Room Bertie, the library's resident spirit, sometimes seen as a glowing blue orb in the library's inner sanctums. Calling the second spirit the Librarian was Marian's way of not honoring her long ago predecessor, whose selfish actions resulted in her own death and lovelorn Bertie's earthbound existence. Karma . . . it was sometimes a harsh teacher. Sometimes a final one. In Marian's estimation, the Librarian didn't deserve to be remembered by name.

"Marcus told me what happened last night."

I glanced up from my reverie in surprise. "He did?"

"He did. He thought I might be interested from a historical perspective." She tilted her head toward me. "He was right, you know. As the head chronicler for the county historical society, this is exactly the sort of thing I should be covering."

"You mean the murder?"

"That, yes. But the cave-in, too. That hidden room.

What a find. Who knows what might be in there. I'm going to go straight out to the Baptist church and have me a chat with the minister."

"Oh, I don't know if today will be the best time for that." I could just see Marian's purple-spotted boobs leading the charge against the Stony Mill PD. I don't think even Tom could stand up to that. Actually, that *could* be entertaining . . .

"I'm not going to get in the way . . . but I'm not going to let them ruin the find while they process the scene for that poor young woman's death, either. They're just going to have to do what they can to keep it from coming to harm," she said as the rest of the girls streamed out from the back office.

"Hi, Aunt Marian," Tara said. I saw the lift of her eyebrows at Marian's outfit, but honestly, Tara had a few doozies in her wardrobe, too. Jump boots and leprechaun green tights, anyone? I rest my case.

"Marian! How lovely to see you," Liss said. "Have some tea? Tara, why don't you get your aunt a cup of whatever she wants."

Evie just waved shyly with a pretty smile.

"No tea for me, thanks. I just polished off a jumbo coffee and don't want to float out of here before I show you my goodies. Oh, and I brought your paper in for you. The boy just delivered it," Marian said, taking it from where she'd looped it through the handles of her canvas tote bag—a lovely, tasteful, imitation giraffe. She slid the newspaper across the scarred but polished wooden countertop.

"A newspaper, today? It's not Tuesday." Our so-called daily paper was printed daily, per its publishing schedule . . . all except for Mondays, Wednesdays, Thursdays, Fridays, Saturdays, and Sundays. The owner's idea of a joke. A little lame perhaps, but hey, we're a small town. We have limited material to work with.

"It's a special early edition, according to the headlines. And somewhere here in *this* mess," Marian said, digging deep within her roomy carryall, "is a tidbit of information I came across the other day while I was cataloguing some vintage books and files that were part of an estate that was deeded to the historical museum. I thought Liss would find it particularly interesting. Ah. Here it is. I photo-copied it for you."

Minnie leaped down from Evie's shoulders and walked over to the folded newspaper, pawing at it as a test, then attacking it with great abandon. While Liss began to read the photocopy Marian had brought for her, I scooted the newspaper over to Tara before Minnie could either shred it or make a bed out of it . . . both of which had been known to happen.

"Fascinating," Liss murmured, pursing her lips thought-fully.

"What is it?" Evie asked, peeking over Liss's shoulder.

"It's a clipping I found saved between the leaves of an old diary," Marian told the rest of us, "about a devastat-ing fire that happened here in the county over a hundred years ago."

"If this is true," Liss said, the intrigue in her tone readily apparent, "then the property my home now sits on once housed a kind of spiritual commune back in the 1800s. A spiritual center of great renown for its time. But which came first, the spiritualists or the energy? Did the spiritualists raise the energy that I feel there now, or were they drawn to the area by preexisting conditions that are a natural part of the land's makeup? That, my dears, is the question." She shook her head and looked up at us, her hand flat on the photocopy. "Fascinating, just fascinating."

"This is pretty fascinating, too," Tara said. Except the flatness in her voice sent my wariness levels soaring. Tara had spread out the newspaper on the counter so that the front page was now readable.

"What is it?"

"Oh, just an article about the murder of that woman last night. Pretty fast work, if you ask me."

"Why's it so interesting?" Evie asked. "We were all there last night. We know what we found."

"It's not so much the murder as the other little details they put in there."

# Chapter 10

We all crowded around the paper. Front and center on the page was a lurid photo of the crime scene with its yellow Do Not Cross tape and red flags of evidence markers. The photo was taken in daylight, so they must have gone out as soon as the sun came up this morning. Very industrious of them.

*U-L-C . . .*

The memory of the Ouija spirit rose fresh and unbidden in my mind.

"They shouldn't have put that picture out there for just anyone to see," Evie said, grimacing. "It's just not right."

"I don't think the press—even the small-town variety— have any understanding of callousness, you know," Marian said. "It's regrettable, but they seem to think their quest for readers justifies their sensationalizing the facts."

Sensationalizing. That was a good word, I decided as I read the article. The facts presented about the crime itself seemed to be fairly straightforward. It was the additional information they had dug up that was questionable.

"Did anyone *here* talk to anyone associated with the newspaper?" I asked. Everyone present shook their heads in the negative. "Hm. I'm sure Marcus didn't, either. Which leads me to wonder where they got their information."

"There was any number of people there last night that could've spilled the beans."

"Yes, but how many of them knew that Marcus is a knife maker?" I asked.

"It says that in there?" Evie asked, her eyes widening with sudden nervousness.

"That and a whole lot of other things."

The "other things" included the fact that one Charles Howell, an employee of the Furlow Construction Company, which had been hired by the church for its recent renovation plans, had discovered the body, along with me (*Maggie O'Neill, an employee of downtown area gift shop Enchantments*, it read), Marcus (described as *a part-time musician and independent knife maker*), two female minors who would not be named in order to protect their identity, and Mrs. Letty Clark, mother-in-law to the minister of the church. Was I the only one who thought the inclusion of our places of employment ventured a little too far into our privacy? Also included was the fact that I had witnessed Veronica Maddox there with Tyler T. Bennett of the Little Turtle Trailer Court out on the State Road. Mr. Bennett was currently being questioned by authorities, the article stated; more information would be forthcoming, but it did appear that an arrest was possible.

I couldn't say that I was happy to have my witness statement exposed to the world at large. It seemed an awful lot of information to let out in an open murder investigation, and it surprised me. I wondered if Tom or Chief Boggs had vetted the flow of information to the reporter. Somehow, I didn't think so.

The rest of the article was dedicated to a thrown-together recap of the victim's life. A poor life, raised by a single mother. Where her father was, who knew? No one they interviewed. A friend, a former teacher, and her mother chimed in about poor Ronnie, each with their own take on the girl's psyche. The one characteristic each person agreed on was ambition and a desire to have it all. Ronnie's mother told the reporter that "Ronnie was always a little bit wild. She was a good girl, though. She knew right from wrong. She just had a streak of the honeybee in her, always buzzin' from this 'un to that 'un. Stirring things up a little, sure. But she was fixin' herself up right good, finding a path with God and doin' her best to straighten herself out. This didn't have to happen. She was just a poor girl trying to make good in the world."

"The poor woman," Liss murmured.

Marian agreed. "I know Harriet Maddox from the library. She comes in regularly to pick up the newly arrived romance novels. A simple woman with a quiet life. I feel bad for her. Ronnie was her only child."

A mother should never lose her child, at any age, for any reason. The thought to me was unthinkable, and I didn't even have kids. And yet it happened every day, all over the world. To have them taken away at the hands of another, though, without rhyme or reason? That had to be the ultimate in parental heartache.

The rest of the front page was taken up by a speculative letter to the editor titled "Chaos In Our Midst?" and proved to be a recap of the string of bad luck—murders, that is—the town had suffered in the last nine months. It was not pretty. It wasn't even polite. And it pretty much called out the police department for being inadequate and even unequipped to cope.

The letter writer seemed to have a dual purpose: It suggested that there were more insidious, behind-the-scenes threats to the town's well-being that others might not be aware of. The readers were hereby advised that there was now a group of ghost hunters in Stony Mill, headed up by self-professed witch Ms. Felicity Dow, owner of Enchantments, with the author opining that the group's conversing with spirits might be a reason that the town's luck had been changing. Furthermore, it was revealed that Ms. Dow had been personally involved in a ritual "clearing" of a demon at an unnamed Stony Mill residence within the last month. The author of the letter suggested that, while the witches in question purported themselves to be performing a beneficial service by clearing away evil spirits, there was no reason to trust that claim. Witches in Stony Mill, demons on the loose, murders on our doorsteps. Was this the sort of future we wanted for our town? Readers were advised to contact their local clergy and ask what they could do to help ensure the spiritual well-being of their families and the community at large.

It was signed by Anonymous, but I knew, I just *knew* it must be Margo Dickerson-Craig. Putting her gossip to good use, I see. Who else could have been timely enough to make the "Special Edition" with her own personal brand of spew?

My stomach burned when I saw that Tom was singled out by reputation, if not by name. *Even the addition of a Special Task Force Investigator to the city budget cannot squelch the violence in our town*, was the specific charge. Well, of course having Tom take on the additional duties of the cross-departmental task force wasn't going to stop the violence from occurring. The murders that we had endured weren't in any way related. They were random, separate, without ties in any way. Completely unpredictable. All of the murders that had happened had been solved . . . I couldn't for the life of me understand what more dear Anonymous (cough, cough) thought could be done.

"What she wants is impossible," I protested, stabbing a finger down at the op-ed piece.

"You didn't finish reading it, Magster. She's calling out Tom for his ties to this store. Through you, obviously."

*"What?!"*

It was true. I read the words myself. "She has *way* overstepped her bounds."

"She's gone completely mental," Tara corrected. "I mean, I'm not exactly Tom's number-one fan, but even I can see what's what, and what's what definitely doesn't include him not doing his job. Sometimes he does it only too well."

Well, she would say that, having been busted by the man in question down at the hanging gardens at the old quarry, a favorite make-out destination among the local teenagers and so-not-teenaged. And that's pretty much what Evie told her. With glee.

"Bite me, Evil."

I was going to have to find Tom and get his take on all of this. That much was obvious. What wasn't obvious was how he was going to take the news that I had been with Marcus when I once again found myself in the thick of trouble. Not trouble that I had caused, and yet trouble nonetheless.

And then there was the information about Tom that Annie had helpfully passed on.

Marian left, saying that she had a lunch meeting with a judge on behalf of the county historical society. I decided to follow her lead. With a nervous twinge in the pit of my stomach, I told Liss I was going to take my lunch just a little bit early. After promising to bring Tara and Evie each a large order of fries and a strawberry milkshake from the drive-up Coney Dog restaurant and giving Minnie a kiss between her ears, I took myself off to find Tom. There was no answer on his cell, so I headed over to the police station.

His car was there, parked in its usual spot. I pulled into a visitor slot and popped the gearshift into first gear to hold the car in place, since Christine's emergency brake was a little unreliable. Then I flipped down the visor to check my appearance in the vanity mirror I'd Velcroed there long ago. My hair had absorbed the steam from the air, even though it had been clipped and moussed into place. I ran my palms over the front and plucked at the bangs, hoping to make it appear that I had at least tried to be tidy. I wished I understood the fundamentals of a Glamour charm better. I might be tempted to try it, if I thought beauty would be enough to distract Tom from the real issues at hand.

Just my luck that Tom had ethics.

Still, a woman knows instinctively that her wiles can get her out of a tight spot here and there, and it certainly doesn't hurt to employ the arsenal, even when uncertain of the effectiveness of it. So, I grabbed my lip gloss from my purse and applied it liberally. The slick of rosy gloss on lips can have a distracting effect on even the sternest of men, doncha know. So does adjusting the boobage upward, back from the sad state of affairs gravity drags them into. Getting out of my car, I smoothed my sundress as best I could—steamy heat makes the worst, limp wrinkles—and closed my door, not bothering with either locks or windows. Anyone who would steal a car without air-conditioning on a day like this was welcome to it.

Jeanette was behind the counter window when I walked in. She opened it as soon as she saw me. "Hey there, Maggie. Long time no see."

I smiled uncomfortably. Even Jeanette had noticed. "Hey, Jeanette. I don't suppose Tom is around, is he?"

Her smile stiffened as, from an office down the hall, raised voices came thundering out. "Get the hell out of my office, Reed!"

"Now, Hiram . . . don't get your gun belt in a twist—"

"You come in here and accuse me of spilling my guts to the local fish wrap, then tell me to calm down? You've got some nerve, you ham-handed excuse for a politician. You're not a lawman. All you care about is catering to the city council and being their whipping boy when it comes to budgets and protocol."

"There's no need for you to get personal about this. I only said—"

"You accused me of giving the Gazette all of the details about the crime. Do I look that stupid? Do I look like I've never handled a case before? Jesus-H.-Christ-in-a-box."

Jeanette sent me an apologetic shrug. She and I both knew that all we could do was wait out the storm.

"I asked you whether you talked with them. They've been alarmingly close with their information all year long. Too close. I just thought—"

"Well, you can just think again. You got problems with the way I do things, tell me. But only when you got your facts straight."

Sheriff Reed said something low that I couldn't quite make out. I was really trying not to look too much like I was eavesdropping, even though Jeanette and I both had our ears open and we both knew what we were doing.

"Fielding!" Boggs barked. "You find out who spilled the beans to the Gazette."

"Sir, with all due respect"—Tom's voice, obviously in conference with the two of them—"it's not against the law to talk to the press when you're a civilian."

"Not illegal, maybe . . . but someone knows an awful lot."

"Sir . . ." The faint rustle of papers. "According to Johnson's report and yours, there were a number of people on site at the crime scene. Professionals as well as civilians. Any one of them could have—"

"You're right. Any one of them could have. So be sure you talk to all of them. You can start with that girlfriend of yours."

Jeanette's eyes flicked to mine. She opened her mouth, then closed it again and stared down at the stack of papers in front of her, extra attentive and conscientious, then reached out and silently slid the window closed, a too-late gesture for the sake of discretion. I turned my back to the window entirely and leaned against the wall to wait. I didn't blame Jeanette—she was only doing her job. At that moment I was strongly considering sneaking out and calling Tom later from my cell phone.

Why did I have to come here *now*? I was beginning to wonder at my usual stellar timing.

"And while you're doing that," Boggs continued, his voice muffled by the glass but certainly not inaudible, "you get Ty Bennett in here. We know he's the one who did it. Do your job and get the dirt needed to put him away."

They really needed to look into soundproofing this window. Closing it didn't make a bit of difference.

"Yes, sir."

"I want him in custody before the end of the week. Before he has a chance to fly the coop."

"We're keeping an eye on him, Chief."

So they suspected Ty Bennett, to the point of exclusion? I wasn't sure how I felt about that. I knew what I had witnessed yesterday was the truth—the first argument had been heated. And who else could the second argument have been between but Ty and Ronnie? In fact, the very thrust of the second exchange suddenly made sense. She'd said herself that their relationship had been very sexual and that she wasn't ready to give that up when he had cut her loose. Whoever had been in that room with her—because clearly it had been Ronnie who'd come out of that second confrontation with angry tears—had been the prey to her predatory thrust. So to speak. The man in question had been trying to fend her off. That much was certain. Given that bit of insight, I knew I had no real reason to think the man of that moment wasn't yet again Ty Bennett.

And yet . . .

*Oh, stop it, Maggie*, I thought to myself. *Who else could it have been?* At least Ty was a good place for them to start.

Unfortunately, he also seemed to be a stopping point for the Stony Mill PD. Or, should I say, for Chief Boggs. Was that right? Was it fair? Worse yet, was that my fault? I just didn't know.

"What are we hearing from the engineering crew? Anything?"

Reed said, "They're still getting safety measures set

up so they can send down a scope and take a look. The dirt should have settled enough by now from the actual collapse to take a good gander."

"Don't matter, I don't guess. We aren't going to find anything down there relatable to the murder itself."

"Maybe. Maybe not," Reed said. "But did you stop to think, Hiram, why the victim was in that hole to begin with?"

"Nope," Boggs said stubbornly.

"She wasn't killed there. We know that much from the shortage of physical evidence."

This was news to me.

*U-L-C . . .*

Again the memory of the Ouija reading came to me. What? What would I see?

"And there was no murder weapon found," Reed went on. "Maybe . . . just maybe it's down in that hole, where we haven't searched yet."

"Any clues as to what caused the puncture marks?" That was Tom.

"Nothin' that we saw," Boggs admitted. "They didn't resemble anything I recognized. Some triangular object with blunt points seems to be the best guess from preliminary examinations. Whatever it was tore through the skin and bone pretty roughly. Definitely not clean marks, that's for sure."

Abruptly the image of the girl's crumpled body tore into my head, unbidden. Just a flash, but enough to make me flinch and cause my head to ache. Biting my lip, I closed my eyes and leaned against the counter to keep myself upright. I was seeing stars, and it was all I could do to breathe deeply, purposefully, steadily, until the expanding pinpoints of light had diminished to a manageable level. I thought I felt a tingle along my cheek, a warm tracing of something. I brushed my hand there, not sure why I half expected to find blood . . . but my fingertips came away clean.

Linking to a subject was something that an adept clairvoyant or medium could do at will, given the right circumstances. I wasn't adept at anything except for finding ways to include chocolate in my life. Instead, when I made a connection of the psychic kind, it tended to be random, erratic, and completely unpredictable, like a stereo receiver that suddenly and temporarily picked up a broadcast from distant lands where before there was nothing but dead airspace.

An accidental empath, that was me in a nutshell.

Nut*shell*, not nut*house*. Big difference.

I was so caught up in the moment that I didn't realize the meeting had ended until the door opened to my right, catching me unawares.

"I was wondering when I'd see you."

Tom stood in the doorway, a grim look on his ruggedly handsome face, his gray-green eyes clouded. I raised a hand and waved at him. "Hi."

"Hi yourself." Without another word, he grabbed my wrist in an unyielding grip and pulled me toward the door. Off balance the entire way, I just barely managed to keep from stumbling along behind him.

Outside, I blinked against the blinding glare of the sun. I would have reached for my sunglasses, but before I could, Tom whipped me around to face him.

Someone was not happy.

"So."

I fluttered my eyelashes. I couldn't help it. The sun was making my eyes water. "So?" I asked innocently.

He stared at me a long moment, then let his breath out in a long-suffering sigh. "I can't wait to hear the whole story. I really can't. I just know that the truth is so fascinating and unexpected that you couldn't wait to share it with me, so you rushed over here at your first available break from the store. Am I right?"

Well, now he was just being insulting. I pulled my wrist out of his grasp and started to rub the blood back into it. "You seem to know everything already. Why don't you tell me?"

"Cut the crap, Maggie. Yeah, I know it all. I read the report." He paused, waiting for the words to sink in. "Did you hear me? I read. The freaking. Report."

In my dreams, my tongue was as witty and sharp as they come. My reality rarely lived up to that, more's the pity. I stared him down, feeling a twitch of annoyance start at my temple. "And?"

He closed his eyes. Probably praying for self-control. "What was it this time, Maggie? Just your lucky day? Bad timing? Bad karma? What?"

Suddenly I was feeling the need for self-control just as much as he was. "I was helping a friend," I grated out.

"Oh, well, that makes all the difference in the world. Helping a friend. Would that friend be Marcus Quinn?"

I wasn't going to rise to his bait. I wasn't. "No."

"And yet there he was with you. Helping your friend."

"It was all completely innocent, Tom."

"Huh. I'll bet. You are found in an out-of-the-way place, late, with a man who I know for a fact is out to get into your pants—"

"Oh, that is so unfair!" I fumed. "You don't know Marcus—"

Tom cut me off with a steely gaze. "Maggie, he's a

guy. He's single. He's hanging around you of your own free will. Of course he's trying to get into your pants."

I wasn't about to argue that point further with him. I actually wasn't completely sure what Marcus wanted from me, but I did know that he was my friend, no matter what we chose to do or not do in a physical sense. And I knew that he was okay with that.

Or at least I thought I did.

"We were there," I told him flatly, "to find Tara's cell phone. She lost it when we went to the church fundraiser yesterday afternoon."

"You're all about being in the wrong place at the wrong time, aren't you?" His mouth had not relented from the hard line it often took when he was put out. "It's amazing, this innate ability you have."

"If you're insinuating that I *want* to be involved in all of this, you're out of your mind!"

"I'm not insinuating anything. I'm telling you, it's awfully strange that you keep ending up in the middle of things. And I'm not the only one who's noticed."

I knew who he meant. But he didn't know that, and I wanted him to spell it out. No tricks, nothing left unsaid.

I crossed my arms over my chest. "I don't know what you mean."

He crossed his, too. His display was more impressive than mine, because it pushed out the already taut muscles in his arms. "The whole town is talking about your boss."

"Yes, I know. All thanks to my sister, who should know better, but who has never heard a rumor she hasn't wanted to spread."

"So it's just a rumor that Felicity Dow's a witch, then. Is that how you're spinning it to everyone?"

"I'm not spinning anything! I don't need to spin anything. What Liss is or is not is no one's business but her own."

"Maggie. We live in a small town—"

"A provincial small town," I corrected him.

"No more provincial than any other," Tom shot back. "You know how things are done here, and you know the way people are. You can't just make them change longtime behaviors and attitudes just because you want them to."

"How about because it's not right to be so judgmental? The Bible says we should love our neighbors—"

"It also says, 'Thou shalt not suffer a witch to live,'" he said, a touch too quickly for me to think he'd not rehearsed it a hundred times.

"Actually, it was mistranslated," I had to correct him, yet again. "Liss says some scholars believe the translation was altered intentionally during King James's reign to reinforce feelings of the time into the text. The original word in Hebrew should have been translated as 'poisoner,' not 'witch.' And there are other instances in the Bible where godly men have consulted with seers and diviners. Hence, witches. The Witch of Endor ring a bell? Good old Saul went to her for help, you know."

He stared at me as though I had just told him I had been born on the planet Valron and my parents were blue. Long enough that my annoyance had a chance to rise to new and improved heights. "Just how much time have you been putting into studying stuff like that? Good Lord almighty, Maggie. Do you even hear yourself? I thought the crap you were spouting before was bad enough—all that psychic touchy-feely mumbo jumbo—but *this* . . . this goes way over the top. Do you hear what being around that woman has changed in you?"

"You think I've changed?" Actually, he had no idea the true depth of the changes I've felt within myself. If he knew, he might just go off a-running.

"Yes."

"And you don't like the changes."

Now he looked harassed. "Yes . . . No . . . I didn't say that. But I want you to be very clear on what's going on in that store. With that woman. Now, I know you like Liss. I know you consider her a friend—"

"The best of friends."

"—and I know you like your job. But Maggie, you've got to see the truth in this. Things are spiraling around here—and Enchantments, it's smack in the line of fire. You think you've seen backlash before, maybe in other situations? I have a feeling it's nothing compared to what your boss is going to see when people start reading their newspaper tonight."

Hm. There was a nugget of truth in that.

"People are conservative in this town"—and there was an entire gold mine of truth there—"and that's not likely to change anytime soon. The river of public opinion's about to turn, in a big way. The question is, are you going to be standing upstream or down?"

I drew myself up and faced him down. "I'll be standing beside my friend. Because that's what friends do. And I don't care that people will associate me with her. I'm proud to be Liss's friend. I'm proud of her, I'm proud of the store, and I'm proud of what we, the N.I.G.H.T.S., do. Besides, I'm already in the middle of things now that the article's come out, aren't I? There's no turning back the clock now."

He shrugged and said, "People aren't going to like the fact that your boss is a witch."

"Liss is an upright member of the community. And this conversation is going nowhere."

And the two of us were at a crossroads. It might as well have been there in the physical world, etched into the concrete between our feet.

He scowled and pinched his eyes shut, sighing heavily as he struggled for words. "Maggie, Chief Boggs is not happy about this whole situation. There's a lot of public frustration and fear about all the things we've seen here in town. And with another murder on our hands . . . public opinion is only going to get worse. People are afraid. They want answers. The chief has to give them answers. And I . . . I'm the one who's going to have to provide them to all. I don't even know where to start. How do you explain to people that some of them have just been going temporarily crazy for no real reason?"

But was that it? Temporary insanity? Caused by what? Something in the water? Something in our food supply? If only it were that simple. Oh, I had no doubts that there was a thread of something winding its way around and through our town, finding its way into the farthest corners, lodging its way into the tightest crevices, but I also sensed it wasn't going to be easy to pin down. A sickness of sorts, but in what way? And how to know where it would touch next?

Too many questions, too few answers.

All we could do was keep our senses open and our feelers out.

"Chief is, uh, also putting pressure on me to dig into the ghost-hunting group you're involved with."

I blinked and raised my brows. I hadn't expected to hear *that*. "Excuse me?"

" 'The nutters' is how he put it, I think. People have relayed their concerns about that element to him, too. Not that there's anything illegal in what you all are doing. I told him that much myself—"

"Thanks," I snapped.

"At least, there had better not be," he said, oblivious to the way that sounded. "Not sure Chief liked that, but there you have it. He'd prefer that the N.I.G.H.T.S. disband, just to remove that question from people's minds."

"Disband."

"People in town are nervous, Maggie. Can you blame 'em? All these deaths. It's unnerving the hell out of them. Out of all of us. People are watching each other, now more than ever. They're looking for differences. They're looking for reasons. They're hoping for reassurance. They're looking to us to keep them safe from all the bad guys out there. Any unknown at this stage of the game is bound to make them uneasy."

"Like the N.I.G.H.T.S."

"Yeah. Wouldn't it be nice if I could reassure people once and for all that there's nothing untoward going on with your group?"

"Do you really need to 'look into things' in order to do that?"

"Well, no, not as such, but—"

"Because you know better than I do that there is no connection whatsoever between any of the deaths that have taken place . . . let alone throwing the N.I.G.H.T.S. into the equation."

"I didn't have to," he pointed out. "The Gazette did that for me."

Ouch. The Gazette and Margo. Which was pretty much the same thing.

"It's just for appearances," he said, trying the appeasement route. Too little, too late. "It's no big deal."

"Yeah. Right. Of course it isn't." Because why should disloyalty be a big deal?

He frowned owlishly. "I'm trying to look out for you, Maggie. And for the people of this town."

*Try again.* He was looking out for himself, his job, and trying to preserve his sense of order. "Fine. Reassure away."

"It doesn't mean anything."

Except it did. To me.

I didn't say anything.

"So . . . I guess we're at a standoff."

It was the way he said it more than the words themselves that gave me pause. "Yeah. I guess so."

He nodded grimly. The muscles in his jaw were popping in and out, so I knew he was gritting his teeth. Not in anger—more and more I was feeling his confusion. "Dammit, Maggie. I don't know why we always have to go through this. We just can't seem to catch a break. Why can't you find a different job? It would make all the difference in the world. It's just retail . . ." His voice trailed off as he saw in my stony face that he'd made a mistake.

"It's not *just* retail!" I shot back. "Why should I leave? I love it at the store. I enjoy what I do. I belong there. Did you know I've searched my whole adult life to find a job where I felt like I really and truly belonged? Why should I have to give that up just to play to *your* boss's stupid prejudices?"

"You could do it for me."

It was a mind game, a passive-aggressive play for domination within the relationship, and completely unfair. I knew that. So why did it still manage to work its guilt magick on me?

*Be careful, Margaret. A man, once he knows he has you in this way, will be tenacious. You'll never be free.*

*Point taken, Grandma C*, I thought to the voice of conscience in my head. *And thanks for watching my back.*

I shook my head at him, holding steadfast to my cause. "I shouldn't have to change who I am to satisfy you, Tom. And you know it. If you wanted me, you'd take me as I am."

I wasn't going to bring up the even sorer subject of the mystery woman Annie had seen Tom with. For all I knew the cozy scene Annie had witnessed could have been something innocent; adding it into the mix today would be overkill. We had enough hurdles on the path in front of us without that, too.

"But—"

I started backing away, determined that this time my emotions wouldn't let me back down from what I knew was right. "Do your job, Tom. Do what you have to do. And I'll do the same."

Frustration stretched and contorted the lines of his face as he struggled for footing amid his feelings. It was just as painful for me. Finally I could stand it no more and turned and walked quickly the rest of the way to my car, cursing myself for not having the keys in my hand.

"Maggie," I heard Tom call out.

I turned slowly. Tom was still standing where I'd left him, his only movement to put on his mirrored aviators— against the sun, or as a shield against me? I couldn't be sure, but I thought I knew.

"Are we okay?"

The words were softly spoken, and yet I heard them as

if he was standing right in front of me and not fifteen feet away. I dropped my gaze, protecting myself much in the way that he had with his shades. "We'll talk later, okay?"

I could tell it wasn't the answer he wanted, but it was the only one I could give him for now.

You know what killed me the most? Finally it was Tom doing the asking . . . and I was the one pulling my energy back.

Life. It just wasn't fair. Pet Peeve #27.

# Chapter 11

I had no stomach for lunch after the argument with Tom had ended so badly, so I drove around town for a little while to calm my beleaguered emotions, stopping only by the Stop & Shop for a giganto frozen Coke to cool down. Eventually the heat of the day chased me back to the store, where I hoped that the rest of the afternoon would pass by without incident.

That hope was in vain.

When I pulled into my usual parking space, there were flyers tucked under the windshield wipers on Liss's car and under the seat strap on Tara's scooter, which I guessed Marcus had been able to fix. Juggling my handbag and two paper sacks from the Coney Dog place, I pulled the closest sheet out to take a peek. Flamboyant in a particularly obnoxious shade of chartreuse was a copy of the petition notice that Reverend Martin's First Evangelical Church of Light had brought to the Baptist fundraiser. A glance around me showed that the cars parked behind the stores surrounding us had all been papered as well. A lovely example of small-town togetherness philosophy, I thought, making a face. Not a surprise, though, since we'd already seen the preview out at Grace Baptist. Evidently they were picking up steam. Pity.

Across the alley, a door opened. Out popped the owner of the scrapbooking store on the next block. I didn't know her name—I'd seen her only once or twice. I lifted my hand to wave at her, as was the custom around these parts. Then I noticed the folded newspaper held beneath her arm. Crap. The woman made her way to her car, pausing to snag the chartreuse paper from beneath her wiper blade. Her mouth tightened. She lifted her gaze to mine . . . and then she began to walk purposely in my direction.

Double crap.

To my surprise she stopped at the recycling bin at the back edge of the store parking, just before entering the alley. With her eyes still on mine, she took the ugly, bile-filled flyer, tore it neatly in half, and stuffed it into the paper bin. "Just taking out the trash," she said to me. "Have a good lunch."

And with that she headed back to her car, waving as she drove off calmly toward her own destination.

People in this town never stopped amazing me. In more ways than one.

Smiling to myself in spite of everything the morning had presented to me, I took Liss's and Tara's flyers inside with me. Minnie came flying beneath the velvet curtain when she heard the jangling of my keys. She launched herself at me in a three-point attack: chair, desk, shoulder. I reached up and gave her ears a rub and a nuzzle up against my neck. "Hello, little one. Did you miss me?"

"That you, Maggie?" Evie called from the main room.

"Yes, it's me. I'm back."

I pushed through the curtains with Minnie wobbling slightly on my shoulders. The girls were seated on the high-backed stools at the beverage bar, with Liss playing the part of barista behind the counter. On the bar top between them were several thick felt-tip pens and a piece of graph paper marked with several hatch marks. "What are you all up to?"

The phone rang at their elbows. Tara held up her hand. "My turn."

I watched in curiosity as Tara went through the usual, "Good afternoon, Enchantments Antiques and Fine Gifts," followed by an "Uh-huh," a "Huh-uh," an "I suppose that's your prerogative," a "We're sorry you feel that way," a "You'd really like us if you got to know us," and a final, "All righty, then. Thank you for calling." She hung up the phone with a smug expression. "How'd I do?"

Evie held up her fingers in the universal A-OK sign. "Purrrrfect." She picked up a black marker and added another hatch mark to those already on the paper.

I tilted my head to look at the sheet. "Thirteen?"

"Calls," Tara confirmed. "All snotty."

"And what are these other hatch marks?" I asked, pointing to the few marked in blue felt-tip.

"Those calls were more positive. They wanted to know the types of gift items we carry and our store hours."

"And the yellow?" Seven of those.

"Possible future investigation sites. Worried people with strange experiences they can't explain who thought maybe we'd have answers. I figure they could count as possible customers, too."

I stared at the sheet and shook my head. "And all this . . ."

"Is a result of the article, yes. I'm fairly certain," Liss answered.

Wow. And to think, most of the town hadn't finished work for the day and wouldn't see the paper until later this evening.

"No customers?"

Liss shook her head. "A few. But don't you worry. Things will smooth out and return to normal before you know it, just as soon as the next scandal hits."

Normal. In Stony Mill. Nothing about the last nine months had been normal actually, though I supposed there was always room for hope.

My cell phone rang, muffled in the depths of my bag. I pulled it out. "Mom" flashed on the small glass window. Hm. That couldn't be good. She never called me at work in the middle of the day unless it was important, or unless I had been ignoring her for days . . . which I hadn't. I pushed the button to send the call to voice mail, then glanced up to find everyone watching me. I shrugged.

"So, how was your lunch date, ducks?" Liss asked.

"How did you—what makes you think I had a lunch date?"

Liss smiled. "Just intuition, I suppose."

"Actually, I went to the police department to talk to Tom," I said, pretending nonchalance. "And I, um, happened to hear a few interesting things." Knowing they

wouldn't tell anyone outside of our small circle, I proceeded to describe what I'd heard.

"So they're going to investigate us?" Tara scoffed.
"Good for them. Maybe they'll learn a thing or two."

"That's not the point, Tara," I told her. "The point is,
we've obviously come under a bit of scrutiny, no thanks
to my sister, and now this murder and this article. The
calls today confirm that, obviously . . . but I don't know. I
have a feeling this is just the beginning."

"She's right," Evie said, looking thoughtful. "I mean,
we were having a bit of fun with the calls this afternoon, but there was an . . . undercurrent, I guess, to
them that wasn't exactly comfortable, if you know what
I mean."

Liss had remained silent until just then. "It is troubling . . .
but not the end of the world. I have faith in the good people
of this town. And in your Tom, for that matter. There
might be some who will speak out of fear without just
cause, but I think the good, the light in the human heart,
will prevail."

I hoped so. I truly did. But a part of me worried that
she was allowing idealism to override reality.

"What I'm most curious about is the woman we found,"
Tara said. "Who killed her and why they put her there in
that hole."

"The police seem to think it really was Ty Bennett."

"I've been around Ty a little bit this summer. He never
struck me as dangerous at all. In fact, he's kind of a softhearted guy."

Even softhearted guys could have a dark side, though,
couldn't they? Of course they could. The only problem
with that theory was, without knowing he had an audience,

Ty had resisted lashing out at Ronnie throughout her entire tirade. Even when she got up in his face. Shouldn't there have been some hint of that dark side yesterday afternoon? Instead, what I'd seen had really been a sort of grace under pressure. But if not Ty, then who? Any one of the hundreds of men at the fundraiser? The thought gave me a headache.

*Then it's a good thing it's none of your bother, Margaret Mary-Catherine O'Neill. Not your concern.*

No, it wasn't. It was just my curious, trying-to-make-sense-of-my-world mind.

The phone rang again. Evie picked it up immediately. "Good afternoon, Enchantments Antiques and Fine Gifts . . ."

While the girls played their phone game, I lead Liss off to one side. "I really think we need to take this seriously. I'm getting a very bad feeling about it. I want you to promise me that you'll be careful and take additional precautions."

"Ah, Maggie, my dear." She patted me on the cheek. "I'll be quite fine. Never fear. My Guides will take care of me. That and an effective protection spell or two."

Not as well as a good security system, some pepper spray, and a personal stun gun, perhaps, but it was a start. "At least keep your cell phone on you at all times."

"All right. I will. Promise. Better?"

I nodded.

"But I don't think there will be a problem. No worries, ducks."

No worries. Unfortunately I was a worrying kinda girl. Telling me not to worry was like telling a chocoholic not to indulge in a Godiva store. It just wasn't going to happen.

"This Ty Bennett," Liss said conversationally, watching my face, "you don't think he killed her."

I had thought about it and thought about it since last night, but . . . "I'm not sure. On the one hand, the arguments they had were suspicious in light of what happened. On the other hand . . . oh, I just don't know. It's probably nothing. Just my guilt getting the better of me."

"Guilt?"

"Because I'm the one who saw them arguing, and I'm the one who told the police about it, and now the investigation seems to be focusing solely on him."

"But . . . if he is indeed guilty, surely that's a good thing."

She was right. I was being foolish. Because being in the wrong place at the wrong time almost always meant guilt. Because bad relationships often did go terribly wrong when the decision to end things wasn't mutual.

"I spoke to Ronnie. The victim. I spoke to her yesterday afternoon—and it seems like forever ago now. I came upon them while they were arguing, and it was so fierce, so ferocious, I couldn't allow myself to walk away. Just in case. But Liss . . . in case of what? What did I see in their body language that made me stay . . . but didn't make me realize what was going to happen?" Minnie was reacting to my frustration, twitching her tail and trying to head-butt my ear. "You say that my intuitive abilities are expanding. I can feel it happening, little by little. So why can't it work on someone's behalf? Why can't I help to prevent some of these things from happening?"

"Because we're sensitives, Maggie. We're not gods. Look at Evie. She has a very clear connection the more that she works to understand her gift. But has she been given the ability to prevent an event that is meant to happen? No. You seem to think that being a sensitive means being superhuman, capable of fighting crime and solving world hunger and leaping skyscrapers in a single bound. I rather think that we are *extra*human. We've been given an amazing gift to help us to traverse the rougher waters of life, an additional sense of understanding of the world and of people that most will never have."

"Then why sense these things at all, if it's not meant to help?"

"Whoever says it's not helping you?" At my confusion, she gave me a sad smile. "Maggie, darling. There are things in this world that are meant to be. They are written for us on the pages of time. Those of us who believe in the reincarnation of souls believe also that we choose these predestined lessons for ourselves and then proceed to make our lives what we will. And our actions and decisions along the path of life decide the rest . . . good or bad.

"As a sensitive," she continued, "one is able to see connections and signs that provide a deeper understanding of the true nature of the world, of people, of the universe. I don't know about you, but I wouldn't want to have to live without it."

Would I? If I could actually choose to go back to the way I was, gifted but clueless, would I do it? It was a fair question. It would mean reacting to my environment and to the emotions of others, being buffeted by them and feeling out of control. And then I thought of the way I had felt since discovering the truth about myself. Empowered. Strong and growing stronger. Knowledge replacing uncertainty.

I was better off now. I knew it. I just needed to trust that knowledge, and trust myself.

"By the way," I said, "these were left on your car and Tara's scooter." I handed her the flyers.

She lifted her half-moon glasses to scan the page. "Oh. Oh my."

"The Reverend Baxter Martin is a nutcase. But he has a following," I told her. "Yet another reason to be careful. He seems to think that having a witch in residence"—I winked at her—"is the cause of our problems. The poor guy. He doesn't seem to realize he's looking for sin in all the wrong places. None of the victims have had anything to do with magick, the N.I.G.H.T.S., or the store."

She refolded the paper, calmly slipped it beneath a notepad beside the cash register, then removed her glasses with a sigh. "I've faced people like him before. And I'm quite certain he won't be the last. One must wonder what kind of personal hell someone like that puts themselves through and what kind of unhappiness must be at the root of it all. It's sad, really."

And on that happy note . . .

Minnie had fallen asleep on my shoulders. I tiptoed to the back office and gently lifted her down, setting her in her pen for her afternoon siesta. She opened one eye—the blue one—and blinked at me twice, then stretched her legs out, yawned, and curled herself back into a tight ball. Smiling, I stroked her tiny whiskers as she drifted back off into the oblivion, then tiptoed back up to the front.

Tara and Evie were at it again with the homemade Ouija.

I put my hands on my hips. "I thought you'd left those sticky notes behind at my apartment."

Tara smirked up at me. "What, you think you got the corner on sticky notes?"

"Are you sure that's a good idea?"

"It's not like business is hopping this afternoon," Tara pointed out. "It's either this or Scrabble, and Evil has this truly unfair advantage of kickin' my ass every single time."

Liss looked over from where she was turning down the heat on the coffee carafes and shook her head indulgently. "There's nothing to worry about here, Maggie. If they're intent on experimenting with the Ouija, there's no safer place for it. The wards I use for the store are strong. It is a sacred space. No dark entities can get through here—I'm sure of it."

"All right." I gave in. "I suppose it's okay—I mean, we're both here, and if you say there can't be any trouble, I believe you." To the girls I called out, "Just as long as you keep the questions about my personal life out of it, thank you very much."

Evie giggled. "Should we withdraw that last question, then?"

"What? Evie! You, too?" I pretended indignation, but I was okay with it because I was pretty sure they weren't going to get any valid answers anyway. At least, not about me or my love life. Besides, I was a teenage girl once, too. I knew how important these meaningless, giggling, girly games were. I looked over her shoulder. "And stop pushing that pointer to 'M'!"

"I didn't push it this time either, Maggie, honestly," protested Evie.

I eyed Tara, but she just shrugged. "Me, either."

"Hm. Well, cut it out anyway."

"Maybe it's just 'M' for 'marry.' You know, as in yes, you will get married someday."

The pointer slid to "no."

"No?" I groaned good-naturedly. "Even worse!"

The grin that broke out on Tara's face could not be considered anything but wicked. "All right, then. Let's clarify this. Will Maggie get married?"

The pointer glided to "yes."

"Thanks, girls," I said, my voice laced with irony. "I'm so glad that some unknown spirit energy knows the ins and outs of my social agenda."

"And *who* will Maggie marry?" Tara asked, not looking up from the homemade Ouija.

A slick, quick flick to "M." I reached over and put my hand over the glass before it could spell out anything else.

"Hey! Not fair!" Tara protested. "Just when it was getting interesting!"

"Play nice, children."

I didn't pay much attention to the girls after that. I fielded a few phone calls myself, did a thorough cleaning of the beverage area, and swept the wooden floor beneath the old oak barrels filled with hard candies imported from the UK and the apothecary bins of bulk spices.

"U . . . L . . . C . . ." Evie's voice calling out the letters caught my attention as I puttered around the store.

"Hey! Didn't the spirit at your apartment call out those same letters, Maggie?" Evie asked.

"Yeah, it did," Tara answered for me. "Don't you remember? *'You'll see'*?"

Surely not . . .

Had the spirit followed me here? Was that why the letters U-L-C kept resounding through my mind during the quieter moments of the day?

It was far more likely that the girls were influencing the pointer again without realizing it.

"W . . . A . . ."

Oh good. A new word. Not the same spirit, I was right.

"T . . . C . . . H . . ."

"Watch . . ." Tara said, drawing the word out in the way people do when they're expecting more information that's slow in coming.

"S . . . I . . . S . . . T . . . E . . . R . . . Sister. Watch *and* sister? Or watch sister?"

I froze again. Sister. My sister? My sister was majorly pregnant. She still had an entity that lurked in the laundry room in her basement. Was she in danger in some way? Or, I thought, maybe it meant I needed to watch her penchant for spreading gossip. Argh. Why couldn't these things be clearer?

"Is this Elias?" Evie asked.

"Yes," Tara read off.

"Why are you here, Elias?"

"W . . . A . . . R . . . N . . . Warn."

"Warn who? Us? All of us? Or just one of us?"

"Yes. Talk about a muddled question, Evie."

"*Pfft.* Fine. Elias, do you know who killed Veronica Maddox?"

"Yes. Yes!"

Excitement made Evie's voice quiver. "Can you spell the name of the person who killed Veronica Maddox?"

"Yes."

There was a long pause. I glanced over. The overturned glass they were using for a pointer was circling around, their fingertips gently but firmly affixed to its bottom, but it didn't move to point at anything.

Then, without further provocation from them it began
to move once more.

"W . . . A . . . R . . . N . . . Y . . . O . . . U . . ."

"Warn *you*. Who, Elias?"

"M . . . A . . . G . . . Maggie, I think he means you!"

Liss was paying attention now, a frown tugging her
brows together. She peered down at the counter where
the glass was moving in circles. "Do you two believe this
is the same spirit who followed Maggie home yesterday?"

Their responses were excitable babbling, obviously
affirmative.

"I won't add my energy to the glass," Liss said, "but I
want you girls to ask this spirit—"

"Elias," Evie provided.

"Elias, whether he has been staying with Maggie."

I shook my head. "I don't think so. I think that Minnie
drove him aw—"

But the pointer slid to "yes."

I closed my mouth, trying not to feel creeped out. "An
attachment? You mean, Minnie didn't successfully drive
him away? He's planning to stay?"

"It happens to the best of us," Liss said soothingly.
"But don't worry too much. It's quite likely he was just
attracted by your energy. I'm sure he'll soon be ready to
cross over, now that his spirit has been released."

"Released. From the cave-in?"

She met my gaze. "It makes sense, now, doesn't it?"

That it did. A little too much for my taste.

I was about to say more when the front door opened,
sending the brass welcome bells into a cacophony of

jangling action. The girls were engrossed in their game and scarcely noticed. I made my way toward the woman whose high heels were clicking across the waxed plank floor, ready to welcome her. She slid her bag farther up on her shoulder as it began to slip.

"Hello and welcome to Ench—oh. You're Evie's mom, aren't you?"

Janet Carpenter had an air of authority about her that was common in highly successful corporate professionals. A sleek blonde with a French manicure and a corner office at one of the most high-profile executive staffing firms in the Midwest, she was as far from the Donna Reed version of homemaking femininity as a woman could get. Every ounce of that authority was in evidence as she strode down the aisle in her expensive suit, somehow managing to look crisp and cool even though the lined, fitted blazer she was wearing amounted to the equivalent of a fall jacket.

"Hello, Maggie. Where can I find my daughter?" Polite enough but there was a terse edge to her voice that was at odds with her controlled expression.

"Hello there, Mrs. Carpenter. Evie?" I called back to the beverage counter. "Your mom's here."

Evie's head popped up suddenly, and she peeped around the corner of the shelves, her china blue eyes wide and decidedly nervous. "Uh, hi, Mom. What are you doing here?"

Mrs. Carpenter veered left past the shelves. Her tasteful brown stiletto sling backs—alligator—squeaked to a halt as her gaze fell upon the counter. "I've come to take you home. What is this?"

"Take me home?" Evie looked confused. "But I'm working all day today—"

"No, you're not. Say good-bye to your friends, Evie." Mrs. Carpenter paused, then said, "I'm afraid you won't be seeing them again."

"What? Mom! What are you talking about? You can't be serious."

Mrs. Carpenter didn't look at the rest of us, who were gaping openly at the scene unfolding before our eyes. "I'm perfectly serious. Now go get your things. We'll talk about this later."

Tara started to open her mouth, and I gave her a quick, negative jerk of my head. She snapped her mouth shut again, but in her eyes mutiny reigned.

Mrs. Carpenter expected her daughter to comply without a peep. With good reason—as a well-loved and nurtured only child, Evie had always been a model daughter. In the nine months I'd known her, I'd never seen a rebellious side to Evie. But the Evie before me appeared downright seditious. Perhaps she took after her mother more than was apparent at first glance. "Mother, you tell me all the time that appearances and etiquette matter. It would be unprofessional of me to leave the store high and dry without adequate personnel."

Mrs. Carpenter's eyes glittered with annoyance, but she stood her ground. With carefully controlled precision, she said, "Evie, I will absolutely not be dictated to by my own daughter. I have my reasons for removing you from this environment. I want you to get your things and come with me."

Evie didn't move as she transferred her attention to me and Liss, then back to her mom, battling against her divided loyalties. She was so open and transparent that every nuance of her thinking process was reflected in her expression. Finally a sigh of resignation left her lips and her shoulders drooped. "Just a second. I'll get my stuff."

She avoided Tara's gaze completely as she made her way back to the office. Liss, Tara, and I looked at each other uncomfortably.

Finally, Mrs. Carpenter broke the silence. "I meant what I said. She will not be back. I won't allow my only daughter to be swayed away from the teachings of her parents and church by those who choose a path of darkness. You all ought to be ashamed of yourselves."

Liss shook her head sadly. "Mrs. Carpenter, your daughter has a natural gift"—she caught the sudden violent shaking of my head—"of being able to relate to customers instantly, and she is a ray of sunshine to be around. I fear you have the wrong idea about us here. I do hope you'll reconsider."

"I won't. I wish I could say I'm sorry, but I'm not. I'd like to invite you all to our church to learn the truth about occult activities. Feel free to come and bring all of your friends—I'm sure our pastor would be thrilled to minister to you all in a special session to help you renounce your sins." Evidently being a modern woman did not necessarily equate to being open-minded or even tolerant.

"Oh," Liss said. "Oh, I see."

"And if not, well then, I can only pray and hope you come to see the error of your ways before it's too late."

"Too late for . . . ?"

But Evie had returned, her backpack slung over her shoulder, her gaze low. "I'm ready."

Her mother pivoted on her well-turned heel and led

the way out of the store, leaving no option but for Evie to follow. Her only sign of defiance was to wave at each of us and morosely mouth "Bye," before scurrying off in her mother's footsteps.

# Chapter 12

The silence that followed was overwhelming.

"Well," Liss said. "Well."

I knew it was perfectly within Evie's mother's rights to do what she had done, but still . . . the prospect of Evie's bright presence being absent from the store left me feeling deeply sad.

The three of us knocked around the store so quietly for the rest of the afternoon that you would have thought someone had died. Even Minnie didn't seem to know what to do with herself, walking relentlessly up and down the aisles as though she recognized even at her young age that something had changed for the worst.

It was a relief when Liss decided to close the doors early in the hopes of warding off a few of the worst kinds of phone calls. "Not that avoidance is a favorable response in most situations, but in light of everything, perhaps in this case it might be beneficial to all."

After the usual end-of-day tasks were complete, I

loaded Minnie into her carrier and waved to Liss. "See you tomorrow."

Liss nodded. "Don't worry about Evie too much, Maggie. I have a feeling she'll be back with us."

I didn't know what to think, other than that the last twenty-four hours had been completely emotionally exhausting.

I set the carrier on the ground as I searched for my car keys, which seemed to be hiding from me again. I really needed a better way of managing them, I thought for perhaps the thousandth time.

The crunch of gravel rolling around under tires in the alley behind me alerted me to the presence of a car. When I heard the whirr of an electric window going down, I glanced back.

Tom.

"Hey."

"Hey back," I said, biting my lip. The argument we'd had was still fresh on my mind. After all that had happened, my nerves were feeling just a bit raw.

"Can we talk?"

A part of me wanted to say no. The day had just been a bit much. I wanted to plead weariness and go on home to a piece of leftover pizza and a spot in front of the TV for some one-on-one with Magnum. Magnum was a single girl's best friend. With his bluer-than-blue eyes and deeply drawn laugh lines, he never failed to make the day brighter. Especially when the day had proven one's kind-of, sort-of, but in-no-way-certain boyfriend to be a spineless, judgmental jerk.

But sure. We could talk.

I nodded my acceptance, if not willingness.

"Good. Get in."

Into the cruiser. Yay for me. "I have Minnie," I said, pointing to the carrier by my feet.

"She can come, too."

Once in my seat, I stared straight ahead at the alley. "So. I'm in."

"Click it or ticket."

Sighing in annoyance at his idea of levity—at least I assumed it was a joke—I grabbed the seat belt and fastened it, balancing Minnie's carrier on my knees. "Satisfied, Mr. Big Time Investigator?"

"Yup." He stepped on the accelerator hard enough to make gravel spew. Not the safest way to get out of an alley that had a brick building on either side, but this was an aggravated man we were talking about.

"Where are we going?"

"Just driving. Want to talk about what happened earlier today?"

"I don't know. Care to apologize?"

"What? Apologize? For doing my job?"

"Well, I could say it's for being an asshole, but I don't think that would be kindly accepted, either."

His lips twisted into a grimace. "You're really angry."

"Yup." Hey, if he could do it, so could I.

"Maggie, that's ridiculous. I'm a deputy. It's my job. You know this."

"Yeah. I know."

"I do what the chief tells me to do, even when—as in this case—there's nothing to investigate. Despite the fact that there's nothing illegal in the works. But I'll tell you this much. If I thought there *was* anything there to worry about . . . I'd have been after you myself. No question about it."

"You know full well there's nothing here for anyone to worry about!" I hissed.

If he weren't driving, he'd have thrown both hands up in the air, I just knew it. "Well, then, what the hell difference does it make anyway?"

"Because . . . it's the principle of the thing." *You didn't stand up to your boss on my behalf* was my more specific answer. Unfortunately for him, I was just irritated enough to make him dig for it.

From the looks of it, he was just as irritable as I was. "The principle of the thing."

"Yeah."

The police radio squawked and called out Tom's badge number. The distraction was just enough to cut through the intensity of the moment. Tom reached over and yanked the mouthpiece from the clip. "Go ahead, Dispatch."

"We've got a situation brewing out at the Grace Baptist Church." The dispatcher read off the address, then added, "10-96 possible."

"En route, Dispatch."

I didn't have time to protest. He flipped on the lights and siren and wheeled the cruiser around in a wide U-turn once traffic had stopped to allow the movement, speeding off in the direction of the church, which was as far across town from where we were as you could get. "So, I'm going along for the ride, huh? What's a 10-96?"

"Possible crazy person. Er, person with a mental condition or disorder," he amended.

"At Grace Baptist? Criminey, what is going *on* out there?"

We were about to see.

The fact that a disturbance of some sort was underway

was completely apparent the moment we pulled into the parking lot. Up on the hill to the back of the church, a number of people had gathered—none recognizable from this distance.

Tom went through his usual split-second routine of unsnapping his gun and stun-gun holsters. "You stay here while I take care of this. Lock the doors." He reached into his pocket and pulled out a pocket knife, which he tossed to me. "For protection."

It was a ritual I knew by rote by now. Tom headed off up the hill toward the small gathering of people, one of whom seemed to be flailing arms at the others. I shook my head, bemused. Was it just me, or did Grace Baptist just have the kind of energy that drew drama and trauma to its doors? But maybe that was unfair. Certainly there had been plenty of people in attendance yesterday afternoon who didn't seem to fit into that category.

The car was getting hot already. I pressed the button to roll down the window as perspiration broke out on my forehead. Voices filtered down to me, muffled by distance. I turned to watch the proceedings. The 10-96 arm-flailer seemed to be a large woman, facing down four men, a couple of them wearing hard hats and some sort of electronic equipment. She held a small stack of papers in her hand that flapped when she shoved them at the men. They showed up really nicely against her purple-spotted shirt . . .

Uh-oh.

I got out of the car quickly, clutching Minnie's carrier, and began to hurry up the gradual hill toward the site of the cave-in, which seemed to be a pretty popular place of late. I stopped to place Minnie's carrier under a shady tree.

As I came into earshot, I could hear Marian Tabor holding forth. "I have an order here, signed and sealed by Judge Maywater, that says you have to stop any and all progress to clear, move earth, or construct any structure until the historical society can have a chance to inspect the site in order to ascertain the historical value of its contents, if any." Marian Tabor waved the papers again. "And this fool here tells me he's not stopping the progress without the consent of all interested parties. Where's that pastor? I want to talk to the pastor."

The two men in business casual exchanged a glance, and as I approached I thought I saw one of them roll his eyes. The two men in hard hats with the equipment didn't seem to care—they were standing back, waiting for their next order. One of them yawned.

"Now, Mrs. Tabor—" Tom began.

"Ms."

"Ms. Tabor. May I see the paperwork, please? And while we're at it, could everyone please back away from the crime scene tape. You are not to cross that line."

Marian handed it over with a flourish and a haughty sniff at the men, who complied with Tom's order by edging away from the yellow-and-black tape, but not by much. "I'm sure you can see clearly that the order is, well, in order."

Tom scanned the document, then glanced up at one of the two business casuals. "The document does appear to be legal and binding."

Business Casual Number Two's face reddened. "Now, that can't be! What legal claim can the historical society have anyway? There's not been enough time for a judge to be consulted and sign off on a written order!"

Tom checked the last page and shrugged. "Judge Maywater signed it at three fifteen this afternoon."

All looked at Marian, who had just noticed me coming up from the cruiser. She winked at me, looking smug as she advised them, "Judge Maywater is a good friend and benefactor of the county historical society. And a good thing, too! Otherwise who knows how many historical sites would be at risk? We have to preserve these things for our children and our children's children."

Business Casual Number Two sputtered, "Dirt? We're gonna preserve dirt? Our men are already sitting idle because of the—"

His partner shut him up with a wave of his hand.

Tom took charge. "May I ask what business you have out this way?"

Business Casual Number One pulled out his card. "David Furlow, Furlow Construction Company. My company is handling the excavation and construction of the new wing for the church. And Steve here is right. Per our findings, the rest of the site is structurally sound, enough to allow us to do what we need to do. And time, as you know, is money."

"Money, *pfft*. That the site was left open to air overnight is regrettable—especially in light of what happened here last night, I must say—but at least we are able to do something now. This is a site that could have historical significance," Marian stated firmly. "All we require is to be allowed the time to have someone come out to take a look down in the buried room so that anything of historical value might be catalogued and preserved. That's all. Surely this can be done expediently enough to satisfy all concerned."

Footfalls on the sidewalk leading from the church alerted us all to someone else's approach. I glanced over my shoulder. Pastor Bob was hurrying over; the only variation in his uniform of a suit and hard-soled shoes was the color: black today.

"I hope this flurry of activity today means we can soon get underway again with the construction?" he asked in his flowery, effusive manner. He rocked back on his heels and rubbed his hands together, waiting for someone to answer.

Tom did the honors. "I'm afraid not, Reverend. There has been a hiccup, one that I'm sure you'll understand. Judge Maywater has granted a stay on proceeding with the expansion until such a time as the newly exposed site can be properly assessed for historical value."

No one said a word about the inappropriateness of rushing to move forward with a construction plan when a corpse had just been discovered on the site less than twenty-four hours previously. This evident lack of concern really troubled me in a person who was supposed to be a man of God. It just seemed somehow wrong.

"You ought to be ashamed of yourself, Reverend. With a woman dead on scene, you want to press on? Tsk, tsk, tsk." Trust Marian to have her say. Not that she didn't have her own agenda with the site . . .

Pastor Bob drew himself up, now all bluster and uncertainty. "Well, of course we wouldn't move ahead until such a time as was good and proper," he backtracked as Business Casual Number Two—Steve, was it?—groaned and grumbled. "We wouldn't wish to offend or seem insensitive to the poor deceased woman—"

"And neither would the historical society, of course," Marian purred. "I know that there has already been a letter sent to Chief Boggs and Special Investigator Fielding here"—she smiled blindingly at Tom—"requesting that the society be informed of the right to proceed just as soon as the crime scene has been wholly processed. Once our experts are satisfied, you will be more than free to proceed with your plans."

Tom stepped in to take over. "If everyone could please evacuate the crime scene area, I would appreciate it. Mr. Furlow, if you could have the results of your safety inspection forwarded to me at the police station for our investigation, that would be extremely helpful—"

Furlow whipped out a leather-bound folder. "I have a preliminary carbon right here. Everything should be in order. I will, of course, have my assistant forward a more professional copy when I get back to the office, but this should get you started." He handed Tom a yellow sheet of paper, scribbled over with a bold hand.

Tom nodded. "Thank you, sir. I'll forward it on to the public building inspector's office as well. If you and your men are done here, you're free to leave."

Understanding they had been summarily dismissed, the four men looked at each other, then quietly and mutually made the decision to leave.

To Marian, Tom said, "Ms. Tabor, I'll check with the office and will let you know when you can have your experts come in."

"Thank you, Deputy Fielding. I trust there will be no further trouble on that end."

"Well . . ." Tom cleared his throat. "Forgive me for saying so, ma'am, but had you waited for the sheriff's department to issue the order as per procedure, there wouldn't have been trouble to begin with. It would have been handled."

Marian laughed, not at all put out by the admonishment. She was too strong-willed to care much. "Ah, but what fun would that have been? A librarian has to take her excitement where she can get it, Deputy. Besides," she said, "if I'd waited, they might have been readying up their crew before the sheriff's department could even get out here."

"Not with the crime scene investigation enforced," Tom reminded her. "Else they would risk legal proceedings against them and their company."

Marian just smiled. "Well, that being the case . . . I'll just toddle off, then." She waved to me and began to walk slowly back to her vehicle. Much more slowly than I would have expected. From her gait one would think she had suddenly tacked an additional thirty years on to her age. A pretense so that she could take her time and absorb everything around her? That was my guess . . . and she wasn't missing a single detail, by the looks of things. Truth be told? I don't think she ever did. Mind like a steel trap, that woman.

Tom turned his attentions to Pastor Bob, who was standing by. "Reverend, I'm sorry your plans have been interrupted, but I'm sure you understand the seriousness of the issue we are dealing with."

Pastor Bob nodded distractedly. "Certainly I do. It is a tragedy what happened here, with Miss Maddox. A life cut short. A real shame. Of course I didn't know her very well—she had only recently joined the church as I recall."

"Nine months ago."

Pastor Bob paused. "Come again?"

Tom consulted his notebook. "According to your wife, who graciously checked for me this morning, church records show that Veronica Maddox first started attending services regularly about nine months ago."

"Oh. Oh, I see. I didn't realize it had been that long. So many parishioners. You understand. Of course I do try my best to acquaint myself with as many as possible, but sometimes that's just not feasible in the short term."

Tom nodded, his mirrored aviators hiding any sign of emotion. "Of course."

Something was troubling me, nudging me in the back of my mind. *U-L-C* . . . The letters whispered through my mind again. *You'll see, you'll see.* We'll see what?

"Well, thank you for coming out, Deputy. Do you have any idea when the crime scene investigation will be complete? We really would like to get moving on things as soon as we can."

"Not long, I shouldn't think. We'll be in touch. Oh, one more thing. Our investigation didn't turn up much in the way of physical evidence at the crime scene itself. There is a possibility that the young woman was killed elsewhere—on site or off, we don't know—and dumped there. If you notice anything suspicious elsewhere on the church grounds, let us know. You know how things usually look around here, and my investigators don't."

Pastor Bob nodded his head like a great shaggy dog with big, woeful eyes and sighed. "Of course. A tragedy. Just a tragedy." After a moment's pause, he brightened. "Well, if you won't need me any further, I have next week's sermon to work on."

"If you don't mind, sir, I'll just take a look around. Make sure everything's secure."

"Feel free. I'll be in my office if you should need me."

Tom watched him go, his face expressionless behind the shades. When the good pastor was out of earshot, he turned to me, keeping his voice low. "Thought I told you to stay in the car."

I shrugged, not ready to apologize. "It was hot in there."

"You could have switched the engine and the AC both on."

"I didn't want to be accused of tampering with police property."

He gave me a look, the kind he always gave me when he thought I was being dramatic. "You're doing it again, you know."

I didn't say anything. What was there to say? I knew exactly what I was doing . . . just as he knew what he was doing. Moreover, I couldn't even say I was particularly sorry. Bitchy? Maybe. But every girl has her moments. It hadn't exactly been the most stellar day in the history of dating.

"I have to go check on a few things. Are you staying put?"

"Are you kidding?"

He sighed. "Come on, then."

I did pause to check on Minnie, but she was tucked up in a little ball in her mesh-sided carrier, snoozing away in the shade of the thickly-leafed maple tree, so I tiptoed away to follow Tom as he made his investigatory rounds. "What are we checking on?" I asked him curiously.

"*I* am going to walk the property to look for likely points of interest that might have been missed in the dark last night. *You* are going to stand back and observe and not touch anything or get in the way at all."

It was his right as a deputy to tell me what to do . . . but the attitude still irked me.

So I followed as he circumnavigated the church, getting down on his knees to search through thicker tufts of sun-fried grass, walking the halls of the church itself, walking back out to where Veronica's body had lain crumpled down in the cave-in itself, then turning to do a complete one-eighty. He stopped, mid-pivot, squinted, cocked his head thoughtfully, then began to walk back up toward the church.

"What is it?" I couldn't help myself. The silence was getting old.

He glanced over as though he'd forgotten I'd been his shadow for the last thirty minutes. "Well, it occurs to me that if the Maddox woman's body was dumped in the hole over there—and that's a given—then someone would have had to carry or transport her body from wherever it was that her murder took place."

It was the same thing he'd been discussing with Chief Boggs and Sheriff Reed at the police department. "Makes sense to me."

"So . . . I don't know if you know this, but the human body, when it isn't controlled or helped along by the person themselves, isn't exactly easy to lift. It's not just a matter of weight, but of balance and heft and flopping body parts—"

"Nice visual."

"Thanks. As I was saying, it makes sense to me that the easiest way to move a body would be to drag it or to use some kind of transport."

I frowned, looking around at the ground. The grass in the vicinity, where it hadn't been scraped away by the payloader before the cave-in had occurred, had been trampled down so much during the beginning of the excavation process by both feet and machinery that I didn't see how anything could be pinpointed as evidence of someone having dragged or transported a dead body. And if the murderer were strong enough, surely the weight of the body wouldn't matter.

"So," Tom continued, "what I'm thinking is that they would have looked for something to help them to do it."

"Like a hospital gurney," I quipped.

"Yeah, like a gurney. Smart-ass."

"Always here to help."

"Actually, what I was thinking of would be more like a lawn cart or a lawnmower of some sort. You know, gardening implements. And with the church's flower garden just up the hill . . ."

Without another word he started tromping up said gentle slope, leaving me to follow or not.

# Chapter 13

The garden's old-fashioned iron gate was closed. As Tom pushed it inward, it squeaked on its hinges, like a crow cawing harshly in protest at an outsider's intrusion. He looked around the garden, his eyes taking in everything. The shadows were beginning to extend outward where the sky-high sanctuary banked the space with its soaring stained glass window. The sun was beginning its downward path in the sky, giving the place a welcome respite with an at least ten-degree drop in temperature from outside the space. In the bigger picture, it was not much . . . but I was grateful.

"Nice here," he commented off-handedly.

"It has a couple of very dedicated keepers," I said. At the lift of his brows, I told him, "The pastor's mother-in-law, Letty Clark, and his wife . . . whose name I don't recall."

Tom consulted his spiral pocket notebook. "Emily Angelis. Very nice woman. A little on the quiet side . . ."

"I met her. 'Fey,' my grandmother would have said."

"Tetched," he agreed. "But nice."

He began to make his way around the garden, pausing to bend over to eye the winding paths of pea gravel and mulch. Nothing looked out of order.

"Quite a lot of plants," Tom said. "But no broken ones that I can see. I guess I was hoping I'd find something here. Signs of a struggle or something."

I nodded. "What about inside the church itself?"

"I don't know. I can't rule it out right now. It seems a long shot, with the threat of discovery high, especially considering that the pastor and his family live right there on church property . . . but then, everything about this particular murder says unplanned to me. I mean, who plots to kill someone when any number of people who had attended the fundraiser could still be lingering around? I do know I didn't see anything on our walk through, but it seems to be a little too twisted to kill someone in a fit of anger in a church. I mean, we'd have to be dealing with a psychopath or sociopath. Someone without any regard for the sensibilities of others."

Touché. But we couldn't rule that out, either.

We? What was I talking about? Tom couldn't afford to rule that out. I was not a part of the equation.

And if I wasn't mistaken, that wasn't the only equation I didn't seem to be a part of. And that's what was causing us so much trouble to begin with.

But that was another worry entirely.

"Let's go back this way through the church," he said, waving toward the rear exit, "do another walkthrough, and then we'll go."

" 'Kay."

We made our way toward the very end of the west

wing. The heavy, utilitarian metal door with its narrow peep window of wire-threaded glass stood open wide, showing a long hall with doors leading off to each side. Tucked up against the building just next to the entrance was a small, prefab shed, securely chained and padlocked against intruders. Inside the church, the lights in the hall itself were off, but the fading daylight cast geometric shapes of illumination here and there from the open doors. From somewhere nearby came the sound of running water.

Tom stepped over the threshold and glanced into the first room on the left, pausing in the doorway. "Hello there, ma'am. Sorry about that. I didn't mean to startle you. Do you remember me from last night? Special Investigator Fielding."

I heard Letty Clark's voice respond. "Yes, of course. No, you didn't frighten me overmuch. I just wasn't expecting anyone to be standing there, that's all."

As I came up beside Tom, I saw Letty standing at a utility sink in what appeared to be a multifunction service room, a hose sprayer in her yellow-gloved hand, a stiff scrub brush in her other. She'd been scrubbing mulch and dirt clumps from her pronged weeding tools. I used to think my mom had long ago cornered the market on her version of OCD—Obsessive Cleaning Disorder. After all, once I'd even caught her ironing my dad's socks. So this new evidence clinched it for me: A little bit of craziness must run in all Stony Mill families.

"Don't mind me," she said. "Just doing a bit of tool maintenance. My daddy always said a tool not cared for is a tool that's wasted. But I just can't stand getting all that muck and mud on my hands, either. Never could. Thank goodness they make these things." She stripped off the rubber glove with a snap and laid it over the faucet to drip dry while she rinsed out the sink and sprayed it with an industrial-strength bleach cleaner. She glanced up at us with a quirky smile on her face. "Some gardener, afraid of a little dirt. Silly, I know." Her gaze flicked sideward as she caught sight of me hovering in the hall. "Oh, hello there. Back again?"

No smile of welcome. I couldn't help wondering if she was remembering Chief Boggs's question about my ties to Enchantments . . . and if she had read the article in the Gazette. Sigh.

I held up my hand in a friendly wave. "Hello, Mrs. Clark. It's nice to see you. We were just in your lovely garden."

Her face relaxed a smidge. It was obvious the garden was her pride and joy. "It's a nice place for a little courting, that's for sure."

I stammered something inane and glanced away, embarrassed by her assumption. There hadn't been much to assume about when it came to Tom and me.

"Mrs. Clark, I'd like to ask you a couple of questions, if you don't mind," Tom said.

"Sure, shoot."

"Did you spend the morning in the garden today?"

"Yes, I spend every morning in the garden. Best time of day to work. It's quite large, if you haven't noticed. It requires constant supervision, constant care. My daughter and I are very attentive to its needs."

"So, you worked on the entire garden or only a section of it?"

"Oh, let's see here. My daughter was feeling a bit under the weather—not sleeping well, you understand—so I worked on my own this morning. I did a bit of weeding around the roses and raked all of the paths. Threw down a bit of new mulch where erosion has taken a toll. Did my usual watering and deadheading. That sort of thing. I guess with all of that I covered most, if not all, of the garden."

"And did you notice anything out of the ordinary about anything? Anything out of place, or broken, or missing?"

She frowned and pursed her lips, thinking. "No, sir. Nothing at all."

"You're sure?"

She chuckled. "I know my garden, every inch of it. Nothing was out of place." She squinted at him. "Why do you ask? Something to do with the murder of that poor girl?"

"Yes, ma'am, maybe so. I'm just muddling things out and trying to put them together. It's kind of like working a puzzle. You try a piece here, a piece there, and pretty soon, if you get your foundation right, it all just kind of falls into place."

She nodded her approval. "Good analogy, that. Makes sense to me. Only, what happens if there are pieces to your foundation missing?"

"You put it together as best you can and hope it doesn't all come tumbling down on you later."

"Funny you should say that. We once had a wall come down when we built this church. It was a horrible mess." She wrinkled her nose and shook her head to demonstrate just how much she didn't approve. "My daddy worked day and night on fixing up that mess with the help of a whole lot of good, decent people, praise the Lord. It's a shame the behavior of a few bad apples has to put a blight on this church's good name."

"It must be upsetting," Tom commented noncommittally.

"A real shame. Though I heard through the grapevine that you have a suspect nearly in custody. Some young man that the girl had been seeing? Did you know, my son-in-law went out to visit the girl's mother this morning, to pass along our condolences. The poor woman is beside herself with grief . . . but worse still must be the worry that somehow her daughter had brought it on herself." She leaned toward Tom and lowered her voice to a loud whisper that was somehow meant to excuse the gossip. "You know how some young women are. Flitting about from man to man without a care for who they hurt along the way. Getting into all sorts of trouble with drugs and I don't know what." She straightened again, staring confidently down her nose with an air of pious judgment common in these parts for anyone who steps over the line of propriety. "You know the type. So, while I say it's a shame, I can't say it should come as a surprise to anyone who knew her." And then, as if she realized how insensitive that made her sound, she shook her head sadly. "Regrettable. A real, real tragedy. I pray she finds rest and forgiveness at the feet of Jesus."

Amen.

"One more thing," Tom said. "I saw a shed just outside. I'll bet that's where you keep your lawn and garden supplies."

"Yes, lawnmowers, gasoline, sprayers, leaf blowers. The usual."

Tom nodded. "I thought as much. Is that shed always padlocked?"

She raised a brow. "Of course. I am nothing if not precise, Officer. Everything has a place, and everything in its place. It's the way I was raised."

"I'd like to take a look at it, all the same, if you don't mind?"

Letty led the way outside to the shed, unlocking the padlock with a key she pulled from her pocket and swinging the door open. Inside the ten-by-twelve shed, items were shelved and stored with an almost militaristic precision. At first glance, most things appeared brand new. Closer inspection showed a few scrapes, a few scratches, but everything was incredibly clean and oiled to perfection. Even the riding lawnmower, the push mowers, and the garden cart. Letty was right—she was nothing if not precise.

Tom and I waited while she locked up again.

"Thank you, ma'am, for answering my questions," Tom said as Letty paused with us once again beside the open door leading inside the church. "I'll be heading on up now to let your son-in-law know we'll be on our way. You have yourself a nice evening."

"And you. Both of you." She flicked her gaze to me with none of the warmth of yesterday afternoon in the garden. Somehow I suspected that her initial opinion of me had been adversely affected by the good chief of police.

We left her to return to her cleanup efforts while we walked along the silent hallway, each of us attempting to soften footfalls that seemed overly loud. There was something about the hush of a church that begged respect from anyone over the age of sixteen, even when it came to one's footsteps. My flats didn't make much of a dent in the silence, but Tom's heavy lug-soled boots could make enough noise to raise the dead. Crossing the sanctuary wasn't much better. The acoustics in the vaulted space were fantastic.

We found Pastor Bob in his office, just as he'd said he'd be. Tom knocked on the door.

"Come in."

Tom pushed the white paneled door inward. "We're nearly done, sir."

The pastor's office wasn't quite what I'd expected. For some reason I saw Pastor Bob as a man who would be into comfort and ease. His office was a large enough space but so sparsely furnished as to be almost utilitarian in nature. His too-small desk was scarred with nicks and scratches along the skirting, its varnished oak faded into an orangey yellow. The desk chair was a simple, bow-backed wooden chair with a thin pad that would have left my behind numb after ten minutes. A pair of old-fashioned paintings of biblical scenes adorned the walls, bordered by sconces on either side of the antiqued gold frames. Opposite the pastor's desk stood the only extra seating—a deacon's bench, also wooden, also thinly padded. That left a short bookcase—no leather-bound heirlooms here—adorned with a number of framed old black-and-white photos and a number of giveaway Bibles, both child and adult versions.

Not quite the utmost in comfort. Working in this office day after day would seem almost like self-enforced penance. I found it bleak and somehow utterly depressing.

Pastor Bob waved us in. "Good, good. Did you find what you were looking for, Deputy?"

"No, unfortunately," Tom replied. "No tracks in the grass, no evidence of blood, no trails marking where a body"—Pastor Bob winced at this—"might have been dragged over the ground."

"That *is* unfortunate. That poor girl. When I think that this . . . this *heinous* crime was committed on church property . . . well, I just don't know what to think. It's just terrible. Awful." He shook his head back and forth as he leaned into the hard wooden back of his chair and formed his hands into a steeple over his heart. "I only wish I had known her better, that I might have foreseen something, some person or circumstance in her life that might indicate this kind of end for her. That I might have been able to counsel her away from . . . whatever element it was that precipitated this. That young man who everyone is saying is guilty, for instance. I will pray for him, too. Young people these days lead such tangled lives, and they don't seem to know how to disentangle themselves when things go wrong. It's a confusing world we live in, full of vice and temptation."

"I would agree with that, sir," Tom said politely.

*Counsel . . .*

There was something about that word that was bothering me. But what?

Tom sat down on the deacon's bench and shifted his bulky gun belt across his middle for maximum comfort. "Mrs. Clark mentioned that you went to visit Harriet Maddox this morning."

"I did."

"A courtesy call?"

"Condolence call is what I like to call it. Just paying my respects to the victim's family, as is only right."

"Mrs. Clark also mentioned that Mrs. Maddox mentioned Veronica's drug use and . . . promiscuity."

Pastor Bob grimaced. "Well, I'm not sure whether they call the propensity for sexual freedom promiscuity in a thirty-year-old woman these days . . . but that about sums it up, from what her mother told me."

"And the drugs?"

"Apparently so. Mrs. Maddox believes she's been clean since she's been attending services at Grace—that made me proud, quite the feather in our cap, I dare say, if it's true . . . or it would be, if she'd not lost her life so precipitously. It's a sad state of affairs that such things affect the lives of our young people more and more these days."

"Did she tell you anything about Veronica's most recent love affairs?"

Pastor Bob hesitated, clearing his throat. "Well, honestly, Deputy—wouldn't it be better to ask Mrs. Maddox herself these questions? If you don't mind my saying."

Tom's lips curved in a hard nonsmile. "I don't mind. But I've already spoken with Mrs. Maddox. I'm just reaffirming what she told me. Now, as you were saying?"

Having the grace to look abashed didn't get him off the hook. "Her mother said she didn't know who Veronica's recent men were. She knew that Veronica had someone lately—or possibly more than one someone—but she was at a loss as to his identity. Apparently Veronica wasn't always forthcoming about her love life. The last one Mrs. Maddox knew of was Tyler Bennett. According to Mrs. Maddox, Veronica's breakup with the young man sent her into a spiral of drug use that was almost the end of her. That was when she found God."

Yet another vote for Ty Bennett. It was looking more and more like Ty might have been the end of Ronnie Maddox after all.

I frowned, not sure why that revelation was making a knot form in the pit of my stomach. Why was my sense of guilt so strong when it came to fingering Ty? Why did it matter? Everything was pointing in his direction. Just because he didn't seem like the psychopathic type didn't mean he wasn't responsible for her death. Maybe it was an accident and he freaked out and hid her body. I mean, just because a person kills someone doesn't make him a monster necessarily . . . um, right?

Anyone?

*Bueller?*

Hm.

While Tom and Pastor Bob hashed out the rest of the details of his visit with Veronica Maddox's mother, I drifted over to the window and the bookshelves beside it. Outside, the shadows from the trees were getting longer. One of them drew a finger of shadow across the plain white sign that was the church's signatory presence: GRACE BAPTIST CHURCH, EST. 1872, PASTOR ROBERT ANGELIS PRESIDING. Eighteen seventy-two, wow. That would make it . . . I calculated the math in my head . . . one hundred and thirty-seven years old. With the county having been formalized no earlier than 1855, that would make this one of the oldest standing buildings in the area. I commented on that to Pastor Bob.

"Actually, no," he said. "Take a look at the photos next to you."

I did. Many of the framed pictures were black-and-white, some of them actual tintypes dating back to the latter quarter of the nineteenth century. I noticed something in them, though. "That's not the church we're in today!" I exclaimed.

Pastor Bob chuckled. "Good eye. This is actually the second Grace Baptist Church on this property. The first Grace Baptist burned to the ground in 1959, and it was rebuilt where we are standing today."

The buildings were similar but not the same. This

church, for instance, was much larger. Only the general shape was the same, that ubiquitous sprawling, white steepled church.

"Come to think of it, your mother-in-law mentioned that her father worked on the church. Apparently a wall must have fallen down while they were in the process of rebuilding."

"He did indeed. As pastor at the time of the fire, that was only fitting."

"Pastor?" I frowned. "But how—"

"Old Zeke Christiansen, that was my mother-in-law's father. He was pastor here for almost forty-five years. Yes, sir. I took over from him the year he retired—I guess that would be fifteen years ago now. He died that next year, you know. Just plum wore out."

I picked up a picture frame. "This must be him." I could see a resemblance to Letty, especially through the eyes and the bridge of the nose. Letty's iron gray pin curls, though, did not come from him. Probably her mother.

Pastor Bob had come up behind me, and he took the frame from my hand to look at it himself. "Yes, that's him. Poor man, lost his son in that fire, and that after having lost his wife when Letty was born. Just a whole lot of tragedy for that family for quite a while, but somehow he managed to see through it all to be a shining example for folks here. Letty took care of him after, you know. She was always good about that. A real nurturer, she is. She's had a hard lot in life, too, what with growing up without a mother, losing her brother so young, and then her losing her husband later on, too. Just like her father. Some people can't seem to catch any breaks. But all that is water under the bridge now. She has a nice home with me and Emily here, and she will 'til the day she dies."

Ah, but had her life changed as much as Pastor Bob suggested? It seemed to me, in the limited bits I'd witnessed of their lives, that Letty was still taking care of people. She must be one of those kind, unassuming souls who isn't happy unless she's nurturing the bejesus out of someone. I'd known a lot of them in my day. They crept out of the woodwork at family reunions and church functions, force-feeding you their latest culinary creation until it was coming out your ears, asking if you were warm enough, pinching your cheeks until they were bruised, or noticing your developing bosoms until you were tempted to resort to leis of garlic flowers and a chestload of crucifixes to keep them away.

While I was lost in my reverie, Tom decided enough was enough and bid Pastor Bob farewell. By the time we made it back to the cruiser (after retrieving Minnie and giving her a drink) we were arguing again. I couldn't help it. Tom went right back to voicing his opinion about the situation with Liss and how it would really be helpful to him if I could just find another job or at the very least convince Liss to scale back on the woo-woo factor until things settled back to normal—which just went to prove that he didn't consider anyone with "those kinds" of abilities to be normal. Which would include me lumped right in there by default. Things escalated from bad to worse pretty fast. By the time we got to my car back at Enchantments, we'd been giving each other the silent treatment for a good seven minutes. I got out of the cruiser without a word and put Minnie safely in the passenger seat. I was going to just get in my car when he stopped me.

"Maggie."

I turned stiffly back and lifted my brow in implied inquiry.

"At least think about what I said, okay? The pressure I'm getting from the chief . . . it's coming from all quarters, and it's not going to be getting better anytime soon."

He drove off, leaving me to fume in irritation, annoyance, and not a little bit of unease. I knew the backlash he was worried about might be forthcoming. I knew this town and its people like a person knows her family's dysfunctional quirks and foibles, and the thing with the petition and the newspaper could very well be the tip of the iceberg. Even the *Titanic* tried to reverse engines. Too late, but it did make the attempt. On the other hand, I'd always wondered what would have happened if they'd just rammed the damned thing and been done with it.

Maybe it was time I did that with Tom, too. So to speak.

Long past time?

I didn't realize until I got home minutes later that I still hadn't broached the topic of his weekend . . . date.

# Chapter 14

Nothing much happened for a couple of days ... and when I say nothing, I mean nothing. The store's business had slowed to a crawl since Margo's op-ed piece came out. Tara, Liss, and I had done our best to keep ourselves busy updating inventory records, following up on errant merchandise orders, dusting, sweeping, polishing the crystal, and any number of other necessary but mindless duties. But a little bit of light had gone out of our day with Evie missing, and by Wednesday afternoon we were all floating around the space looking for things to do. When a customer did come in, Tara and I nearly knocked each other over to be the first to offer our assistance. Most left quickly. I wouldn't be surprised if our overexcited zeal scared them off.

Not even Marcus was around to break up the monotony. "Maybe if someone gave him a reason to be," Tara snarked when I casually asked about him.

Everyone's a critic ...

Then she relented. "He had to go meet with someone about some contracts for his knife stuff. Said he'd be gone a couple of days. He'll be back by Monday for sure."

Which meant the rest of the week and the weekend itself would be a bust. Thank heaven for girlfriends on standby.

Through the ever-active grapevine, Tara had heard whispers that Reverend Martin had something brewing, but for the most part the offensive phone calls had died down. Unfortunately the diminished calls took away our last-ditch hopes for outside entertainment as the scorecard sat idle by the phone, gathering dust. It also gave me no excuse whatsoever for avoiding my mother's calls, and she did finally get through when I let down my guard.

"Good afternoon, Enchantments Antiques and Fine Gifts. How can I help you?"

"Well, for starters, you can stop avoiding your mother's calls. How many would you say that is this week?" she complained into my ear.

"Hi, Mom. How are you? I'm fine, Maggie, how are things going for you? Great, fantastic, just wonderful," I intoned, mocking up a representation of the kind of phone calls most girls receive from their mothers. We'd been doing better for a time, especially while I was helping out with Mel. Maybe that's what this was all about. Maybe she blamed me for Mel's decision to bring the home nurse in. Mel had told me that Mom and the nurse had clashed more than once.

"Don't get smart with me, missy. I'm in no mood."

That would make two of us. I was still smarting over my argument with Tom, whom I'd seen neither hide nor hair of since Monday evening.

"I've been thinking, Margaret—"

Oh no. Not that.

"—that it might be nice to get you in to see Father Tom for some . . . family counseling."

Wait . . . what?

My grip tightened around the phone receiver. "I don't think I heard you correctly."

"It's nothing to worry about, dear. But since you seem so determined to remain by the side of your boss—who, it has not escaped my notice, has been enjoying a bit of notoriety in the past week, wouldn't you say?—I feel it's important that you hear the truth about her occult practices from a man of God."

Man of God? Father Tom was the last person I wanted to hear "truth" from. I had lost all respect for him years ago. How he still remained at the helm of St. Catherine's, I would never understand. I mean, I'd heard of forgive and forget, but that was ridiculous.

"So I've made an appointment for you."

"You *what*?" My explosion was loud enough that Tara paused in the middle of her lotus meditation on top of the checkout counter and looked over to see what I was doing. Minnie stopped running with the strip of satin ribbon she'd found and jumped up on the bookshelf I was trying to dust to gaze intently into my eyes, her whiskers twitching.

"Next week. Wednesday."

"Mom, you can't just go around trying to run my life. I can't go to your family counseling session."

"Do you want me to talk to your boss for you?"

Exasperation, full-blown, did not allow much room for niceties. "No, I do *not* want you to talk to my boss! Jeez, Mom. I am not sixteen years old. Nothing that Liss is doing or not doing is causing me emotional distress or trauma. And I'm *not* going to your meeting with Father Tom, so you can get that notion right out of your head. I know what your feelings are on the subject, and I respect that, but there is nothing in the Bible that says that I have to feel or believe the same as you. Now, I'm going to have to say good-bye. I really have to get back to work."

There was a sigh on the other end of the line. "You hurt me, Maggie. You really do. But we can talk about this more on Sunday."

You see, that was my mother. Woman of a thousand sneaky tactics. When one didn't work, she'd switch gears on a dime. Guilt was always a fave. Probably because it was so effective.

Still fuming, and because I had nothing better to do, I decided a little sisterly commiseration *might* be in order. It was a long shot—sometimes Mel just didn't get the whole sisterly support thing—but there was always a chance. Yes, I was still exasperated with her for spilling the beans about Liss and Marcus to Margo and thereby getting us into the mess we were now facing . . . but a part of me blamed myself for that, too. I knew Mel's propensity for gossip. I should have known she'd view her spook situation as an opportunity to reassert herself as High Queen of the gossip chain. Besides, blood was thicker than water, as the old saying goes, and since the Ouija board spirit had spelled out the word "sister," and Mel was still lying preggers and vulnerable on bed rest under doctor's orders, I was determined to understand what it had meant. I didn't see how Mel could be a further threat to be careful of; hadn't she already done her worst?

I dialed up her home number and waited. Mel picked up on the first ring.

"Margo?"

"Um, no," I replied flatly. It still irked that Mel had taken up with Margo. Sometimes I wondered if Mel—or Margo, for that matter—was using the friendship as a way of being a thorn in my side. Probably not, but that thought made me feel better on days when I saw Mel and Margo together, thick as thieves, and I was forced to grin and bear it. Today, though, I had other things on my mind. "How's Mommy and baby?"

"Oh. Hi, Maggie. Good, good. Bored as all get-out, but I guess that's to be expected. Not much longer now; I keep telling myself that. I hear *you've* been in a little trouble lately."

"Oh?" I asked, playing dumb. Of course, I was in trouble *because* of Mel. Still. Here was another reason I wanted to talk to Mel. Her friendship with Margo might be a cross I'd have to bear, but maybe I could use it to my advantage in this situation. "Just what have you heard?"

"Plenty," Mel said with a smug tone in her voice that made me sigh. But then she switched gears and did something completely unexpected. "You need to watch your back, Sis. Seriously. Courtney AnneMarie Craven, get down off that chair this instant, or I'll have to call Grandma upstairs to have her get you down, and I'm pretty sure you won't be happy about that."

"What are you talking about, Mel?" I asked, trying to get her back on track. "The whole Gazette opinion piece? Yeah, that was a surprise. But after the first rush, things have quieted down here." Boy, had they ever. A little too much for my comfort.

"I have a feeling it's only a lull."

"A feeling?" Mel didn't do feelings. Really. She had the sensitivity of a teaspoon, without even a drop of honey to sweeten the deal. "Or a scoop?"

"Does it matter? The important thing is, you need to take care of you. Have you talked to Mom?"

"Yeah."

"Not good?"

"Got it in one."

"Well . . . I knew it wouldn't be good. She's really been on a warpath lately. Between you and me, I think she's feeling displaced here since we brought the nurse in to help."

I agreed. "She's come to the conclusion the only option is a full-on occult intervention." It sounded so ridiculous. I started feeling giggles bubbling up. "She wants me . . . to go to family counseling . . . with Father Tom."

The laughter proved contagious, crossing longtime barriers and boundaries, bridging the great divide. The two of us burst out in a fit of giggles in a way we hadn't since we were preteens playing a trick on our older brother, Marshall. Before teenage squabbles over boys, clothes, and attention came into play.

It felt good.

"Father Tom needs an intervention of his own," Mel said once she could breathe again. "Seriously. He doesn't have the right to give counsel to anyone else. Why doesn't Mom see that? She would defend him with her last breath, despite his . . . proclivities. That being said, you should go to mass more often. It would smooth things over with her."

That was just the thing. I didn't want to be forced to do anything purely for the sake of smoothing things over. I wanted to make my own decisions, live my own life, and I wanted my mother to accept me for myself.

"Mel . . ." It had to be asked. "You haven't been telling

Margo anything else, have you? About Liss and Marcus and that night?"

"Oh, you know me. Just a couple of little things. Nothing earth-shattering. I mean, they did help me out. I wouldn't want to do anything to hurt them, and . . . well, you know."

*Just a couple of things.* The evasiveness gave me the answer I had been seeking. She'd told Margo everything. Every last detail. It *was* my fault. I alone knew Mel's nature, her inherent inability to keep from spreading the scoop every time she got near one. And the secret about Liss being a witch . . . that was a biggie. There was no way she wouldn't have passed that around the second we were out of sight. I should have known. I should have . . .

That must be the meaning behind the *Sister* clue the Ouija spirit had given us. *Be careful*, it had also said. Point well taken. I had to make sure that whatever came, Mel was kept out of the loop.

That was if there were any more secrets to keep out of the public eye.

I rang off with Mel feeling even more uncertain than I had been before.

I wandered over to where the girls—well, Liss and Tara, at least—were now seated at the counter. Liss had apparently decided to coax Tara out of her ever-deepening state of mourning over Evie's absence with a bit of controlled exploration using Tara's favorite tool of late, the homemade Ouija.

"Hey, Maggie, guess what," Tara said.

"What?"

"We got your Elias back again."

"Did you, now." I wasn't sure how I was supposed to feel about the fact that some nebulous energy from a hole in the ground was playing follow-the-leader with me. I'd really been hoping it was just a fluke, a fly-by spirit that had dropped into the home and life of a sensitive for a little look-see. At least if he had been loitering around me at home, he wasn't making a nuisance of himself. Or maybe it was Minnie that was keeping him at bay. I couldn't know for sure, but I made a mental note then and there to buy a white sage bundle from Liss's herb stores to do a cleansing this weekend. A little bit of spiritual housekeeping certainly wouldn't hurt.

"Uh-huh. Check it out." Tara beckoned me over. "Elias, I have Maggie here. Do you know Maggie?"

The pointer moved to the sticky note marked "yes," then slid through a sequence of letters to spell out my name, one letter at a time.

"Yes. Maggie," I read. *Wonderful.* I glanced up around the tall, tin-plated ceilings, wondering where the energy was lurking. I held up my hand and waved weakly. "Hi, Elias."

"Oh, there's more. Look."

*M-A-G-G-I-E*, the glass spelled out again.

Maggie, yeah. We got that part.

But then it spelled out something entirely different.

*U-N-I-C-E*

"Aww. How cute. He thinks you're nice. Isn't that sweet? Something tells me our Magster has an admirer."

Sweet. Not only did I live in a basement apartment, I now had a spirit who had decided I was his very own bright light in the darkness.

*S-I-S-T-E-R*

"I just spoke with Mel," I told Liss and Tara. "She swears she's not making more trouble for us here."

*B-E-C-A-R-E-F-U-L*

"Of course, there's always the chance that she could be downplaying her role," I conceded. "But what can I do except keep an eye on her?"

*U-L-C*

Unfortunately, none of this was helping us to understand.

The bell at the front of the store jingled, heralding the arrival of a customer—at last! And with Tara behind the counter, this one was mine. I went over to issue a welcome and found to my surprise that the fey wife of Pastor Bob had walked through our front door, looking ever so pallid and drab in a gray-and-white checked shirt-dress and sensible shoes, her only spot of color a quilted Vera Bradley handbag in paisley swirls of blue and yellow. Onto her other arm clung a short, somewhat rough-looking woman whose skin and hair had seen better days. I'd never seen the woman before, at least that I knew of.

"Oh, hello," said the pastor's wife. "I remember you from the other day. You probably don't recognize me without my towel and robe."

I nodded, holding out my hand in greeting. "Of course I do. You're Pastor Bob's wife, yes?"

"Emily Angelis, yes."

I shook her hand. "Maggie O'Neill."

"You're exactly who we were coming to see. You and the young ladies and the gentleman who were with you the other night when Ronnie Maddox was found."

"Oh?" I transferred my attention to the woman by her

side, who was intently sizing me up through big eighties-style plastic lenses, her pursed lips cratered by smoker's lines.

"This is Veronica Maddox's mother," Emily said gently. "Harriet Maddox."

Instantly I felt my heart melt for her. "Oh, Mrs. Maddox. I'm so sorry for your loss. Here, come sit down, both of you. Have a cup of tea, my treat."

Thankfully Tara heard me and managed to have every last sticky note cleared off the counter before I escorted the ladies over.

Harriet Maddox sat down with a sigh and ran her hands through her thinning, frazzled gray hair. Her grief was weighing down upon her like a heavy barbell balanced on her shoulders, crushing, crushing. I turned away from her, stricken as the sheer force of her emotions nudged at my own personal energies, and tried to catch my breath as I muddled over the shelf of teas, trying to decide which would be best. My hand hovered over the canister for chamomile, a good, all-around soothing tea. Then Liss's hand was there, guiding my own to one shelf above to the canister for borage.

"For grief," she murmured for my ears alone, "and sadness."

I prepared a nice, big cup the usual way, then set it down steaming in front of Mrs. Maddox. For Mrs. Angelis I chose a fruity herbal blend that smelled as good as it tasted. She smiled as I placed it before her.

"Thank you. You're too kind."

I slid the honeypot out to let them drizzle to their heart's content. Off by the cleanup sink, I saw Liss measuring out several teacups' worth of borage and scooping the herb into a small cheesecloth bag, which she tied with a pink satin ribbon. A gift for Mrs. Maddox, no doubt. I felt a rush of warmth for my bighearted boss, who never let sadness go without kindness to counter it. I had a sneaking suspicion she was saying a few words over the herbs as well.

"Now, what can I do for you ladies?" I asked once they'd had a chance to sample their tea.

"Mrs. Maddox," Emily Angelis said, "wanted to thank you—"

"I can do the talking from here, Emily, thanks," Harriet Maddox rasped, clutching the cup in both hands and staring up at me over the rising steam. "I wanted to come in and thank you, girly, for coming forward to speak to the police about what you saw that day. Some people wouldn'ta done that, so I thank you for doing your civic duty. Mrs. Angelis here said she'd met you out at the church that very night, and then with the article in the paper and whatnot, well . . . when Mrs. Angelis offered to bring me over to pay my thanks, I jumped at it. So thanks."

"Oh, Mrs. Maddox," I said, never very comfortable when confronted with gratitude. "Well, you're very welcome. I didn't do anything special. I guess I just happened to be in the wrong place at the wrong time."

"No. Never think it," Harriet said, adamant. "My girl, she's gone, but maybe this way the man what got her will be put away, not to harm anyone else. That's what I hope and pray, anyways. Some good's got to come of him taking my Ronnie before her time. That's how I feel."

Mrs. Angelis leaned forward in her seat. "They've picked up Tyler Bennett, you see. Just this afternoon."

So, it was a done deal, then. I wondered if Tyler would have the means to pay for his own lawyer, or if he was to be assigned a public defender. Something told me that the latter was more likely.

Assuming they could make the charge stick.

Assuming? Now, why was I thinking about it that way?

"May he rot in hell for what he's done," Mrs. Maddox hissed. "I'm sorry, Emily, I know it ain't Christian to wish ill on your neighbor, but that's how I feel."

"Dear, dear," Liss said, coming around the counter and putting her arm around the trembling shoulders of a woman wizened by time and too much hard living. "Come along here and walk with me. Let's give you a chance to collect yourself."

Liss's calming influence was mesmerizing. Mrs. Maddox didn't stand a chance of turning the request away. Blindly she rose and allowed Liss to lead her gently away. Tara had disappeared, up to the loft with Minnie was my guess. She could often be found there if she didn't have anywhere more pressing to be.

"Poor woman." Emily Angelis's soft voice broke through my thoughts. "Thank you for being so kind. When she asked if I'd mind driving her here to thank you in person, I just couldn't say no."

"No need to thank me, honestly. Either of you. I saw what I saw. Whether it helps to put the person who did that to Ronnie away or not, we'll see how things go."

She looked at me, her head tilted curiously. "You don't seem so certain."

I shook my head and smiled. "Don't mind me. Just speaking without thinking."

"I do that sometimes," she said, nodding in understanding. "Mama chides me for letting thoughts fly free like a little girl without a filter, but I can't help it sometimes."

"Everyone does that, I think."

She took a sip of her tea, her fingertips toying with the handle long after she placed it back on the table. Something was on her mind; I could tell.

"May I ask you something?" At my nod, she cleared her throat, taking time to form both thoughts and words. "I read the article in the newspaper on Monday."

Everyone had read that article by now. "Oh?"

"Is it true, then? Do you all really traffic with spirits here?"

I coughed. "Traffic? I guess that depends on your definition. Do we conjure spirits in order to ask them to do our bidding? No. It would be dangerous, not to mention the height of arrogance to suppose that . . . Well, no. If you mean, do we receive information sometimes from spirits, and do we do our best to investigate their world in order to understand our own, then yes. We do do that. Sometimes we also help those spirits who for whatever reason fail to cross over. And we try to help those who live with spirits in their homes, so that they don't have to live in fear all the time." I looked her in the eye. "Does that change your opinion of us?"

She shook her head. "No, not really. I mean, the Bible does say that's a sin . . . but there are also instances in the Good Book where spirits are conjured. My husband might not agree with me, but I happen to believe the sin lies with the intent. If you're doing what you say you're doing, I would have a hard time convincing myself that the Lord would object." She took another sip of her tea. "I . . . um . . . I've actually seen a few things myself. On our property."

"Have you?" I asked, surprised.

She nodded. "Mama . . . well, she often sends me off

to bed early. For my own good, you see," she explained quickly, "because . . . well, because of the . . . female issues I've been having." Blushing, she peeked at me, then in a rush confessed in a whisper, "Miscarriages. Three now."

I didn't know what to say other than, "I'm so very sorry."

"And, well," she rushed on, her cheeks taking on a pink tone for the first time since she'd walked through the door, "sometimes I don't go straight to bed when she thinks I do. Bobby, he's been so busy . . . well, he wants to give me time to heal, you know, before we try again. He's been sleeping in the guest room downstairs. So, I stay up sometimes, just sitting in my window in the dark, watching the shadows move."

I started getting that creepy-shivery feeling. I'd seen the shadows move when they shouldn't. But unlike Emily Angelis, I knew for a fact there was something there that shouldn't be. "Go on."

"I saw something that night. The night that poor Veronica was killed. Just . . . a big, dark shadow that wasn't a part of the larger darkness, but separate. Moving around outside by the church. It frightened me," she said simply. "I didn't tell Mrs. Maddox; I couldn't. I wouldn't want her to think that her daughter might not have moved on to Heaven."

"No. No, she doesn't need to hear that. Thank you for telling me."

She nodded again and went back to her tea, sipping away, lost in thought. As was I.

We watched Liss with Harriet in silence for a while, just drinking in the peace of the store. Liss soon had Harriet confiding all to her, words pouring free in a torrent from a mouth twisted in grief and pain. "She was just a troubled girl, that's all. A poor troubled girl. But it weren't her fault, you see. She had a hard life. No father to teach her how a good man acts towards a woman. She was dealing the best way she knew how. But that meant repeating her mother's own sins, don't you see? Mine. I was the one insisted she see Pastor Bob for counseling for drugs and boozin' and men. That Ty Bennett, he and she was like dynamite together . . . jostle 'em a bit and there'd be an explosion somewhere, somehow. My ferocious baby girl."

She was weeping softly now. Liss dug into her pocket and handed her a fresh white handkerchief, touched with delicate lace at the edges. Harriet took it and wiped her eyes, then covered her nose and honked loudly into it before handing it back to Liss. Liss, bless her heart, took it without comment and tucked it back into her pocket as she soothed Harriet Maddox with warmth and compassion and a steady hand on her shoulder. Eventually her sobs slowed and her breathing calmed. By the time that she was ready to leave, Harriet was leaving not just with a gift of borage tea, but with a measure of peace that she'd not possessed when she entered the store, and that was quite something in my book.

Felicity Dow, witch, friend. Miracle worker?

It worked.

# Chapter 15

"How on earth do you do that?" I asked Liss when she returned to her place behind the counter.

"What's that, dear?"

"Give someone so incredibly down a lift of spirit that they so desperately need?"

Liss smiled. "It's not hard, really. You listen to their spirit, very, very intently, with your own. You can hear all sorts of things that way. Secret things, shameful things, sorrowful things, guilty things, privately joyous things. And then your Guides help you say the right words that they so badly need to hear in order to begin healing."

Reason number 1,048 that Liss is my favorite person in the whole world.

"What did she tell you?" I asked.

"Not much more than you probably heard at the end. There are a lot of repetitive thoughts and concepts that spin through a person's mind as part of the grieving process. Mostly they're just muddling their way through the muck, trying to make sense of their pain. They need to talk, to release the emotion that builds with every passing moment so that they don't feel they're going to explode from it. Harriet is the same as every other mother out there whose child passed before they did, no matter the age. She needed to hear a message of hope. That life is not the end. That there is more out there, and that she will see her child again." She paused, her eyes twinkling. "I daresay, I may have renewed her dedication to her church."

Compassion, a kind and listening ear, and a message of hope. Was it really that simple? Was that all that it took to heal a broken heart?

Oh, but wait. If that's what it took, wouldn't the counseling that Ronnie had been receiving have helped her? Wasn't that what Pastor Bob had been doing for her? Listening? Pointing her in the right direction with a message of hope for her future? Because something seemed to have gone very wrong with his method of counseling, if I wasn't mistaken. Ronnie didn't seem to have lost any of her anger toward Ty, even though it had been nine months since she'd been involved with him. And in her case, the need for healing her heart seemed to have been a matter of life and death.

And now Ty would be paying for that inadequacy with the rest of his.

Perhaps Pastor Bob's methods of healing were a little rusty.

I was mulling this over as I reached into the broom closet for the dust mop to give the floors a quick run that they didn't really need. It was just as I closed the door behind me that the realization hit me.

*Counsel* . . .

Ronnie herself had said that the pastor had been counseling her to help her get past the demons of her past relationship: sex, drugs, and booze.

But what had Pastor Bob said when Tom questioned him? He had claimed not to know her enough to place a face with a name. Too many parishioners to know each and every one, or something like that.

But I had been there that afternoon, when Ronnie asked him for counsel.

The plain truth seemed to be . . . he lied.

The question was, why?

After a few minutes of indecision, I texted the information to Tom, as clearly as I could, before I lost my nerve. *Every bit of information helps*, I reasoned. Maybe I'd call him about it later. Maybe we could talk and set a few things straight. Clear the air with grace and humanity, and maybe, just maybe clear the way in our lives for someone else.

*Marcus?* my mind couldn't help inserting.

Perhaps.

I heard the back door to the office open, barely preceding a flurry of voices, both male and female. I peeked through the velvet curtains.

Charlie came through first, dressed in dusty jeans and T-shirt. "Bad *ass*!" he was saying. "Crosses everywhere, man! That just rocked!"

Devon McAllister, fellow N.I.G.H.T.S. member and resident conspiracy theorist, was right behind him. A surprise, because I didn't know he even knew Charlie. He waved at me, grinning. "Hey, Maggie."

And bringing up the rear was your favorite angelic blonde and mine, Evie Carpenter. She did a little Snoopy dance when she saw me. "Maggie!"

"Evie! What are you doing here?" I wondered if Devon's presence could be explained by Evie's. Or was I the only one who'd noticed our young techno-geek had a serious thing for her, despite his being five years older?

Evie lifted a finger to her lips and grinned. "Shhh."

Tara came running into the office from the front, her face alight. She thrust Minnie at me and threw herself into Charlie's arms. Looked like whatever issues they had been having had been resolved, I noticed, smiling. "Charlie! What are you doing here? I thought you were working." She kissed him soundly in a free-spirited, uninhibited, completely un-Tara-like fashion.

Ah, love.

"And Evie!" she continued, throwing her free arm around Evie's shoulder and kissing her soundly on the cheek for good measure. "Oh my *Gawddess*, it has been slow here without you!"

Maybe it was just boredom, but Tara really seemed to be mellowing. Good for her.

"Did I hear voices?" Liss popped her head into the office, too. "Goodness. I see my hearing hasn't forsaken me. Hello, happy young people." She beamed when she caught sight of Evie.

"Tell them, Charlie," Devon urged.

Charlie didn't need much in the way of convincing, but Liss thought everyone might be more comfortable sitting rather than standing in the crowded office. We all played follow-the-leader out to the beverage counter, where my cup of Lemon Ginger Zing was cooling. Liss, Tara, and Evie brought out the cups and a tray of blueberry scones that hadn't quite sold yet.

"We wouldn't want these to go to waste, now would we?" Liss said with a twinkle.

Charlie got right down to relating the tale of how he'd come to be helping the experts for the historical society. With the labor crew grounded until the historical investigation concluded, Charlie was desperate to find a way to put some extra cash in his pockets, so Tara had approached her Aunt Marian to see if the investigation would need additional manpower to help with lifting and hauling. With the go-ahead from the Special Investigation Task Force that very morning, Charlie had received the call he was waiting for. They'd been out all day in the hot sun, first setting up the equipment to safely lower the experts into the pit and then beginning the historical survey of the site. At first Charlie was kept up top while the pair of experts assessed the stability of the underground room, but once absolute safety was established, Charlie was allowed to come down as well to help.

"It was really bad ass," he said, repeating himself with his favorite phrase of the month in that habit common among teenagers the world over. "There were crosses everywhere, a couple of really rough-looking old tables, pages from an old Bible, a kid's book of animals. And even creepier than the crosses? A couple of animal skeletons. They'd been killed, you could tell, and it kind of looked like it was on purpose. That was the creepy part. Other than that, though, the place was pretty bare. Dusty, but empty. I think it was kind of a disappointment to the guys from the historical society." He grinned. "But it was still bad ass."

What was it about teenage boys that made them adore adventure so much? Show them a mountain, and they want to climb it. Show them a ledge, and they want to jump from it. Show them a rope, and they want to swing from it. Show them a dark, scary place, and they want to investigate. And then they grew up to be men, who also never met a mountain they didn't want to climb, a ledge too high to jump from, a rope that didn't whisper their name . . . and so on . . . and so on . . .

It was hopeless, really.

"Man, I wish I'd been on the crew, too. My dad, though . . . he'd have a cow," a gloomy Devon told him. He shook his shaggy brown hair out of his eyes, but it flopped back in. "He's already telling me I'd better have my degree by the end of this next school year, or he's cutting me off. It wasn't bad enough that he made me attend Grace with their strict rules, rather than IU like I wanted."

Devon was our perpetual college student, who had more interests in and fascinations with the world than you could shake a stick at. He also had a banker father who would never understand his geeky, studious, underground rebel of a son, who would much rather hunt ghosts than hunt for errors in a spreadsheet, and who never met a conspiracy theory he didn't like.

Evie gave him a loop-armed hug over the shoulders from behind, the way a kid sister would hug her older brother, and Devon's cheeks went scarlet. "Poor Dev. Your dad and my mom are two of a kind. I'm not supposed to be here. Mom thinks that Maggie and Liss are going to lead me over to the Dark Side."

Tara raised a dark brow. "You still haven't told them about your abilities, have you?"

"Are you kidding? I'd be packed off to boarding school before you could say 'witch hunt.' You all would never see me again. I'd return someday, maybe five years down the road, a pale shell of my former self, with all life stamped out of me."

Obviously Tara had been teaching Evie a thing or two about melodrama.

"The kid's book actually had a name written in side it," Charlie said off-handedly, "which I guess is good for the historical society because then they can look up whatever information they can find on his life. Elias C. is what it said."

Liss, Tara, Evie, and I all crossed glances. The guys noticed. "Hey, what's going on?" Devon asked, just as Charlie said, "What?"

"Maggie's being visited by a spirit that calls itself Elias," Tara said carefully.

"Hey! Cool coincidence," Charlie said.

Tara shook her head. "It started visiting her the day of the fundraiser. Right after the cave-in."

A shiver ran through the room, seemingly passed on from one body to another like a bolt of electricity.

"Could it be the same entity?" Devon asked.

How could it not be? It was a question I kept asking myself over and over again as I secretly made a phone call to Marian later that afternoon.

"Stony Mill Public Library, Marian Tabor speaking, how can I help you?"

"Hi Marian. Maggie."

"Oh, hey, Maggie. What's up, girl?"

"I just heard about the items that the survey team found in the cave-in room."

"Fascinating, isn't it? Of course we were hoping there would be much more down there, but at least we were able to take photos of the room intact, with all of its articles in their original positions. The same way it must have been left decades ago. Why it was buried, I don't know. I don't suppose we'll have an easy time of deciphering that mystery, either, especially if Pastor Angelis isn't aware of such an event in the church's history."

"It isn't the first Grace Baptist," I commented, lost in thought, "so maybe it was closed down at that period in time. Pastor Bob has photos of the original building. I guess it burned down in the fifties. The pastor at the time lost a son in the fire. Pastor Zeke Christiansen."

"No, you're right about the fire," Marian began to confirm. "Of course I was only a child at the time . . ."

Her voice trailed off. Not really, but bells were going off in my head, *ding-ding-ding*! It took me a moment of reflection to understand why.

"Elias C.," I whispered without thinking. "Elias. My Elias. Elias Christiansen?"

Marian heard me, despite waxing factual on the historic fire. "You mean the son, I take it. Is that just an educated guess?"

"It's a long story. Marian, do you have any way of checking that?"

"I can check census records, when I get a chance. Call you back later?"

"You'd better."

"Good. And then you can tell me why I'm getting cold chills up my spine."

"Agreed."

"The crosses, though, Maggie. The crosses are fascinating. A few of them are church quality and appear to have been store bought, but many of them are just two sticks of wood nailed together against the wall or fastened together with a length of rough twine. Some even with colored ribbon, like I used to wear on my ponytail. I have no idea what purpose they really served, other than they seem to indicate that someone was very, very afraid of something."

Poor Elias. A child, lost in a tragic fire. It must have been horrific, if it was bad enough to take out the entire original building.

The air around me was changing as I stood there with the portable phone in my hands. I closed my eyes, testing it. Energy moving in. Spirit energy. I felt a crowning pressure at the top of my head, like a headband that was on too tight, pressing ever inward. It wasn't painful or even unpleasant . . . it was just there, and it made me a little lightheaded. "Elias? Is that you?" I asked aloud.

The swirling of the air around me continued. I saw a silvery sparkle, just a flash really, out of the corner of my eye.

"That *is* you, isn't it?" I breathed. My chest felt tight, like the squeezing was continuing down from my head. I gave up trying to talk and thought-projected my questions instead, the way I did when asking questions of my spirit guide. It was worth a try.

*Do you want something from me, Elias? Is that why you haven't moved on? Do you need someone to do something for you? Do you need . . . me . . . to do something for you?*

Minnie bumped up against my ankles and twirled her body around them. Or at least I thought she did. When I glanced down, no one was there. But then, a wave of sadness flooded through me, enough that I wanted to dissolve into tears there and then. Somehow I choked them back.

*Is that it? You're sad? You want comfort? Oh, Elias, I*

*really wish you'd gone to a stronger sensitive than me for help. I want to help you; I do. I'm just not sure I can.*

And then, suddenly, unexpectedly, into my brain popped the letter clues he'd been giving us all along. Once more, with feeling: *U-L-C.*

I'll see. I'll see what? I was getting frustrated. I was really and truly afraid I wasn't going to see at all. That I wouldn't be able to help. That little Elias would stick around. As much as I liked kids, I just wasn't sure I was ready to be a surrogate mother to a fifty-year-old phantom child.

Not to mention what that would do to my already lackluster love life.

*U . . . N . . . I . . . C . . . E . . .* filtered into my thoughts. I was seeing the letters in my head as I'd seen them counted out on the Ouija board.

Oh, great, now I was getting guilt trips from spirits, too? As much as the thought was appreciated—I mean, who wouldn't like having their own personal admiration society?—it just served to make me feel even more a heel for wanting to send him packing to the Great Boy Scout Camp in the Sky.

*You're going to have to do better than that, I'm afraid, Elias,* I told him.

*S-I-S-T-E-R*

*And that's not helping me, either. I already know my sister's a pain. I'm watching her like a hawk. It's all I can do.*

*M-A-G-G-I-E-B-E-C-A-R-E-F-U-L*

He merged his previous Ouija board messages together in my head, two blips of thought, one directly on the heels of the other.

A warning?

And then he was gone, the sense of him, the pressure all around me. Gone. In an instant. And I was left feeling more lost and oblivious than ever, and missing that fleeting point of connection.

# Chapter 16

I couldn't stop thinking of Elias all afternoon. I also couldn't stop thinking of the shadowy figure that Emily Angelis had seen flitting about the dark recesses of the property the night that Veronica Maddox was murdered. Was it the shade of Elias that she'd seen, released from the room that his spirit was imprisoned in? Or was Veronica Maddox herself hanging out around the site of her own murder, waiting her turn to be able to connect with someone in the physical?

Marian called me back just before closing time. "I have that information for you. Made a copy of it for myself, too, for the historical files," she said.

I laughed at her efficiency. "I would have expected no less of you."

"I aim to please. You know, because I'm a librarian. It's what I do."

We both dissolved into giggles.

"Now that that's out of the way," she said, "here you

are. Elias Leonard Christiansen. Born to Ezekiel Lucas Christiansen and Elva Alice Fuehrer, June twelfth, 1948. Sister Eunace Letitia born to the couple the following year, June fifteenth, 1949. Death notice for Elva Alice Christiansen dated June sixteenth. Cause of death, postnatal hemorrhaging."

Somehow knowing his identity and his history made Elias's failure to cross over after death even sadder. Poor boy, dead in a fire at the tender age of eleven. A child, not even on the brink of puberty. Innocent of the world.

The sadness lingered for me as I locked down the front of the store and placed dust covers over the glass items. We hadn't been working the evening hours this week—it seemed rather pointless to keep the store open when we'd had fewer than a dozen customers all week during the daytime hours, an unfortunate side effect of the Gazette's opinion piece, which I hoped would be forgotten just as soon as the next scandal hit . . . probably sometime next week, knowing this town.

Was it too much to hope the next scandal wouldn't somehow involve one of the N.I.G.H.T.S.?

I packed Minnie into the passenger seat of my car and started off for home. I hadn't noticed it throughout the afternoon, but the sky appeared to be clouding up overhead for the first time in weeks. Maybe we'd soon be getting a respite from this heat wave after all. We could definitely use some rain and cooler weather. Of course, with my luck, all it would do is spit at us just enough to make the air really steam and the poor hapless folks who lived here in this one-horse town really swelter.

Home to my apartment I went, still feeling out of sorts and puzzling over what I was supposed to do, or think, or feel. The one thing I disliked most about being a lower-level sensitive is the confusion that comes along with the package. It was very difficult to gain both experience and confidence without feeling like an inept dope along the way.

One thing I didn't understand—one thing among many—was why Elias's spirit was bound to that secret, buried room to begin with. I knew that earthbound spirits who passed via an unexpected or traumatic death sometimes remained behind due to their own confusion that death had befallen them, and were often found in the places where their deaths occurred . . . but that wasn't entirely the case with Elias. While dying in a tragic fire certainly qualified as a precipitous death, the buried room didn't seem to have been a part of that 1950s catastrophe. His skeletal remains were not found down in that pit—only those of a couple of small animals. So why was he there? Why did he stay behind?

And the room was a mystery, too. Why didn't Pastor Bob know of it? Why was it buried to begin with?

Why were there so many secrets in this town?

I settled Minnie in with a dish of her favorite Tuna Surprise Kitty Buffet and a healthy helping of milk—warmed, of course, I was a good kitty mommy—and went off to strip out of my work clothes and into something a little more comfortable. Comfortable and cool, that was the goal. I settled on a pair of stretchy yoga pants—not that I did yoga, but they were good for the occasional Buns of Steel–style workout I did sometimes while happily ensconced in front of a really good (*as if there are any that aren't*) episode of *Magnum, P.I.*—and a soft, fitted tank top, then slid my hair back from my face with a cotton headband. While I was at it, I washed off my makeup and decided tonight would be the perfect opportunity to apply a cool, deep-cleaning, pore-tightening mask. Nature's Bounty, the label read, made with all natural ingredients that were guaranteed to leave behind a soft, dewy glow. I couldn't help thinking it made me resemble some sort of swamp monster instead. But it was worth it. A girl can never be too vigilant about her skin care, especially in the kind of heat we'd been having. Besides, it's not like I had anything better (*read: male companionship imminent*) to do with my time.

Minnie glanced at me as I came out of the bedroom, then did a double-take and crouched down, ears flat against her head, as I walked by. Not exactly a vote of confidence for her ever-loving human, but she'd just have to get used to it.

I wasn't in the mood to eat yet, but I did grab a Diet Coke from the fridge and then settled back in my big, yuck-green wingback to meditate. Maybe if my mind was clear, I'd be able to make some kind of sense out of what I'd been perceiving. Drawing my knees up Indian-style, I closed my eyes and began to breathe deeply, in through my nose, out through my mouth, over and over again until the calm and serenity of being in The Zone began to descend upon me.

And that was when I was yanked rudely out of said Zone by the sound of the phone ringing.

Frowning, I dragged my eyelids open, blinking away the trance hangover until I felt my own energies return full force.

I picked up, expecting Steff or maybe even Liss. But a very male voice came down the line instead. Marcus. "Hey, Mags. What's doing?"

"Well. Not much," I said automatically, then realized that of course wasn't the case. A lot was doing. So even though my heart had begun to flutter the moment I heard his low-pitched rumble on the other end and my cheeks were warm with a flush of pleasure because he had thought to check in with me, I proceeded to tell him all that I'd learned about the identity of my little shadow and the history of Grace Baptist Church.

"They found a book down in the caved-in room that had the name Elias C. written inside. We already knew that the former pastor at Grace Baptist was Zeke Christiansen, and Tom and I found out through Pastor Bob himself that this Grace Baptist wasn't the original Grace, and that the pastor had lost a son in the fire. Marian did some research checking the census reports and found records for Elias Christiansen. That aunt of yours is really amazing."

He listened to it all—really, really listened.

"Tom, huh? How is the good officer?" Marcus asked, his tone a little playful but with a seriousness behind it.

I paused. How to answer? The pause seemed to be the answer Marcus was looking for.

"Not great, I'm guessing?"

Guessing? Or hoping? I laughed noncommittally and moved on to telling him about Marian's showdown with the construction crew at the scene of the crime.

We were laughing hard enough that tears were running down my cheeks when I reluctantly hung up the phone. I wanted to talk to him more about Tom and, well, everything, but I didn't want it to be over the telephone. I needed to be able to see him, to look in his eyes, to judge his reactions. I needed to be certain . . . and I definitely needed to have that talk with Tom, as well. The sooner, the better.

Fifteen minutes later I was settling down for a snuggle

with Minnie when a knock sounded at the door. Then another. The knock was firm but not insistent. Guess it wasn't going to be such a relaxing evening after all. With a sigh, I got up and went to answer.

Who should be standing on the other side of the threshold but Marcus in all his glory, his hand lifted to knock again. My mouth fell open as my heart began to beat clumsily within my chest. A blank stare was all I could manage.

He grinned at me as his gaze flashed in an instant over my person, taking in my workout casuals. "Hey, sweetness. Hope you don't mind. I was in the neighborhood, and since you didn't have any company, I, well, I thought I'd drop by."

In the neighborhood? He couldn't have mentioned that fifteen minutes ago? But he was supposed to be out of town for a few more days still! Not that I minded. Hell, no! I mean, it was good to see him. Really good. Gosh, was it ever. How on earth did he manage to make a roughed-up pair of jeans and a plain T-shirt look so . . .

His grin spread even wider. Sillier.

I forced myself back to the world of the mentally functioning. "Well, of course I don't mind. Want to come in?"

"Yeah. Sure." He hadn't taken his eyes off me. His lips twitched in . . .

Amusement?

"What?" I asked, lifting my hand to touch my cheek . . . and coming away with fingertips slimed with sticky blue-green goo. Immediately I felt my cheeks go hot beneath the cooling mask I'd forgotten about. "Oh. Oh, fudge."

He reached for my hand and brought it to his mouth slowly. Somehow I knew what he was going to do. I had my chance to pull away. But I didn't. He caught my fingertip lightly between his teeth, and his lips closed around it. "Mmm. Nope," he murmured, his breath warm on my palm. "Seaweed and honey, maybe, but not fudge."

He straightened again to stare down at me with those eyes that had a way of stripping me bare of all masks, all pretenses, and his lips curved in a smile that would have rivaled the superiority of the Cheshire Cat. I think he'd realized that I'd stopped breathing the moment he took my hand, and that I still hadn't started back up again. It wasn't fair for a man to know how off balance he could make you feel . . . was it? Clearly, I was at a disadvantage, because he seemed to be still very much in control of his faculties, and I was having difficulty finding the wherewithal to string words together to form a sentence.

I could find my feet, at least. I stumbled backward. "'Scuse me," I mumbled, then turned and ran to the bathroom, flipping on the faucet before I even had the door closed behind me. Minnie kept trying to pry it open with her tiny hooked claws but had to settle for rattling it incessantly instead.

"Don't feel you have to take that off on my account," Marcus called from the living room.

I could hear the undercurrent of laughter in his voice. The brat. I should never have let him in.

But something made me glad that I had.

I checked myself in the mirror to make sure I had rinsed completely, then checked my smile, too. As an afterthought, I grabbed the mouthwash and swished it around a few times for good measure, then spat it out and rinsed. A quick sweep of cherry-flavored lip balm, and I was done.

*What are you doing, Maggie?*

Damned if I knew.

Marcus was sitting in my chair when I came back out, kicked back with his big boots up and hands folded across his middle, looking very much like he owned the place. He smiled when he saw me. "Very pretty. Fresh."

I was trying not to succumb to the pleasure his compliment gave me.

"Like a sweet little piglet that's been scrubbed with milk."

*Screech!* Crash. Burn.

He laughed when he saw my face. "Just kidding, sweetness. You're beautiful and you know it."

I turned my face away, because I knew he must just be pulling my leg still, and I didn't want him to know that he'd struck a nerve. Not trusting myself to speak, I walked wordlessly past him to take a seat on the sofa, but he caught my hand and tugged me down onto his lap. My breath left me in a whoosh.

For one precious moment, I didn't move, I just sat there with the warmth of his arms looped loosely around me, held captive by the light in his eyes. Then I came to my senses and cleared my throat, nervously pushing against his chest for leverage to get back up.

"Don't go . . ." His hand came up, framing my jaw with his palm. Long fingers traced delicate shapes just behind my earlobe. "Beautiful. Sweet. Maggie," he said, his voice a husky whisper in the quiet room. And then his mouth dipped into my own, and there was not a single thing I could do about it but close my eyes and enjoy. My hands, needing a task to keep them out of trouble, closed around the soft front of his T-shirt . . . but I only succeeded in pulling him closer to me.

For some reason, I was fine with that.

Things blazed quickly out of my control.

I could say that I realized instantly that I had no right to be kissing him like that, at least not yet. I could say that I serenely rose and put distance between us, in order to preserve my good-relationship karma. I could even say that I allowed myself to slip a moment—I am only human, after all—and then drew from some heretofore unknown reserves of strength to do the honorable thing and rally my flagging restraint, all the while conscientiously reassuring him of his appeal for me.

I did none of those things.

*I* kissed him back.

Good.

And hard.

Repeatedly, even.

It was Minnie who saved the day and my self-respect. She leapt from the kitchen table all the way to the kitchen counter, knocking the toaster to the floor with a clamoring crash, then double jumping the rest of the way to the back of the chair. Within seconds we both had cat fur in our mouths as she forced her little body between us, purring to give the devil his due. In the next moment, as I leaned back precious body-cooling inches, Marcus had a sleek black tail beneath his nose in some weird imitation of a moustache, and a pretty, glistening pink tongue liberally applying itself to his earlobe.

And no, it wasn't mine.

He looked scared.

"Um, wow. Does she do this often?"

I giggled and shook my head. "She doesn't get the chance."

Probably not the wisest thing to say, now that I think of it. His eyes flashed blue fire, and I nearly ended up sprawled back across his lap. Again. And I'm pretty sure we all know where that might have led.

Somehow, some vestige of respectability lived on inside of me, though, because when I saw the flash, I knew I'd better get out of the fire before I got burned.

I scrambled off his lap, ignoring his growl of protest and evading the grab of his hands. Swallowing hard against the insistent twirling of desire that was having its way with me, I backed away, just so that I could keep my eye on him.

Some of the tension left his shoulders. He met my gaze. "No?" he asked simply.

I shook my head. "No. Not . . . yet."

It was all I could offer, and yet it seemed to be enough. Marcus sprang up out of the chair, his lean body all taut muscle and masculine vigor, not to grab me again but to head for the door.

"Where are you going?" I couldn't help myself. I couldn't not ask.

"We."

"Oh." I couldn't seem to summon a single protest. Not that I really wanted to.

Allowing Minnie the run of the place, I slipped on my Mary-Jane tennies, grabbed my cell from my purse, slid my stretchy wristband of keys over my hand, and followed him out the door. At that point, I think I might have followed him anywhere.

Yes, the kisses were that good.

Outside the sky had darkened considerably. Marcus lead me to his motorcycle and handed me the spare helmet he kept strapped onto the back. I glanced up at the sky. "Looks like it's going to rain."

"Nah. It's not supposed to rain until after midnight. There's plenty of time to take you for a ride."

Oh, now if that didn't give me all kinds of forbidden ideas . . .

He strapped on his own helmet, then swung one long leg over the back of the bike. Looking back at me, he patted the seat behind him. "Hop on."

I eased onto the seat, shimmying up close to him. Hey, I had an excuse. One pothole and I'd have road rash if I didn't.

He reached around and drew my arms around his waist, giving me even more of an excuse. Turning my face to one side, I smiled against his shoulder and tried not to hold on too tightly.

Something told me he was using excuses, too, because every once in a while he would take his hand off the handlebar and curve his fingers around my knee, holding my leg tightly in place next to his.

At a stoplight, I pulled my cell phone out of my pocket to check the time. Six fifty-seven. I also noticed I had two text messages. Making sure that the light was still red, I clicked the first, from Steff: *I saw that, you hussy.* I grinned, and texted back, *I don't know what you're talking about.* The next text was from Tom, sent only five minutes before. I started getting a sinking feeling in the pit of my stomach before I clicked on it. Had he seen us out on the bike? My nervousness proved all for naught, though. It read only, *Thx.* Short, not so sweet, and to the point. Not even a sorry, a we-need-to-talk, or a have-a-good-evening. It was beginning to crystallize just where I stood with him, and I didn't think it was by his side. Tom's questionable weekend activities only added fuel to that already smoking fire.

And then there was Marcus, my own secret flame-thrower.

Marcus patted my leg to let me know the light was about to change. I flipped the phone closed and tucked it back into the fold-over waistband of my yoga pants, determined not to give Tom another thought. At least not for the time being.

We rode up and down city streets and county roads, letting the early evening air cool our bodies and our thoughts. But when we somehow ended up on the road that Grace Baptist Church was on, an undeniable urge overcame me. I leaned forward, plastering my body along Marcus's back in order to shout over the air whipping past us: "Can we stop?"

He shouted back over his shoulder, "We can stop anywhere you like if you're going to do that."

He pulled the bike into the parking lot, his body moving as one with it, leaning into the curve. I rather enjoyed that. After we'd removed our helmets and I had shaken out my helmet hair, he took my hand, linking his fingers with mine. I tried not to smile too much, but . . . yeah, it was a struggle.

A light was on in the church office. We walked up that way and tried the door. "Hellooooo?" I called up the hall. "Anyone here?"

I heard the scrape of a chair on hard floor, and in the next moment Emily Angelis poked her head out of the doorway to her husband's office. "Oh, hello there," she said as though wondering what we must be doing there at that time of the evening.

I cleared my throat and offered a friendly wave. "I hope you don't mind. We were out in the neighborhood, and I thought I'd show Marcus your lovely flower garden."

Her face brightened. "Oh, of course not. Spend as much time as you like. It does look like rain, though, so just keep an eye on the sky."

"Thanks. Would you mind if we walk straight through to the back? I'm sure Marcus would love to see your sanctuary as well. It's so beautiful."

How could she not give her permission? "I'll probably not be here when you are through—Mother will have me off to bath and bed soon, I'm sure. I'll let her know to check in on you later, to be sure you got off all right."

"Fine. Thank you," I told her with a smile.

"The flower garden?" Marcus said as we meandered down the hall.

"Well, not really. Hush," I said, as we entered the cavernous sanctuary. I paused and pulled his head down to whisper in his ear: "Voices carry like crazy in here."

"But we're not saying anything important," he whispered back, taking the opportunity to nuzzle my neck.

I swatted him playfully. "Come on."

Through a door on the opposite side of the sanctuary, we found our way to the church's first expansion wing, the one the new addition would mirror to create Pastor Bob's "Y for Yahweh" layout. Most of the doors along the hall stood open. But which one might it have been? I paused in each one, trying to see out the windows into the garden beyond in order to pinpoint . . .

"This one," I said, gazing into a comfortable lounge room fitted with several mismatched sofas arranged in a circle. Even through the dense screens in the open windows I could easily see across the garden to the rose arbor where I had sat the day of the fundraiser. "I'm almost sure of it. We would have had perfect acoustics out there—there isn't much stuff in here to absorb sound."

"Hm. Sounds like an intriguing assessment. Want to tell me what we're talking about here?"

"Well . . . I just wanted to be sure of something. It's been bothering me off and on ever since that day. Pieces just weren't fitting together."

He chucked me lightly under the chin. "You're talking in circles."

"Not really. You remember what I told Chief Boggs about that day?"

"About seeing Ty Bennett arguing with Ronnie Maddox?" he asked.

I nodded. "And I did. And it was vicious, ferocious, everything you don't want to witness in an argument between two people. For a moment, I was really afraid that she was going to go off on him in a big way . . . but never him," I said, musing along with a troubled brow. "Oh, he was mad all right, and I'll bet he had some fairly large bursts of testosterone running through those veins, egging him on to give as good as he got, but he remained in control. He stood his ground. He never once reacted in a physical way to her taunts or even to her attacks." I met Marcus's gaze. "And they didn't know I was there until the end. They were inside the church, away from prying eyes. They had no reason to censor themselves."

"You don't think he did it?"

"I don't think he did, no."

He paused, thinking. "They have him in custody right now."

"Presumably on eyewitness testimony placing him at the site in an altercation with the victim. Mine. But how many other people were on site that day as well?"

"Not everyone could have done it. Not everyone had a reason to kill her. If not Ty, then who?"

"Who even said a reason was needed?" I argued, playing devil's advocate. "Sociopaths don't always need a reason, do they?"

"You're thinking a sociopath showed up out of the blue at the church fundraiser and selected Veronica Maddox out of hundreds of other women to be his next victim?"

"Well . . . no," even I was forced to concede. "But there's something else."

"Something that involves the garden."

I nodded, pleased by his perceptiveness. "After that first fight, they went their separate ways. Ty disappeared into the church to meet up with his buddies on the construction crew. Ronnie wheedled her way into an impromptu counseling session with Pastor Bob. The two of them went off to Pastor Bob's office."

"Uh-huh."

"It didn't occur to me until today that Pastor Bob's office is on this side of the sanctuary—you saw so yourself tonight. It was the room that his wife was working in. That day, the two of them—I would swear to this, even though I only saw it in passing—paused at his office, then continued on through the sanctuary. And then I left and went to sit in the garden."

He was beginning to see my point; I could see it in his eyes. "And then you overheard the second argument from the garden sometime later."

"Yes. I think from this very room. And that's not the only thing that's strange," I said as I watched Marcus more closely assess the room we were in.

"There's more?"

"Pastor Bob told Tom that he didn't know Ronnie well. That he had too many parishioners to keep track of them all, he said. It was a lie, Marcus. He'd counseled her that very day, however briefly. Why would he lie?"

"People lie for all sorts of reasons, most of which don't make sense to anyone but themselves. Maybe he thought he would be involved in the investigation and didn't want the negative publicity."

"Maybe. But a man who will lie to protect himself might also act accordingly, mightn't he? Because I think it was Pastor Bob in this room with Ronnie. I don't think it was Ty at all. Letty Clark, the pastor's mother-in-law, had come around back to try to catch up with whoever it was, but they were long gone. I had gone around to the front door and saw Ronnie leave the church in a hurry, wiping tears from her eyes. I went inside to try to head off Mrs. Clark at the pass, and Ty was coming up the stairs from the basement at that time. He hadn't seen anyone."

"So . . . if Ty was downstairs . . ."

"Someone else had to be in this room with Ronnie. It makes sense, doesn't it?"

"You know what? I'm starting to get an uneasy feeling about this."

"Join the club. I *knew* something was wrong. I just didn't know what."

He took my hand. "Let's get out of this room."

In the hall, I said, "That way. To the right. I want to go out to the garden for a sec to see if I can get Elias to connect with me again." I smiled up at him as I grabbed the doorknob and pushed . . .

And nearly bowled over Letty Clark, who had been reaching for the doorknob from the outside.

"Oh my goodness! Mrs. Clark, are you all right?" I reached out to steady the older woman, as it appeared she was wobbling on the edge of the concrete slab ready to topple. "I'm so sorry. I didn't know anyone was there, and—"

"Thank you, dear. Yes, of course I'm all right. What on earth are you doing in here? I just came to check on the two of you to see if you needed anything. My daughter said you'd be in the garden." Her lips pursed almost accusingly.

"We're sorry about that. I guess we just got to talking," I told her as Marcus gripped my hand harder. Why, I wondered. "By the way, have you seen Pastor Bob? I was hoping to be able to talk to him for a moment before we leave. I saw your daughter just a little while ago."

"They're both off to beddy-byes by now, dear. A touch early, but poor Robert has been so overwhelmed by things, he's been allowing himself to get a bit under the weather. I sent them off to get some much needed rest." She glanced up at the sky. "Well, if you're going to have a little look-see at the garden with your beau there, you'd best be doing it now," she told us. "The wind is starting to pick up. I have a feeling we're going to get that rain earlier than the weatherman told us."

"We're on our way out there now. Thanks for letting us know."

"I think she was listening to us," Marcus whispered as we rounded the corner toward the garden.

"Mrs. Clark? Why would she do that?"

*U-L-C*

The thought prodded its way into my brain, unbidden.

"I don't know. But I got that feeling—you know, the quick, look-over-your-shoulder, someone's-there feeling. And then there she was."

I frowned. "Hm. You could be right. Maybe she's just bored. You know, one of those old ladies who likes to stick her nose way too deeply into other people's business."

Out in the garden again, I noticed Mrs. Clark was right. The wind really *had* picked up. It was whipping the trees in the wooded patches at the far edges of the field, not to mention the big maples in the windbreak along the church sidewalk. Dried leaves, crisped by too little rain, drifted down from them and were tossed around by vicious air currents. At least it would be harder to hear us now; the roar of the wind was pretty constant.

"I think he's with us," I told Marcus. "Elias. Back there, I heard one of his usual Ouija clues in my head. U-L-C. Maybe we can tap into him out here, closer to the cave-in. You're a medium. You should be able to zoom right in, shouldn't you?"

"I could try. But Maggie, for whatever reason, he's chosen you to come through to. He might not feel comfortable with me."

"But why?" I wailed, distraught. That wasn't what I wanted to hear at all. "He has to realize I can't help him. I'm not clairvoyant. I'm not a medium like you. He has to see that I'm just a plain old empath, hardly of any use to him at all."

"Plain old . . . come here." He spun me around to face him and took both my hands in his, lifting them to his mouth. "Darlin', you are not a plain old anything. You have a light to you that is so bright. I wish you could see that. I wish you could see yourself the way I see you." He paused, then added, "I do think you're selling your abilities short. If you're getting cues, visual or thought or otherwise, then you do have mediumistic gifts as well.

The way these things present themselves from person to person varies. Few of us are 'just' anything."

*U-N-I-C-E*

*Aw, thanks, Elias,* I thought back in response, *for that vote of confidence. You're pretty nice, too, for someone who doesn't actually have a body anymore. No offense.*

Letty came marching briskly around the corner of the building, carrying two steaming cups in her hands. "I thought you two lovebirds could use a bit of warming up," she said. Never mind that in spite of the wind and impending rainstorm, the temps were still hovering around the eighty-degree mark. A nice drop from the mid-nineties of earlier in the day but hardly one that would inspire the need for hot drinks.

"Thank you," I told her, reaching for the offered mug. I took a sip, grimacing at both the heat and the thick, syrupy quality of the tea. "How sweet of you."

I gave Marcus a pointed look. He quickly followed suit, taking a gulp of his own. His eyes widened and met mine, but he managed to force it down.

She hemmed and hawed a moment, shifting her weight from one foot to another as she watched us. "I, well, I hope you'll forgive me, but I couldn't help but overhear the two of you a little while ago. Do you really believe that Tyler Bennett isn't responsible for Veronica Maddox's death?"

Again Marcus gripped my hand harder, but I couldn't exactly deny what she'd already overheard. "Well, no. I don't believe he is, Mrs. Clark."

"That's impossible. He must be. There's no one else."

I was not going to tell her that it could possibly have been her son-in-law. I had to wonder if she had heard us discussing that possibility. "I'm sure there were lots of people it could have been," I assured her. "So many people were at that fundraiser. It could have been any of them."

"No. No, no, no, it couldn't. There has to have been a reason. It doesn't make sense without a reason. There always has to be a reason."

She was getting more and more upset. I took a deep drink from my tea to mollify her, hoping she'd notice. She seemed to care so deeply about taking care of things—her daughter, Pastor Bob, her father before them. Probably her brother, too, before he died . . .

I frowned as something hovered tantalizingly along the edge of my memory, calling to me. What was it?

"Drink your tea, dears," she said agitatedly, "while I mull this over."

Marcus and I sat on the arbor bench and obediently sipped at our tea as she began to pace, twisting her gloves in her hands. She was back to her old favorites again—grimy, well-worn leather. A man's style but small enough to fit a woman's hands. Finally, she seemed to come to a decision. She tucked her gloves into her waistband, put her hands on her ample hips, and looked around the garden. With a resigned sigh and a resolute straightening of her rather thick body, she walked decisively over to where she had left her garden tools out, placed her spade and a crescent-shaped root-chopping blade across a wheelbarrow, and began to push it down the path toward the garden gate. It seemed an odd thing to do unless she was moving them to the shed for safekeeping—obviously she wasn't planning to do any gardening, not with a storm brewing. But then, some people have to stay busy when they are upset or worried, to take the edge off their distress.

Always taking care of things.

She set the lot of it down, blocking the gate, and turned to look at us, cocking her head to one side. "Not long now," she said.

I glanced up at the sky. "No, not long now. I guess we should be going."

I stood up with a stretch, tipping too far forward as I lost my balance. "Whoops." My head was feeling a little funny. I closed my eyes a moment, waiting for the vertigo to pass, then turned to Marcus. His eyes were unfocused and his head was tipping dangerously to one side. "Marcus? Marcus, are you okay?" Stumbling forward on feet that felt like someone else's, I took his face in my hands. "Hey. Come on, big guy, say something."

His focus cleared a touch for just a moment, and his gaze slid sideways to mine. "Tea," he whispered.

I reached for his cup automatically, closing my hands around his to lift the cup to his mouth.

It was then that it hit me.

*S-I-S-T-E-R*

I turned to look at Letty, who was watching the proceedings with that same intense, birdlike focus. My mouth had fallen open. I didn't think I had the strength to close it. My legs felt as if they weren't going to hold me. I twisted my body as I fell, hoping I would make it into the bench seat. "You . . . you drugged . . . the tea."

She considered my words a long moment, then nodded solemnly.

"You . . ." I closed my eyes, swallowing. My throat felt full, tight. "You're Elias's sister." *U-N-I-C-E.* Not *You're nice.* It had never been that. We had read it wrong and had somehow forgotten that Elias didn't always spell correctly. U-L-C. Unice. "Eunace. Eunace Letitia Christiansen."

She frowned. "Well, of course I am. You needn't state the obvious, dear."

*Sister . . . Be careful . . .*

Had I really been that blind? Not Mel. Well, Mel, too . . . but not in the way that Elias had meant.

With great effort I twisted my head to look up at Marcus. His eyes were closed and he was breathing shallowly.

And then the bottom opened up on my world and I slid off the edge of the bench, down, down, down into endless oblivion.

# Chapter 17

I came to, I don't know when. And I didn't know where. All I knew was that night had fallen and I was somewhere dark and cool. My head was throbbing to beat all hell, and both my shoulder and left hip hurt. I closed my eyes—it didn't help to have them open anyway, I could see nothing—and did a physical self-check. Toes were functioning. Ankles. Knees. Hands, fingers, thumbs. All good. I raised my head off the ground a couple of inches. Other than the wave of nausea that hit me with that ill-advised movement, everything seemed in decent working order.

But where was I?

I was still feeling a bit floaty, so I allowed the sensation to run unchecked. It was almost pleasant, if I didn't pay any attention to the knot on the right side of my head. Ow.

There was warmth there, too, next to me. I stretched out my hand and bumped into something solid but yielding at the same time. I pushed on it again, a little harder.

"A little farther to the right, sweetness, and you're going to be pretty embarrassed."

"Marcus!" I sat up too quickly, and the room—or whatever—swam.

"In the flesh."

I got up on my hands and knees and shifted over toward him. "Where are you? I can't see a thing."

"That would be because . . . it's dark."

"Oh. Thanks. Very helpful. I wouldn't have noticed if not for you." Smart-ass. I found his leg and patted my way up the side of his body.

"Hmm. You could have told me you wanted to play. I would have come prepared."

"Very funny. Stop trying to distract me. This is so not the time." I patted his chest, then slid my hand up to his face. His five o'clock shadow was getting fairly poky, so I knew it must be getting late. I stroked his cheekbone with my fingertips. "Are you okay?"

"My head hurts and my mouth feels like someone stuffed it full of prickly cotton balls, but other than that . . . yeah, I think so."

"Good. Sit up."

I heard movement, so I was pretty sure he was complying with my order.

"I take it she slipped us a mickey."

"Yeah. The tea."

"Wanna fill me in on why? I think I missed some of it."

Briefly I told him what I knew and what I had only just put together. "There are a lot of holes as to the why and the how, but if it's true that Pastor Bob killed Ronnie, maybe she's just trying to hold things together. For her family. For the church." The more I tried to concentrate, the more elusive the details became. "I do know that somehow it has to do with Elias, her brother. Somehow!"

*Please tell me, Elias. Please help me to understand. And while you're at it, if you want to help us get out of wherever we are, that would be good, too.*

To Marcus, I said, "I don't suppose you have your cell phone on you?"

He patted his pockets. "I did. It's not here now."

"Mine either. It was tucked into my waistband earlier. Now all I have left are my keys—" My voice drifted off. "My keys!" I slipped the stretchy wristband over my hand.

"If you're happy to see them, I'm glad, too."

"No, look." I fumbled around until I found the right attachment, then flicked the tiny switch with my thumbnail. Suddenly we had a pinpoint glow of blue-white light that illuminated my hands and a very small portion of our hiding place.

"An LED flashlight? Aren't you the Girl Scout. I could kiss you for that."

He helped me to my feet and, with the flashlight in one hand and my hand tucked in his other, we investigated our space as best we could. It appeared to be some sort of cellar, plain dirt floor that was hard-packed and swept clean, old shelves along the wall. Nothing else.

Nothing else except a pile of dirt and rubble beneath the irregular opening in the ceiling, and what looked like fresh, green planks closing off the only way out.

No ladder.

"We're in the cave-in room, aren't we?" I asked, already sure of the answer.

"I think so, yeah."

"At least all those crosses and animal skeletons are gone. Can you reach the boards?"

He stretched upward while I held on to his waist to steady him. "No. How about if I boost you and you try?"

He had me stand on his knees and use one hand on the wall to keep myself upright. I could just touch the boards with my fingertips. I summoned all of my strength and tried to channel it through my fingers. "They're not moving. I don't know if I'm just not able to push hard enough or what."

A voice came through the crack between the boards, startling me enough that I fell off the ledge formed by Marcus's knees. "Actually, there's something on top of them, dear."

Marcus stood up. His arms went around me protectively. "What do you think you're doing? What do you want from us?" he shouted at the boards.

"Nothing really. Except quiet. Peace and quiet. I can't let you get away with trying to expose Robert to the police, so I'm afraid you're just going to have to stay down there."

"You're going to protect him? When he killed that poor girl?"

The lighthearted titter of her laugh coming through the boards made my blood run cold. "Robert didn't kill Veronica Maddox. He might have played around with her, the swine, but he didn't kill her."

*U-N-I-C-E*

"You did," I said out loud as the horror of the realization struck me. "You did it." Marcus's arms closed even more tightly around me, pulling me up protectively against his body, his warmth, his strength.

"Very astute of you, my dear," she intoned through the crack in the boards.

"But . . . why?"

"Dear, dear. She was so very messy. I can't bear mess. And dirt. She was dirt. Carrying on with married men . . . men of God! . . . right under our church roof. Can you imagine the scandal if that got out? More messes to clean up. More dirt. Did you know she carried out her inclinations right there in our garden that first time with Robert? Religious counseling has certainly changed since I was a girl, let me tell you. I saw them. Right there on that bench you two were sitting on. I talked to him about it after. Warned him against her. And then the girl went after him again, and I could see I was going to have to do something."

"It wasn't the first time you'd killed, was it, Eunace?" The words just popped out of my mouth from nowhere.

"Letty, dear. I don't go by Eunace anymore. And just who have you been talking to?" She sighed. "Secrets. They always seem to get out. People just don't know how to keep from flapping their gums nowadays."

"Did you set the fire that took your brother's life? That claimed the entire church?"

Marcus was looking at me in a whole new light. "Where are you getting this from?" he whispered.

"I don't know," I whispered back. "Elias, I think."

"Fine, then. It won't matter anymore. This is one secret that won't get out. Yes, I set the fire. And I made sure Elias was going to sleep right through it. Happy now?"

"Except he didn't sleep forever."

"No, he . . . what did you say?"

"I said, he didn't sleep forever. He's here with us, here now."

"Stop it."

"He is. He used to spell your name wrong, didn't he?"

"Yes . . . how did you—"

"He used to spell it with a U, not an E."

The silence on the other side of those boards was deafening. "It's starting to rain. I'm going to go now."

"Wait!"

A hesitation and then, "Do mind your manners, dear. It's 'Wait, *please*.'"

"Wait, please, then."

"Much better. Your mother would be proud."

I heard something against the boards. A heavy thud. Dirt sifted down on top of our heads. This was getting serious. "Elias is sad," I told her. "He *is* here. Why did you kill him, Eunace?"

"If he's here, why don't you ask him?"

"He wants you to say it."

She sighed. "It was so long ago. I'm tired."

A whine, like a child would make at the end of a long day.

"Why, Eunace?"

She huffed out her breath. "Because he was a bully. He was always making Daddy happy. I wanted to be the one to make Daddy happy. And because he . . . he said he'd tell on me. About the animals."

*The animal skeletons.* "You hid them here in this room."

"We used to play here sometimes. Found it one day. Nearly broke my leg doing it, too. But I didn't tell anyone. Only Elias. It was our secret place."

Tom had said that only a psychopath or sociopath kills without reason. He didn't know how close he came with that assessment. He might never know, if we didn't get out of here.

"If you let us die, he'll tell. He'll tell your daughter."

She laughed, sadly this time. "My daughter is a foolish, airheaded woman who can't even manage her own body or life, let alone her husband. She stares off into space, hasn't a thought she can call her own, and sees things that aren't there. Why would it matter if Elias told her? Elias is dead. No one would believe her, given her history."

"I believed her," I told her.

"Then you are a fool."

"I believed her when she said she saw you scrambling about in the dark that night. That was when you were moving Ronnie's body, wasn't it? That evening, in the dark, after you gave the pastor something to make him sleep and keep him that way? You gave your daughter something, too, the way you always do, but she outsmarted you. She hasn't been drinking it. And she saw you."

She didn't say anything for several minutes. "You're lying," she said finally.

"She knows, Eunace," I said, not yielding to her request to be called Letty. "She knows, and Elias knows. And sooner or later, everyone else will know that you are a murderer, too. And that is the way your life here will be remembered. Forever."

"You're wrong. No one will know."

"You could change that. You could let us out of here. You could do the right thing."

"Oh no. I can't do that. No, I put you there, and there you'll stay."

"I don't believe you," I countered doggedly, hearing her heap another shovelful of dirt on top of the boards, and then another. "I don't believe you really want to kill us. To let us die."

"Oh, dear, dear. There's something wrong with me, inside, I'm afraid," she said lightly. "Yes, indeed."

It was the last thing we heard her say. For several minutes we heard heaps of dirt and rock hitting the growing
pile on top of the boards. And then, we heard nothing at
all but the sounds of our own breath in the stillness.

Unable to think anymore, I clung to Marcus, drawing
strength from his calm, steady presence. He pressed his
lips into my hair and breathed in my scent, rocking slowly
back and forth with me, like a young, flexible tree bending
in the wind. We stood that way for I don't know how long,
comforting each other, taking comfort. No one would be
coming for us. No one knew where we were. Only Emily
had seen us, and that had been earlier in the evening, before Letty drugged her to oblivion. No one would even
know we were missing at least until morning, and even
then, our absence might be explained away by the mutual
attraction everybody seemed to realize we shared. Would
the construction crew arrive in the morning, I wondered?
Or would Letty find a way to get around that? And even if
they did come out in the morning, could we be certain the
air down here would last that long? Trying hard not to
panic, I thought of Minnie and her beautiful eyes, and of
my nieces Courtney and Jenna and the smiles that could
get me, just like that. I thought of my mom and dad,
Grandpa Gordon, Marshall, even Mel. Tom. I thought of
all my friends. I thought of Liss. I thought of Steff. I
thought of Marcus. That was an easy one.

So many people who loved me. Funny, how we take
that for granted sometimes.

And it occurred to me that giving up, even when it
seemed the only answer, was not the answer.

I pulled myself gently from Marcus's arms and wiped
my face with my hands. "Come on. Let's go over the space
one more time and see if there's anything we can use."

The room had been wiped clean by the historical investigation crew. Not a mousetrap, not a crumb, not even a thumbtack remained. Only the shelves . . .

I walked over to them, pulling on them to test them. They weren't a solid piece of furniture; they were built to the walls, and too far away from the opening to be much good as a ladder.

Marcus grabbed hold of one of the boards and rattled it. It *was* attached to the wall, but it had been built so long ago that the mooring screws pulled right out of the damp wood supporting beams with little effort. Marcus and I looked at each other, and in the next instant we were both tearing at the shelves, yanking and prying, until we had them down.

And now, we had . . . a pile of wood.

Hmm.

"Can we use them for anything?" I asked, breathless with the exertion.

"Got a hammer and nails?" Marcus cracked.

I felt my lip quiver. It had seemed a good idea at the time. Action for the sake of action, I suppose. Busy work. And now, there was nothing we could do with them, except . . .

I grabbed a long piece of wood and held it upright against my body. Staring upward, I aimed it toward the boards above. *Whack . . . Whack . . . Whack . . .* Over and over and over again, like a metronome. Dirt was sifting down all around me, into my eyes, into my hair. I didn't care.

Marcus got up and put his hand on my arm. "Maggie. Maggie, honey. Stop."

"No."

"It's not doing any good."

"I won't stop. I can't. If I stop, I might collapse."

"Then I'll do it for you." He pressed a kiss to my gritty forehead and took the board from my hands. And as I watched, he started the pounding again. Knowing it wasn't doing any good but doing it anyway.

For me.

I went behind him and put my arms around his waist, pressing my cheek to his back.

It took me a moment to recognize the sound that I kept hearing in between thumps. My ears were ringing from the blows of wood on wood. I wasn't even sure that I *was* truly hearing something and not just inventing it for the sake of hope.

Finally I stopped Marcus in midstroke, staying his hand. "Do you hear that? Or am I crazy?"

It was a thudding sound that repeated, much like the pounding of the wood here within. Except this wasn't coming from somewhere inside the room. It was coming from the other side of the wooden barrier.

Marcus and I looked at each other, and then he started banging away in earnest. I grabbed a second length of board and picked up the counterpoint to his upward thrusts, working in rhythm. And when we weren't thumping, we were calling out, "We're here! In here! Down here!"

Finally a single board was pulled away above our heads, and we were hit with a mixture of dirt and rainwater in our faces. I for one didn't care. I was never so glad to see another human face in my life.

It was Pastor Bob.

And Emily, to be fair. She stood by anxiously, wringing her hands as the pastor finished scooping away enough dirt to get enough boards off to haul us both out, one by one. As soon as Marcus was out, I fell on Pastor Bob, holding myself upright with two fisted hands on his muddy bathrobe, and gave him a big, resounding kiss on the cheek.

"Thank you, thank you, thank you, thank you."

Marcus grinned, watching me. "You're mauling him, Mags."

Laughing with relief, I hauled myself off of him and stuck out my hand instead. He took it in his own.

"Thank you," I said again, more sedately.

"My pleasure, Miss O'Neill," he answered with all the dignity of his office. "Now, could someone please explain to me what the devil is going on?"

# Chapter 18

It was Emily Angelis who had raised the call of alarm. Emily who had thwarted the intent of her mother's ritual tea. She'd hidden away in her bedroom, pretending to sleep, until she heard her mother leave the house. Wondering what she was doing heading out into an impending thunderstorm, Emily watched from her window as Letty made her way toward the church. She saw Letty speaking with Marcus and me. And she saw both me and Marcus fall.

What she thought as she watched her own mother load me up onto her wheelbarrow and cart me toward the cave-in, and then drag Marcus over by his boots, inch by precious inch, I don't know. It must have been a shock. An even bigger shock when her mother came back without us and headed into the church utility room to wash up.

Emily had gone then to rouse her husband, only to find him out cold. It took hot coffee, ice, and much talking to get him to wake enough to get dressed. And yet she did it. She got him dressed and out of the house, urging him up to the cave-in before he even had a chance to gather his faculties enough to ask her why in blazes they'd want to go out digging in the dirt in the middle of a monsoon. Blessed woman.

Marcus and I explained everything we knew to Pastor Bob and his wife. No matter how hard it was to say. And then the four of us went looking for *her*, trailing mud and rainwater and muddy rainwater in our wake wherever we went.

She wouldn't like that.

Letty wasn't at the church, where we thought we might find her. She had, however, taken the time to put away her wheelbarrow and tools every bit as neatly as if she had only just ended a day of gardening. Her muddy clothes had been rinsed and thrown into the church's washing machine. Her dirty shoes—gardening clogs—had been rinsed clean and now rested side by side on the floor beneath the coatrack on the wall, as though she expected to be stepping back into them in the morning. Every last bit of mud and water had been wiped clean from every surface.

She was incredibly thorough.

We went up to the parsonage next, and that was where we found her. She'd gotten dressed again in a plain gray street dress and a white cable-knit cardigan, stockings, and sensible shoes, looking every bit as though she intended to go out to market or to the gardening center for supplies. Instead she was lying on her bed, on top of the bedcovers, her feet together, her hands folded over her chest. Her eyes were closed. On the table next to the bed was a cup of tea.

It was the perfect out for her. Always in control of the situation, up to the last.

She opened her eyes once as Emily sat down on the bed next to her and touched her cheek. Her eyelashes fluttered as she recognized her daughter. Her lips moved but only faintly. "Better . . . this way."

"Oh, Mama."

"Be . . . careful. Elias . . ."

And then she stopped. For a moment we thought she had already gone. It was easy to see she was close to that precipice. Then her eyes slitted open again, just for a second. She looked straight at me.

"Elias . . . his cats. Proper . . . burial."

And then she really was gone, before Pastor Bob could even finish giving the emergency operator the street address.

It was fitting, somehow, that Elias connected in the end through Letty, rather than through me. That through Letty's lips came his final request to have a fitting burial for the pets he loved and that were taken away from him by a jealous and unstable younger sister. Fitting, too, that she took her own life in the end. I'm sure somehow it lessened the pain her daughter had to suffer, knowing that her mother's end came, yes, at her own hand in her final demonstration of control, but in what was also perhaps her only truly selfless act throughout her long and twisted existence.

Somehow. At least, I hoped it did.

As for Marcus and me . . . we found our cell phones in the church washroom, lying so sedately side by side. On mine was another text from Tom, saying that we should talk. Boy, were we going to have to talk, and it wasn't something I was going to relish. I hate confrontation, and I will go out of my way to keep from hurting someone's feelings . . . but Marcus and I couldn't stop touching each other after we got out of that hole, and I had a feeling that wasn't going to change anytime soon. It wasn't fair to Tom—not that his weekend outing had been fair to me, either—and I knew I was going to have to tell him that we needed to go our separate ways for a while. Maybe forever. You see, I was ready now. In Marcus I realized at last that I had found something that was pretty special. He supported me, he protected me, he laughed at me and with me, and he made me laugh at myself. And he was an awfully darned good kisser. But one step at a time. No need to jump to forward-thinking assumptions just yet, for either one of us.

The talk with Tom came sooner than I had hoped, since he responded to the call to arms, he and two of Sheriff Reed's men, along with a flotilla of emergency vehicles. The look in his eyes when he saw me there with Marcus, poised yet again on the brink of disaster, Marcus's arm looped protectively around my waist . . . well, it said it all. He avoided my gaze throughout the taking of statements while the EMTs worked with Letty, trying to revive her even though it was obvious she was already gone. When the deputy finally came over to Marcus and me to let us know that we could go home, I knew I was going to have to approach him myself. I squeezed Marcus's hand and eased away.

Tom barely acknowledged me with a grunt when I asked if I could talk to him privately for a moment.

"So," he said, his voice low and proud.

"So," I echoed softly, an admission.

He seemed to understand. He took a deep breath, then let it out slowly, nodding to himself. "I guess this is it, then."

I wished he would look at me, I wished he would feel

my regret, I wished he could know that I never wanted to hurt him. His weekend date didn't even matter now, and I realized that it had been there to help me make a decision. A lesson from my Guides, I supposed. "Tom—"

He lifted his chin, his gaze on the treeline. "You keep yourself out of trouble, Maggie."

I swallowed, hard. "I hope—" I wanted to say, *I hope we can be friends, I'll always be your friend, I hope you can still be mine . . .* but I stopped myself. Now was not the time to offer platitudes of friendship that might not ring true given the roller-coaster emotions of the moment. Time enough for that in weeks to come, I hoped. Time enough for everything.

Who knew what the future would hold?

Marcus kissed me good-bye at my door and held me until I stopped shaking, then touched my cheek and made me lock the door against the night and its inhabitants.

The next morning, we went to see a woman about some cats.

Obtaining the skeletal remains of the cats from the historical society wasn't as difficult as we'd thought it would be. Marcus and I simply explained to Marian the relevance of the request and how it came to be communicated to us. The bones had no real historical value anyway, other than from a novelty perspective. We placed the remains in a box that Marcus built specially for the occasion, then took them out to the Angelises' place. Our gift to them. The four of us saw to it that the remains were properly laid to rest, at long last.

I think Elias was there, in spirit. And I hope now that his spirit can rest. That it can even move on.

And I hope and pray that the pain plaguing this town can come to an end.

It has to sometime. Some way. Somehow.

Are you afraid of the dark? I'm not. Not anymore.

Because even the darkest, scariest places are only dark and scary until you poke a hole through and let a little light inside.

Walk softly, but carry a big stick.

I'll remember that. Trust me.

# Madelyn Alt

# No Rest for the Wiccan

Maggie O'Neill reluctantly volunteers to care for her bedridden, oh-so-perfect sister, Mel, but strange spirits threaten to divert her attention. Then a friend of Mel's loses her husband to a dreadful fall, and the police call it an accidental death. Maggie's not so sure, and sets her second sights on finding a first-degree murderer.

penguin.com

Be bewitched…
# The Bewitching Mysteries
by Madelyn Alt

## The Trouble with Magic

"A fascinating ride…A hint of romance
with much intrigue, mystery, and magic in a small
Midwestern town setting."
—*Roundtable Reviews*

## A Charmed Death

"A magical, spellbinding mystery that enchants
readers with its adorable heroine."
—*The Best Reviews*

## Hex Marks the Spot

"Quirky, enchanting, mystical, and addictive…
Not to be missed."
—Annette Blair, national bestselling author of
*Gone with the Witch*

M306AS0608